THE SURVIVALIST

by **Dalton Keene**

GB

**GLADIUS
BOOKS**

ISBN-13: 978-0-982910-06-1

Design direction by Gunther Rollins

Printed in the United States of America

Library of Congress Control Number: 2016960475

FIRST EDITION

Visit the author on the web at *ww.daltonkeene.com*

*For Mom and Dad, whose love and guidance
inspired me to create.*

THE SURVIVALIST

1

IT IS NEVER EASY to stage one's own death—at least not convincingly. But where Andrei Kovalevsky was concerned, the ruse was foolproof. In the beginning, his co-conspirators had objected on grounds that the plan was too dangerous, that there were too many elements beyond their control: weather conditions, aircraft integrity, impact variables. The list went on. But the lure of great reward, a fortune in diamonds, had ultimately persuaded them to take the risk.

And so for the third time in as many minutes, Andrei Kovalevsky checked his pocket GPS and squinted through the cabin window at the sunlit clouds below. The six-passenger Gulfstream banked left, leveled, then eased into a slow descent. By Andrei's calculation, the time had come to execute the plan.

He turned, gesturing to Viktor who acknowledged with a nod. The two Russians unbuckled their seatbelts and stood up in the aisle. The cabin seated six, but Andrei and his three partners were the aircraft's only passengers. Ahead, Andrei could see the forward cabin opening into a small cockpit, the space squeezed narrow by two control columns and banks of gauges and orange-lighted screens. A lone pilot sluggishly worked the controls.

"Ready, my friend?" Andrei asked Viktor.

The sinewy man met Andrei's gaze with pale blue eyes, his rigid stare answering the question in the affirmative.

Andrei signaled his other two partners, both of whom were shifting anxiously in their seats, and said, "Fedor, Sergey, begin preparations."

Each man nodded and reached for a black, waterproof rucksack lying on the floor at his feet.

Andrei drew his pistol and jerked back the slide, chambering a round. In single file, he and Viktor moved toward the pilot.

Beyond the cockpit windows, Andrei could see the cloud cover beginning to clear, yielding to a landscape of tree-lined ridges and snow-capped peaks—by his estimation, the jet was now cruising twenty thousand feet over the foothills of the Canadian Rockies. While formulating the plan, he had taken great care in studying the area's topography. The Canadian Rockies, he'd learned, were the northernmost mountains in a greater, three thousand mile long chain that extended south as far as New Mexico. Andrei's interest, however, was limited to an area of extreme desolation northwest of their current position.

Viktor took the lead and stepped into the cockpit.

The pilot, a prim black man with closely cropped hair, turned in surprise. "Sorry, gentlemen, but regulations require all passengers to remain—"

"Regulations?" Viktor lowered himself into the empty co-pilot's seat. "Captain, we needn't concern ourselves with tiresome regulations."

Andrei lifted his pistol.

The pilot's eyes widened. "What is this? What are you doing?"

Crowding close, Andrei pressed the barrel against the pilot's chest. "There's been a change in our destination, I'm afraid."

The pilot gaped down at the pistol, then looked up incredulously. "I don't understand. You mean to tell me you're hijacking the aircraft?"

"Hijacking? Oh no, Captain, that's an unfortunate word. And it would imply we've a greater motive: a political cause or ideological grievance, perhaps. I can assure you, we are not hijackers. We harbor no such motivations."

"Then what's the meaning of this?"

"*That* you needn't concern yourself with. Know only that we'll be making an unscheduled landing."

"Impossible," the pilot said. "We have to land in Anchorage for refueling."

"Anchorage, Captain, is no longer part of the flight plan."

"Then where would you have me divert?"

Andrei pointed the barrel of his pistol at the cockpit window, then stabbed downward toward the Earth.

The pilot frowned. "There's nothing down there

but mountains and valleys."

"Quite right, Captain. And nestled in one of those valleys is a very large lake. Perfect for our needs."

"What good is a lake? We couldn't possibly—" The pilot's face blanched. "You mean to say you want me to touch down on water? Are you out of your mind?"

Andrei glanced at the instrument panel. Taped under the navigation display he noticed a small photograph of the pilot and, presumably, his family, enjoying a summer picnic in the park. The woman, a sickly thin Asian, sat next to the pilot on an outstretched blanket, a baby bouncing on one knee. A young boy, maybe ten or twelve, stood nearby holding a half-eaten sandwich, his slanted eyes made all the more narrow by a wide, toothy grin.

Andrei gave the woman a second glance. "Your wife, Captain?"

The pilot lowered his eyes to the photograph.

"Tell me about her," Andrei said.

"My wife? I don't understand."

"What attracted you to her?"

Given current circumstances, Andrei knew, it must have seemed to the pilot like an absurd question. His mouth moved wordlessly as his mind worked to make sense of it all.

"You do love her, do you not, Captain?"

"I—well, yes. But I don't understand the relevance."

"I see she is Asian," Andrei said. "Her race, it does not shame you?"

"Of course not. Look here, mister, do you have a point?"

"I'm curious. How did the two of you meet?" Andrei poked the gun's barrel into the pilot's chest.

The pilot looked down, his eyes darkening with fear. "Hey, buddy, take it easy. You want to know so badly, I'll tell you." He paused as if thinking. "Some years ago I was on a layover in New York City. I stopped in a café for a cup of coffee."

"You met your wife in a café? How charming."

"Not exactly," the pilot said. "I was drinking coffee, staring out the window. Min, that's my wife, she was driving by. A pedestrian stepped into traffic and forced her to swerve. Her front tire hit a curb and had a blowout."

"Ah, the picture is becoming clear. So like a gentleman, you changed it for her?"

A quick glance down at the pistol. "No, no I didn't. But don't get me wrong, I wanted to. I even stood up and headed for the door, but a man on the street beat me to it." The pilot shook his head, his mind becoming wrapped around the memory. "Funny thing is, Min rejected the guy's help. I think she took it as some sort of insult, or maybe she thought that changing the tire herself would be a challenge. Who knows? Either way, I sat there drinking my coffee, watching this ninety-pound woman jacking up a Camry. After fighting the spare out of the trunk, and dirtying her hands getting it mounted, she walked into the café to clean up."

Andrei smiled. "An independent woman."

"Yes." The pilot stared admiringly at the photograph. "When Min finally emerged from the restroom, I had a glass of iced tea waiting for her. I'd been impressed by her determination. I wanted to learn more about her. The rest is history."

The jet shuddered through a pocket of turbulence, disturbing the pilot's memory. Again, he glanced at the pistol.

"A fascinating story," Andrei said. "But unfortunately, we've run out of time, and there's business to keep." He motioned to Viktor, who produced a sheet of paper scrawled with GPS coordinates. "Feed these numbers into the Flight Management System, if you would please, Captain."

Suspiciously, the pilot read the coordinates, then keyed the information into the FMS. When the position came up, he switched the display grid to terrain view. His mouth fell agape. "You weren't kidding. You actually want me to ditch the plane into a lake?"

"You'll do the best you can, of course. Given the circumstances."

"I can't do it," the pilot insisted. "I can't, and I won't. Don't you see the danger?"

Andrei's eyes narrowed. "What I see is a stubborn *durak* not long for this world." He jammed the barrel against the pilot's temple. "It is fortunate your little Min is a resourceful woman. She'll need every bit of that resourcefulness raising two children...without a father."

"Please, this is insane. Don't you understand? Any number of things could go wrong. If I fail to slow to the proper airspeed, or fail to touch down at just the right angle, the force of impact will tear this plane to pieces. Not getting killed is at best…a coin toss."

Andrei smiled, drew back his pistol. "Your estimation is optimistic, Captain. Personally, I would have given us one chance in three."

The pilot loosened his necktie. Beads of sweat ran from his brow. "This is crazy. We'll all be killed."

"Your objections are growing tiresome, Captain," Andrei said. "Tell me, will you or will you not land this plane?"

"You mean am I willing to drop it into a lake and commit suicide?" The pilot glanced at the photograph of his wife and children, then swallowed as if taking down a stone. "I'm sorry, but the answer is no."

Andrei shook his head in disappointment.

Viktor gestured to Fedor, who had been watching the scene from the forward cabin. The hulking man bound forward, rucksack slung over his shoulder.

"Secure the pilot," Viktor ordered in Russian.

Fedor's meaty cheeks rose with a relishing grin.

Andrei holstered his pistol and knelt beside the Captain, whose face now glistened with sweat. "It was a mistake for you to refuse my demand."

The pilot straightened his posture in defiance. "I don't see that I had any other choice."

Fedor removed a roll of duct tape from his bag, then maneuvered behind the pilot. Quickly, he freed the end of the tape and began winding tight loops around the chair, making a dozen circuits over the pilot's chest and arms, securing him to his chair.

When Fedor finished, he tore away and fastened the strip, then repeated the process at the pilot's legs.

"Forgive the inconvenience, Captain," Andrei said, "but I cannot risk you signaling duress with the transponder. That would ruin everything."

"Who's going to fly the plane? Have you thought about that?"

"Given your experience with this aircraft, I was hoping that person would be you. However, your refusal to cooperate forces my hand. I must now initiate a secondary plan. Comrade Viktor here will take the controls. He was a decorated fighter pilot in the Russian Air Force. And although his familiarity with the Gulfstream is limited to a recent study of technical manuals and computer simulations, I trust he will do an adequate job."

"No, you mustn't!" Tendons in the pilot's neck stiffened into ropes. "You're going to kill us all."

"Captain, your lack of faith disturbs me." Andrei leaned over the control column and yanked away the photograph, then tossed it onto the pilot's lap. "Fedor, I've had enough of this bothersome *durak*. Quiet him."

Eager to oblige, Fedor plucked a small plastic bag from his rucksack, then pulled it over the pilot's head. With a quick play of his fingers, he tore free a long strip of duct tape and wound it three times around the man's neck, securing the bag airtight. He stepped back and admired his handy work.

The pilot struggled furiously to breathe. The bag expanded and deflated violently as he sucked in long, panicked breaths. "For the love of God, get it off me!" came his muffled plea. The bag continued to expand and deflate like a plastic lung.

Fedor beamed with excitement.

"Viktor, take the controls," Andrei ordered.

Tightly restrained, the pilot jerked from side to side, crying out a long, frightful scream. His dark hands stiffened. His head whipped in a seesaw motion as a portion of the bag sucked into his open mouth. A moment later, there was an involuntary convulsion, and his body went limp.

Andrei stared at the pilot's lifeless body and chuckled. "And our good pilot was worried about the dangers of a water landing."

2

VIKTOR'S FACE REMAINED stoic as he assumed the flight controls and began verification of the jet's position.

Andrei and Fedor returned to the cabin. Andrei said, "Tie off the inflatable as close as possible to the passenger door. Secure it with a hitch knot. When we hit the water, it must be immediately accessible."

Fedor went to work throwing open storage compartments and retrieving equipment.

Suddenly, the jet's engines whined, and the cabin vibrated. Andrei felt a fluttering sensation in his stomach as the aircraft made a severe drop in altitude.

Andrei looked to Sergey, who had steadied himself against a passenger seat, his face pale as curd. Andrei knew that his companion feared flying. In fact, he had originally protested the plan on grounds that it involved an aircraft. But the prospect of great wealth and a new life far from the reach of the *mafiya* had helped him to reconsider. Sergey, swallowing with an intense look of nausea, peered at Andrei. "All supplies stored and accounted for."

"Excellent." Andrei unzipped his rucksack and removed four flotation vests, tossing one to Fedor, and another to Sergey. "Get these on and strap in."

A false twilight fell over the cabin as the jet dipped into the bowl of a great valley. Andrei stared through the window at the jagged mountainside, now level with the plane as it made its rapid descent. A blanket of aspens covered the rocky slopes, their deep green color nearing black in the shadow.

"Weather conditions moderate. I have visual of the lake," Viktor called out from the cockpit. "Circling to locate optimum approach vector."

Andrei hurried back to the cockpit and handed Viktor a vest. While his partner shrugged it on, Andrei stared through the window at the lake below. In deep shadow, it appeared as an immense pool of oil. Wind blew over its surface, rippling the water and stirring up an occasional whitecap. Andrei turned to Viktor. "I am eager to read our obituaries, my friend."

"We should be so fortunate. You're aware, the pilot was correct when he warned us of the danger. This will be a risky maneuver. Success is not at all guaranteed, I'm afraid."

"I have confidence in you."

"And I in you." Viktor's eyes dropped to Andrei's waist, where he kept secure the belt filled with diamonds.

Andrei noticed the stare. "It would be in your best interest to prevent my sinking to the lake's bottom, comrade. For where *I* go, *they* go." He touched his belt, then turned and patted the shoulder of the dead pilot. "You needn't worry, Captain. Viktor shall bring us down safely."

Viktor turned and gazed through the window. "Given current wind conditions, I think it's best we approach from the north." His serious blue eyes studied the terrain. "Return to the cabin, secure yourself, and speak a prayer. The events of the next three minutes will determine our fate."

•   •   •

Sergey rubbed his clammy hands, but still they continued to sweat. He stared out the cabin window. The earth was rising quickly. Flashes of green caught the corner of his eye. Suddenly, a field of blue appeared. The lake, climbing insanely fast. His ears filled with the sick sound of a whining engine. The cabin shuddered.

Sergey gripped the arms of his chair and shut his eyes tight as a vice. It was all happening too quickly. It hardly seemed real. He could feel the drag, the jet slowing severely.

"Airspeed reduced," Viktor's voice called out from the cockpit, surprisingly indifferent to their impending ruin. How could the man be so calm? Sergey wondered. It was as if his sense of fear had been surgically removed. He was inhuman.

Sergey's mind continued to race. He couldn't help but think that bailing out by parachute and allowing the plane to crash would have been safer. But terrestrial wreckage could be found and inspected,

Andrei had explained. Bodies recovered and counted. Their *mafiya* controllers would soon come to realize they had been double-crossed, their stolen diamonds stolen in turn. Andrei insisted that to guarantee success, the plane must never be found. Which meant putting it in the water. Somewhere remote. Somewhere inaccessible.

The engines suddenly wailed, the thrust reverser system engaged, and they now fought the plane's momentum. The cabin vibrated so intensely Sergey could feel the pressure in his chest.

"Wings level, nose up," Viktor called out.

Sergey squeezed the armrest tighter. His fingertips numbed.

"Brace for impact!"

A foolish plan! He should never have agreed!

Sergey expected a splash, but when the plane impacted, it hit with the sound and feel of crushing metal. Someone let out a low, guttural cry, Fedor possibly. But Sergey couldn't be sure. He had no visual of his friends, only the backs of their seats. And in the confusion of the impact, the cabin had seemed to turn gray, distinct shapes becoming blurs. There came a high-pitched whir, so loud that Sergey felt as if he had been sucked into the heart of a terrible machine.

Another cry, and the cabin tilted at a severe angle, followed by a tremendous jolt. There was a sudden loss of momentum and Sergey jerked forward, then upward, his seatbelt cutting deep into his gut. A cacophony of shredding steel, and the hiss of rushing water filled him with panic. Within seconds, a chill gush swallowed his entire body. Movement stopped, and for an instant he felt weightless, suspended in an icy cocoon.

A foolish plan!

He heard activity, others screaming out a confusion of words.

Sergey's eyes squinted against something blue, something bright, and he quickly realized he was staring at the sky above him through a massive tear in the fuselage. His eyes darted left, then right as he tried to get a sense of his surroundings. Everywhere, the gargle of roiling water filled the cabin. The plane had become a sinking ship, with jets of water spraying in through breaches in its metal hull.

A new wave of panic seized him. He had to free himself.

He clawed at his seatbelt, but the frigid water had numbed his fingers, and he couldn't feel distinctly enough to locate the buckle. Desperately he pulled at the strap, but his effort seemed only to tighten it. Water rose above his chest. He could hear voices, now coming from outside the fuselage: Andrei and the others. No doubt preparing to assist him.

He fought to hold back a growing sense of dizziness.

Water slapped at him from every direction, rising to his neck, brutally cold. He heard his comrades' voices becoming fainter, more distant, his name being called in anguish. Water rose over Sergey's head, forcing him to lunge for a final breath of air. Completely submerged, his arms flailed above him. He clawed uselessly at the bitter currents.

He was sinking with the plane! The thought jolted him with terror.

With greater effort, he fought the restraint, clutching the strap with both hands, pulling, stretching. But still it clung to his waist, ensnaring him as if possessed of a wicked mind. All around water thrashed and bubbles rose. Then, his lungs starved for air, Sergey was overcome by a strange sense of calm. In his exhaustion, he was transported back to his homeland—to his beloved Russia. He was a child again, his beautiful mother sponging him in a basin of soapy water. Bubbles everywhere. She spoke, and he laughed. Her voice was like a sweet melody. *Mother, I have come home.*

Something solid crushed against Sergey's skull, and his senses returned. He stared up through a tear in the fuselage and saw the scattered light of a blue sky. Yet it seemed distant and unreachable, protected by an immense barrier of water. And as he gaped skyward, his body sinking deeper into the abyss, his vision darkened, then darkened still more, until all that remained above him was a canvass of icy black.

The last of Sergey's air escaped his lungs, tiny bubbles rising in the darkness. His chest tightened, and as his mind faded into unconsciousness, a final thought occurred to him: *It had been a foolish plan.*

3

"MOMMY'LL BE THERE soon, sweetheart," Becky Ford said, reaffirming a promise to her daughter Gracie. "Grandma will keep you company till I get there. It'll be later tonight, but don't worry, I *will* be there." Becky listened to her daughter rave about the hospital's macaroni and cheese, then said a painful goodbye. She ended the call and swiped away a tear. Gracie was only eight, but already she had endured more surgeries and hospital stays than most people experience in a lifetime. It broke Becky's heart.

A shadow rose behind her. She turned, sensing a presence.

"You all right, Beck?" It was Hank, a close friend and the show's safety and survival consultant. He studied her with kind, hazel-green eyes.

She forced a smile. "I've had better days."

"Allow me to play Sherlock, if you don't mind." He rested a hand upon her shoulder. "Seeing as you got a phone in your hand and a tear in your eye, I'd say you been talking to an angel."

Becky's smile turned genuine.

"How's Gracie feeling?"

"Surgery is in twenty-four hours, so naturally she's nervous, but she puts on a tough act."

"Did you give her my love?"

"I always do," she said. "And speaking of giving," Becky narrowed her eyes, "Gracie asked when you're bringing her a chipmunk."

"Oh she did, did she?"

"You didn't promise her a chipmunk, did you?"

Hank pulled off his Mariners cap and scratched his head. He was a tall man with a thick build, in his early fifties, and Becky was sure he was good-looking—if only he would shave off his heavy beard and prove it.

"Well, did you?"

"Guilty as charged."

"Hank, you can't promise Gracie something like that. Where would I ever keep a chipmunk?"

"Well, those kinds of critters need open space, plenty of it, and a forest of trees to scamper about in. Tell her as soon as she talks her mommy into giving up the city and moving out old Hank's way, I'll have a hundred of 'em waiting for her."

Becky smiled. Hank always had a way of lifting her spirits. She turned to the helicopter. The crew had finished loading the last of the production equipment, and still Cody was nowhere to be found.

As if sensing her thoughts, Hank said, "Maybe that mollycoddled boss of yours will be a no-show. Then you and I can head into town for a porterhouse."

"I wouldn't count on him not showing," she said. "And remember, he's your boss, too."

"Only on paper, Beck." Hank gazed out over the mountains. "Over the next seven days, out there in the bush, J. Codwell Hobbs III is just another know-nothing, spoiled rich kid." He shook his head. "Jesus, these Hollywood types."

The blare of a car horn ended their wonderings. Becky looked in the distance, where she could see Cody's Hummer fishtailing from around a stand of lodgepole pine, bumping along a rutted road. Its cherry metallic shell glinted under the autumnal sunlight. In an explosion of speed, the vehicle accelerated and made a beeline for the helicopter before skidding to a stop at the edge of the clearing. The car doors opened and a giggly group of blondes spilled out from the interior. Cody Hobbs, host of the reality television show, *The Survivalist*, emerged from the driver's side and quickly joined the mess of fur-lined hoodies and silicone implants. His red-rimmed eyes and pale complexion betrayed a sleepless night.

Becky rolled her eyes. Like Hank, she wasn't a fan of Cody. In her estimation, he was little more than a self-absorbed Englishman with an exaggerated Oxbridge accent. In front of the camera, he worked tirelessly to cultivate a bold and fearless image. Tall, lean, and athletically built, he looked every bit the rugged outdoorsman. But looks, Becky knew, could be misleading, and in the case of J. Codwell Hobbs III, they were outright lies.

"I don't get the guy," Hank said. "We're gearing up for a week's stint into some of the most inhospitable terrain on the face of the planet, and he arrives as if late for a bachelor party."

Cody broke from the pack of she-wolves and jogged over. A grin displayed a rack of white teeth. "Hank, Becky my dear, let's begin this adventure, shall we?"

Becky gestured to the women. "Looks to me like the adventure's already in full swing."

Cody smiled knowingly and turned to regard Hank. "Seems we're in for an exciting jaunt, wouldn't you say, old boy?"

"If that's Hollywood speak for we got a week of hard living ahead of us, then yes, I'd say so."

"Well, it's perspective, isn't it? Where one man sees hard living," he swept his hand to indicate the distant peaks, "another man sees salvation."

"I have no idea what that even means, Codwell."

Becky interrupted, "The production crew is on Chopper One en route to the drop-zone to set up base camp and the opening shot. You and Hank should get moving."

"Indeed," Cody said. "Oh, and I know this may come as a bit of a surprise, last minute and all, but you'll be accompanying us, as well, Becky."

Becky thought she misheard. "I'm sorry?"

"Into the field," Cody said. "You'll be coming."

"Now is not the time for jokes."

"No joke, you're coming along."

"No, we've talked about this," Becky said. "Gracie's in the hospital, another surgery scheduled. This time I'm going to be there for her. I promised her. Besides, you and I agreed I would produce from the studio now."

"A slight change of plans, I'm afraid. I'll need your assistance in the field one more time, until I can find a suitable replacement for you."

"A replacement? What on earth are you talking about? Maloney's my replacement. I'm off-site, studio only. We've had this discussion."

"I've reconsidered," Cody said unapologetically. "This is the shoot for the season finale. It's too important. We must come with our A-game." He turned and gazed toward the helicopter, as if considering something else. "Becky, did you gather my essentials?"

"No, of course not. Why would I? It's Maloney's job now."

Cody's eyes widened. "What! You left something of such import up to Maloney?" He hurried toward the helicopter's open cargo hold, where a production intern with a clipboard was double-checking inventory. Hank and Becky followed.

"Be a gent," Cody said to the intern, "and drive the ladies back to town and park the hummer at the hotel." He tossed him his keys. "And have the interior cleaned and detailed, if you don't mind. A messy night, if you know what I mean."

The intern stared at the keys and shrugged before shuffling away.

"Cody, talk to me," Becky said. "What's going on?"

Cody turned his attention back to the cargo hold and began shifting aside cases until he found his personal pack.

"Maloney's my replacement," Becky repeated. "He left earlier with the crew. In fact, they're probably already on location."

"Yes, but the boy is not my new field producer. His experience is in fitness reality, not survival. He'll need a little in-the-field training. He's been demoted to your assistant."

"He'll have to learn without me."

"I met with him yesterday morning, and may I say, the boy possesses a wit as sharp as a football—British, of course, not that dreadful American thing. And besides, he's Irish of all races, a detestable lot."

Hank interrupted, "Cody, be reasonable. Beck's got Gracie to think about. That little girl will be under the scalpel in a few hours. Beck can't afford to make this trip. She's out."

Cody glared. "She can't afford not to. She's out when I say she's out."

"We had an agreement," Becky said calmly. "As far as I'm concerned, this discussion is over."

Cody ignored her objection. "For the season finale, I'll be taking the show in a new direction, and so I need someone who understands my vision, who has a creative eye and a knack for framing the shot. In short, Becky, I need you...not some half-witted Irishman."

"Well I'm sorry, but you're going to have to do

without me, in the field anyway. I can't afford to leave for a week at a time anymore. Gracie comes first."

"Yes, of course, Gracie." Cody paused and chewed at his lip, calculating in his mind. "You must think of your daughter. Have you considered the cost of medical bills? Without the renewal of your insurance I'd imagine them to be obscene."

"What are you talking about? Why wouldn't my insurance be renewed?"

"If I'm not mistaken, your insurance is paid contingent upon your employment with the studio?"

"Yes...so?"

"So connect the dots. No employment, no insurance."

"No employment?" Becky said incredulously. "You've got to be kidding me."

Cody zipped open his personal pack and began scanning its contents. "See, this is what I'm talking about." He jerked out a box of nutrition bars. "I specifically asked for the Lara brand. They're unprocessed and all-natural. Maloney brought me these imposters." He stared at the box and scoffed. "How can I be expected to perform optimally without the proper fuel? Becky, you never would have made this mistake."

Despite her efforts to remain calm, Becky felt her face beginning to flush. She wanted to take Cody's so-called *imposters* and cram them down his throat. "They're just snacks, for crying out loud. Snacks!"

Cody tossed them back into his pack.

"Plus I don't have the necessary winter gear,"

Becky said. "That alone prevents me from going."

"Already considered and taken care of," Cody said. "I phoned earlier and sent an intern into town, had her pick up everything you'll need."

Becky looked to Hank. The muscles in his jaw had tightened, but he, too, was at a loss for words. "Are you seriously going to threaten me with my job over this?"

Cody zipped up his pack, tossed it to the back of the hold, then turned to Becky. His expression was grim. "I'm sorry, Becky, but this is business. If you're unwilling to accommodate my needs, then I see no other alternative."

Her mind jarred by Cody's sick ultimatum, Becky turned and began walking away.

"Beck, wait," Hank called out after her. "Where you going?"

"Into the wild, apparently," she called back pulling her cell phone from her pocket. "But first I have a little heart to break."

4

ICY WIND HOWLED through the open cabin door. The helicopter pitched and yawed against intermittent gales. Working the control stick, the pilot fought to steady the aircraft, and in a momentary lull, he shouted back over the shriek of the rotors, "No better time than the present, Mr. Hobbs! If ever you're going to jump, I'd suggest you do it now!"

Despite the chaos around her, Becky couldn't shake the pain of disappointing Gracie. Thankfully, at Becky's request, her mother had agreed to take care of her for the week. Still, Becky knew, it wouldn't be the same to Gracie. And it sure as heck wouldn't make up for a broken promise.

Another gale buffeted the chopper. The cabin quaked.

Taking a long, resolving breath, Becky stared across the cabin at Cody, who was bundled in an orange jumpsuit, body harness, and parachute pack. Reaching base camp by dropping in from five thousand feet was his favorite way to open an episode.

"Kick it off with drama," he often lectured the scene coordinators. "The audience needs to know I have balls. It's my willingness to take risks that make them love me."

Shouldering a Sony Betacam, the cameraman signaled Cody, who moved into position and grasped the door's safety rail. Carefully, he turned to face the camera. His dark eyes bulged beneath the lenses of his safety goggles. Wind whipped at his hair. His nostrils flared from the influx of deep breaths.

With three fingers, the cameraman counted down, "Three, two, one, and action!"

Cody peered steely-eyed into the lens and bellowed over the tumult of wind and rotor blades. "I'm a mile above the rugged mountains of the Canadian Rockies, one of the most remote and inhospitable regions on the face of the planet, a wilderness untouched by man."

Becky glanced at Hank, who had turned away from Cody's monologue to gaze pensively out the window. Becky knew it bothered him to hear Cody play up his fraudulent role as a seasoned outdoorsman.

"Over the next seven days," Cody continued, maintaining his granite stare, "I shall venture west into terra incognita, across treacherous terrain, at the mercy of the rugged backcountry. There, I will be forced to endure tortuous elements and overcome unforeseen dangers, many of which in years past have claimed the lives of less-accomplished explorers."

Hank moaned, shook his head.

"With minimal supplies and no food or water, I shall be forced to rely solely upon my acute natural instincts and expert survival skills. My iron will and superior conditioning will carry the day!"

Becky squeezed Hank's forearm. When he turned from the window, she winked.

"And I invite you," Cody announced, "my loyal viewers, to come along with me for an adventure of a lifetime!" His face a mask of courage, he made the sign of the cross and turned to the open door, wind whipping at his hair and jumpsuit. He tightened his grasp on the safety rail and crouched in preparation to jump.

"Cut!" the cameraman cried.

In an instant, Cody fell back from the door to the safety of the inner-cabin and sank into a seat across from Becky and Hank. His breathing was labored. "Bloody hell, that wind is cold!"

"And it's beginning to gust heavier!" the pilot shouted back.

The cameraman motioned to the rear of the cabin, and James Kilpatrick, Cody's stunt double, bound forward and took his position at the door. He turned to mimic Cody's last position.

A strong gale buffeted the helicopter. It pitched violently. Becky could hear supply cases sliding and toppling in the hold.

The pilot struggled with the control stick. "I recommend we postpone the jump, Mr. Hobbs!"

Cody waved a hand to dismiss the pilot's warning. "Out of the question. This is fantastic. The heavy winds will add texture to the shot."

The pilot glanced back incredulously. "You've got one minute, then I'm putting this bird on the ground!"

The cameraman looked to Cody, who gave him a quick nod, then turned back to Kilpatrick and once again held up three fingers. "Three, two, one, rolling!"

In a cat-like burst, Kilpatrick leapt through the door.

Becky watched through the window as he twisted and tumbled earthbound. Strong winds swept his body violently askew. He struggled. A tense moment passed before he was able to right himself and become horizontal again.

Becky's eye followed Kilpatrick's fluorescent form as it streaked earthward, a blemish of orange against a stark gray mountainside. Then, in a rainbow of color, his chute deployed, jerking him vertical. He tugged at the steering line as wind swept him toward a distant prairie, where the remainder of the production crew were gathered waiting. Marshal Leonard, the field videographer, stood in miniature, filming the jump from below. After a series of adjustments, Kilpatrick hit the ground and rolled, his multicolored chute billowing around him.

Wind thrashed the helicopter, and its tail swung in a wide arc. Becky's attention quickly returned to the cabin. Frigid air whistled through its interior.

"I'm putting her down!" the pilot called back before rapidly descending.

Becky's stomach lurched from the sudden drop in elevation. Momentarily, she felt a sense of weightlessness before her body jolted forward in the seat. Her restraint tugged violently against her waist.

A feeling of dread unsettled her.

She grabbed Hank's arm as a psychological lifeline and closed her eyes, wishing she were on the ground.

Hank took her hand, trying to reassure her.

Then as suddenly as the tumultuous winds began, they eased, and the helicopter righted itself and glided earthbound.

Moments later, relaxed and nearing the landing site, Becky observed the production crew's hurried activity. She spoke a silent prayer and thought of Gracie. Seven days in the wilderness, a piece of cake. She'd done it many times before. Seven days and she'd be home looking after her girl. *Seven days.*

Hank squeezed her hand as if knowing her thoughts. "Don't you worry any, Beck. Gracie's strong. She'll hold tough till you get back."

Becky smiled, and the chopper touched ground as if punctuating Hank's promise. The rotors' pitch lowered as the pilot began powering down.

Seven days, Becky thought again.

Piece of cake.

5

The drop-zone was an expansive montane prairie fringed with aspen and lodgepole pine. Already past midday, the sun was low in the sky, casting a golden half-light over the thick blanket of trees that rose sharply to distant peaks. The heavy winds had died, and now only a cool breeze stirred the prairie's creeping wintergreen. In the majesty of it all, Becky felt insignificant. Her problems, too, insignificant. Worlds away from doctors and sterile-smelling hospital rooms, it was the kind of place she could lose herself and her problems.

"Becky?" Cody's voice dispelled her wistful reverie, and she swallowed painfully and thought of Gracie. A pang of guilt wrenched at her gut. What right did she have to wish escape from her problems when Gracie, alone and afraid in the hospital, was unable to escape hers? What kind of mother was she? Becky wondered bitterly.

"Becky?" Cody's voice sounded again, turning

her head. "You *are* a part of this production, are you not?" Becky could see Cody had gathered the crew, each member standing quietly in a line.

She joined next to Hank.

After a moment of dramatic contemplation, Cody began pacing the line, fingertips steepled at his mouth. At length he stopped center, took an exaggerated step back, and spread his hands. "Make no mistake about it," he began, "in terms of artistry, indeed, in terms of ratings, this episode must exceed in quality all that have come before it. But for me to accomplish this task, I will need each and every one of you to perform at your best."

Having heard Cody's spiel before, Becky tuned out. While he droned on about the importance of commitment, she turned her gaze toward the western peaks, where distant clouds scudded in strange relief. They were amassing quickly, thick and silvery gray. The National Weather Service was tracking the first major storm system of the season, and although the skies above the prairie remained a brilliant blue, over the next twenty-four hours, all was sure to change.

"But already I've witnessed complacency and mediocrity," Cody was saying. "And those attributes I simply will not tolerate."

The crew glanced about. Marshal Leonard shrugged. Tasha, his wife and the show's video and sound coordinator, spoke up. "Mediocrity? We arrived here hours ago, double-checked inventory, and erected base camp. All ahead of schedule, I might add. What exactly are you talking about, mediocrity?"

"Oh, sure you've completed the routine, mundane tasks, Mrs. Leonard. Square pegs in square holes, so to speak. Trained orangutans could have accomplished as much. No, I'm referring to the opening shot." Cody gestured to Kilpatrick.

"Me? What did I do?"

"Your jump, Mr. Kilpatrick. I've viewed the ground reel, and I must say your attempt was clumsy and amateurish."

"Clumsy and amateurish? You kidding me, I never should have made the jump in the first place. You were up there, you saw the conditions, the dangerous winds."

"Precisely, Mr. Kilpatrick," Cody answered, meeting his stare. "There were dangerous winds. Don't you see? The environment provided you an opportunity to exploit the shot. You should have fought the currents, stretched the viewers' feelings of suspense, aroused within them a visceral response. You should have forced the question: would Cody Hobbs, the survivalist, right himself in time? Or would he plunge to certain doom? But instead you lost your head and like an amateur panicked and pulled the ripcord far too soon, without even a hint of drama."

"Hey, wait a minute," Marshal said. "You can't be serious. Rule number one is safety first."

"I'll make the rules if you don't mind, Mr. Leonard. And I'll remind you that in *The Survivalist*'s six seasons, the number of viewers has steadily grown—in no small part because of my ever-evolving vision of the show. Therefore, all of you would do well to quiet your objections and heed my advice."

There was grumbling from the crew.

"This is not open for debate," Cody added. "I am, however, willing to forgive and forget, but from here on out I expect a renewed sense of commitment from each of you. *The show comes first.* That must be our new rule number one!"

Hank said, "Way to rally the troops there, Codwell. I'd love to hear more, but we got a heavy storm approaching, and I'd like to review safety procedures with these folks before it gets too late. Afterwards, you and me need to talk."

"Yes, certainly," Cody said. "Do what you must with them. When you're finished you'll find me in the Bubble."

•   •   •

The "Bubble," far from the frail sphere its name suggested, was in fact a state-of-the-art, cuben-fiber reinforced portable shelter, a six-meter geodesic dome engineered to withstand the planet's most extreme environments. Stocked with food, water, medical supplies, and backup production equipment, it served as a base of operations from which the film crew ventured out. During week-long shoots, two production interns and a medical officer remained behind ready to respond to emergencies. Outside of it were four smaller portable domes used in the field by the crew.

Inside the Bubble, Hank and Cody stood at a center table, a topographical area map pinned at its center.

"...and that, in my opinion, is the most favorable route," Hank was saying. "It should take about seven days to reach the extraction point."

Cody peered down at the map suspiciously. "Yes, I trust the route will be a splendid one. What really concerns me are the scenes. All of my criteria must be met. I trust that you saw to it?"

Hank produced an index card from a coat pocket and consulted its contents. "You mean like this one here, triggering an avalanche?"

"That's one, yes."

"In that case, no, not all your criteria will be met. Some of it is just plain foolhardy."

Cody's expression darkened. "Oh, rubbish, Hank. I'll have you know each scene you see there has been thoroughly researched and safety approved by my own pre-production experts."

"Researched and approved by experts, huh? By that you mean you and those necktie producers of yours? What, you fellows met at Starbucks and Googled all this?"

"Excuse me, but Googling is a verified method of research."

"Oh good heavens, Cody."

"Rather than cast dispersions, perhaps you care to elaborate on the problem."

Hank looked again at the index card. "Okay, I have a concern or two."

"Which is it," Cody said impatiently, "one concern or two?"

Hank peered at Cody with narrowed eyes. "It's as many as I decide to get off my chest."

"Very well, quickly then," Cody said, paddling a hand.

"First, you wrote here you want to film an avalanche *escape*. What exactly do you mean by *escape*?"

"I should think the word is elementary. Shall I define it for you?"

Hank's glare turned menacing. "You'd best watch all that smart-ass spilling from your mouth, Codwell. You may get away with it with the folks outside, but with me it won't stand. I hear any more of it and you're liable to get taken to task on your survival skills."

Cody shrank back.

"We clear, Codwell?"

"Yes, of course, we're clear. Just tell me what it is that worries you?"

"Are you planning to have Kilpatrick flee from an avalanche?"

"Indeed I am. I would think it the most dramatic segment of the entire production. We'll build events, with it as the climax."

"You'd best think again," Hank said. "I won't subject a man to that kind of danger."

Cody was nodding agreeably. "A sound policy, usually, but in this case the finale demands it. I need a thrilling, climactic scene, one that will draw my audience to the edge of their seats, that will steal the very air from their lungs and make them yearn for next season's premiere."

"And so your brilliant idea was to trigger an avalanche, with Kilpatrick in its crosshairs."

"Would it be dangerous otherwise?"

Hank laughed mirthlessly. "My God, Codwell, that's madness. Have you any idea what'll result?"

"An Emmy nomination, I should think."

Hank was having a difficult time listening to Cody rationalize his bullshit. The Englishman had always been one to push the envelope, but this was madness, even for him. Hank took a calming breath and said, "You would seriously risk a man's life for a worthless award?"

"Not just any man, a highly trained Hollywood stuntman." Cody raised an index finger for emphasis. "It's what he does."

"There're lines you can't cross, even for a stuntman, and this cockamamie idea of yours is one of them."

Cody thought for a moment. His expression was one of false deliberation. "Well, Hank, I appreciate your input on the matter. It's what I pay you for, after all, but regrettably I must reject your assessment. This is well within the limits of Kilpatrick's skill set."

"C'mon, you have any idea what getting caught under tons of driving rock and snow will do to him?"

"Bury him, I presume?"

"Bury him, alright. Lacerations, ruptured spleen, fractured skull and all."

"Now wait just a minute. I read somewhere that mimicking a freestyle swimming stroke in the midst of an avalanche will prevent such an occurrence. Suffocation is the real culprit."

"You read that, did you? And you believed it?"

"All we'll need to do is dig him out quickly, pat him on the back for his efforts."

Hank's jaw tightened. Reasoning with this fool was pointless. He was getting nowhere. He decided to take a new tack. "Anyway, this discussion is irrelevant. We don't have the means to trigger a slide, even if we wanted to. You need a concussive force. And you yodeling at the top of a mountain ain't gonna do it."

"As I've explained," Cody said smugly, "I've looked into the matter."

"What's that supposed to mean?"

"It means I understand how to trigger an avalanche, theoretically that is, and I've come prepared to do just that."

"What are you saying, Codwell? That you brought along explosives?"

His expression went from smug to downright cocky. "Indeed, a brace of four two-kilogram charges, each double fused to ensure detonation. I can hardly contain my excitement."

At the mention of the charges Hank's blood ran cold. He could scarcely believe what he was hearing. This idiot was going to get 'em all killed! It was time, Hank now realized, to drop the hammer and simply forbid it. Period. End of discussion. "Listen to me carefully, Codwell," he said. "It's simply too risky. I won't allow it. I want whatever it is you brought with you, and I want it now. Any explosives or other dangerous paraphernalia are going to be stored here in the Bubble. None of it goes with us. You got that?"

Cody paused as though considering Hanks objection, then rapped his knuckles on the table. "I'm going to have to pull rank and override you, old boy. The avalanche escape is a non-negotiable, I'm afraid."

Hank guffawed. "A non-negotiable?"

"Yes, a non-negotiable. Figure out a way to make it happen."

"Well, it ain't gonna happen, at least not under my supervision it ain't."

The door unzipped and a chill breeze blew inside. Candi Hammett, Cody's busty, hand-picked production intern, slipped inside clutching a large makeup case. She tapped its top. "Time to prep for the landing shot, Mr. Hobbs. Marshal and Tasha are filming B-roll in the forest. They say the light will be perfect in about half an hour. They would like you ready."

"Certainly, darling." Cody ran his fingers through his hair. "I was thinking something tousled yet sexy." He turned back to Hank. "What do you say we revisit this later?"

"Far as I'm concerned, it's already settled," Hank said. "Those charges are to be in my hands within the hour. If they're not, I'm scrapping the entire production." He put on his sunglasses and ducked out of the Bubble.

6

TASHA LEONARD WALKED along the forest fringe, among dormant stands of buffaloberry, passing between thin shafts of sunlight. Casually she would stop briefly, then start again, studying the environment in deep contemplation.

Shouldering a camera, Marshal followed a few feet behind her. His eyes traced the curves of her body. It was amazing how well her figure revealed itself through three layers of clothing. She was slender, yet possessed an ample bosom. Marshal licked his lips.

"Here will be our best angle, I should think," Tasha finally announced. A faint accent still betrayed her Bulgarian origins. Marshal had met, courted, and married her three years ago while filming an HBO special in Eastern Europe. A year later, they arrived in Los Angeles, where they both landed jobs on *The Survivalist*.

She pointed in the distance. "From long we'll capture the prairie and landing zone through tree-filtered sunlight, then tighten on Cody as he collects his parachute."

"That's one option," Marshal said. "Or we could hold off a few minutes and find something else to keep us busy." He set the camera on the forest floor and began unbuckling his belt.

Tasha turned and blinked. "What are you doing?"

"Thought we might make a movie of our own."

"We're not screwing, if that's what you think."

Marshal turned up his palms, letting his belt dangle from his waist. "Why not? No one's around."

"We have work to do."

"That's a lame reason."

"Why do I need a reason," Tasha said. "You ever hear of a woman's right to choose?"

"Right to choose?" Marshal repeated. "I'm pretty sure that applies to a decision you might have to make *after* the screwing."

"I'm just not in the mood. What more reason do I need?"

"That's always your excuse. Christ, Tasha, we've been married three years and I can count the number of times we've done it on two hands. I'm a man, a young man, I have needs."

"What you need is to stop the whining, pick up your camera and prep for the shot."

"Oh, come on...is there no changing your mind?"

But there came no answer. Tasha had already turned and was walking in the direction of base camp.

•　　•　　•

James Kilpatrick stood at the center of the prairie unfolding his chute. Wind slapped at the nylon fabric, hampering his efforts. He had paused his work to flex the chill out of his fingers when he noticed Hank approaching.

"What do you say, Hank?" Kilpatrick called out above the wind. "Ready for the fun to begin?" He liked Hank, who was always friendly to him and did his job well.

Hank nodded to the chute. "Didn't I see you pack that earlier?"

"You did, but they need me back in the harness for additional footage. The plan is to film me from behind, fighting the chute against the wind. Tasha says she needs it for continuity, or some such nonsense."

"That was quite a jump you made earlier. Risky."

Kilpatrick grinned. "Well, they tell me I'm the stuntman."

"You could have been killed. Think maybe you should have delayed the jump?"

Kilpatrick's answer was a rehearsed one: "I do what the boss says. Bills to pay, a family to support. You know how it is."

Hank nodded. "Speaking of family, how're Patty and the girls?"

"Never been better," Kilpatrick said. He'd yet to mention the news of Patty's pregnancy to anyone outside the family, but he knew Hank would be genuinely pleased. "Patty and I are expecting."

"Expecting what?" Then the light went on in Hank's eyes and he grinned. "Why you devil," Hank said, slapping Kilpatrick on the shoulder. "What are you going to have?"

"Definitely not sex," Kilpatrick said laughing, "at least not for seven or eight more months."

Hank grinned. "Okay, but dopey humor aside, a fourth little princess, maybe?"

"Not according to the ultrasound. Doc says the girls are going to have a little brother. It'll be three against one."

"Well, I'll be. Finally a little stuntman. Congratulations. When you see Patty, give her my blessing."

"I'll be sure to," Kilpatrick said, and then he noticed the darkening clouds on the horizon. "So the storm, is that what you wanted to talk to me about?"

"An uncomfortable few nights, but we'll get through it," Hank said. "No, the storm's second on my list of worries."

"Then what's first?"

"I'd like to talk to you about Hobbs."

"The boss, eh?"

"I'm concerned he's pushing some of the crew too hard. You especially."

Kilpatrick wasn't going to argue the point. He knew Hank was right. It seemed each outing Cody was asking him to perform greater and more dangerous stunts.

"You're a stuntman, not a crash-test dummy.

The man has no right asking you to take unnecessary risks. Like that jump. We could just as easily have waited for conditions to improve."

"Cody doesn't like delays."

"The delay will be permanent if one of us gets badly injured or killed."

"Maybe so, but what do I say to the man who signs my paychecks."

"You say no," Hank said. "There's a limit to how much you have to risk. I just hope when the time comes, you'll recognize that limit."

"Look, Hank, I understand your concern, and I appreciate it. I really do. But at the same time I have mouths to feed. I can't afford to get on the man's bad side."

Hank's eyes showed a reluctant understanding.

"You needn't worry. I'll be careful."

The shriek of a whistle interrupted their conversation. They turned to see Becky standing near the Bubble, waving her arms. She used a whistle to signal the start of a shoot. The crew ceased activity and began gathering on the prairie.

"Guess I better get ready," Kilpatrick said.

"Guess you'd better. Just be safe."

Kilpatrick slapped Hank's shoulder. "Don't think what you've said is unappreciated, because it's not. I'll be fine." He smiled and resumed unpacking his chute.

•   •   •

Becky stood shoulder to shoulder with Cody, studying the master scene card. A newly scribbled notation in the margin caught her attention. It was written in Cody's hand. "What's this about a snow cave?" she asked, looking up at him.

"Yes, a brilliant idea, came to me during makeup. I thought why not use the approaching storm to our advantage. It's sure to drop an abundance of snow."

"So your first thought was to dig a snow cave?"

"No, my first thought was Ms. Hammett's breasts. Natural or artificial? My second thought was the snow cave."

"Let's keep this professional?" Becky said.

"Whatever you say, love."

"Okay, so you want a snow cave?"

"Yes, is that a problem?"

"I shouldn't think so. I'll run it by Hank."

The wind carried the voices of Tasha and Marshal from the prairie. Becky could hear them instructing Kilpatrick.

Becky said to Cody, "Do you have a monologue in mind, or do I need to write something up?"

"Already written."

"Okay, then, I'll discuss it with Hank, see if there are any logistical problems, then get back with you."

"Quiet on the set!" Tasha called out. "And action!"

Becky watched on as Kilpatrick fought against the wind, collecting his chute among the prairie's wildflowers. Gusts dragged him like a ragdoll.

"And cut! That's a keeper!" Tasha hollered. "Cody, You're up!"

Cody flipped open a pocket mirror and checked his teeth. "Be a dear and fetch me a granola bar, would you Becky?" With a smile, he jogged away toward the crew.

•   •   •

Filming had finished by mid-afternoon. Strong westerly winds stirred up earlier than expected, pushing the storm nearer to base camp. Inside his dome, Cody reclined on a sleeping bag draped over a thick layer of memory foam. At his side was a humming generator, and to it attached a portable monitor running dailies. His eyes studied the tiny image of Kilpatrick as he struggled to pack his parachute. His movements were too jerky and his shoulders appeared unnecessarily rounded. A most unflattering look, Cody thought, a look his viewers would attribute to him. He made a mental note to discuss posture with the man.

From somewhere in the distance came a deep boom that Cody could feel resonating in his chest. The light of a small lamp showed the tent shuddering. He flipped on a small pocket radio and adjusted the tuner. Among the static he could hear frequent popping and crackling, a telltale sign the storm was almost upon them—and heavy with lightning.

Lightning. Cody tensed at the thought.

Of all nature's dangerous phenomenon, lightning he loathed the most. Cold could be remedied with heaters; rain with Gore-Tex; animals with rocks and knives. But lightning, lightning was an altogether different threat. Sure, by favoring some terrain and avoiding others, he could decrease his chances of being struck, but in the end, it all came down to probability. Dumb luck.

Cody dismissed the thought and continued his study of the film.

A light rain began to fall. Its pit-a-pat beat played in concert to the rhythm of intermittent winds. But it was the sudden unzipping of the door that pulled his eyes away from the monitor.

From a gray silhouette resolved the figure of Tasha Leonard. She zipped the door closed.

"Mrs. Leonard, you startled me." Cody erected himself.

Tasha turned and lowered the hood of her jacket.

Cody said, "I realize we're far from civilization, but I should still think it proper to announce your presence with a rap."

"My apologies."

"In any event, I'm glad you're here. I'd like a word with you concerning your behavior this afternoon during my address to the crew."

"In fact," Tasha said, "that's why I've come."

"Ah, yes, guilt?"

"Unbearable guilt."

"Then you admit questioning my criticisms were grossly inappropriate?"

"Of course."

"Excellent, you're learning," Cody said. "You

must remember that I am the creative force behind this enterprise, and my opinions are beyond reproach.

Tasha lowered her eyes. "I don't know what came over me."

"When I brought you on board, I did so expecting that you'd heed my advice."

"And I have."

"Yet you spoke out against me."

"It was impulsive, a mistake. I see that now." Tasha removed her jacket and knelt at Cody's bedside.

He reached out and stroked her silky hair. "Perhaps we can attribute your poor judgment to the environment. This insufferable cold can make a person act foolishly."

"Yes, and do things they may later come to regret."

"Indeed." Cody rested a hand on Tasha's knee.

There came a prolonged silence before the two exchanged wry smiles.

"I wasn't expecting you until much later, my dear."

"The storm is moving quickly. I didn't want it to prevent my coming."

"And Marshal?"

"Cleaning lenses and inventorying equipment. He believes I'm scouting camera angles."

Cody smiled and slid his hand gently up her inner thigh. "And your earlier insubordination, it won't happen again?"

"Certainly not." With a slow and seductive

parting of the legs, she mounted Cody. "No question, I was a naughty girl."

"Yes, indeed, very naughty."

Tasha lifted her sweater to reveal firm, alabaster breasts. "Now, how do you intend to punish me?"

•　　•　　•

"If Cody were to build a snow shelter," Becky was asking Hank, "would you suggest a quinzee or a trench?" The two were in the Bubble discussing tomorrow's itinerary. Samantha, the medical officer busied herself organizing the base camp's medical supplies, while Maloney and Kilpatrick sat eating noodles from steaming tins, engaged in quiet conversation. The spice of their ramen filled the air.

"I would think a quinzee," she continued, "I'm not so sure he'd last in a trench."

Hank scratched his beard. "Codwell come up with a new idea for the finale?"

"He did."

"Were you aware he was planning to stage an avalanche?"

"Yes. I figured you'd veto that one."

"Were you aware he brought along explosives?"

Becky frowned. "No, I had no idea."

"Yeah, to trigger the avalanche." Hank's eyes darkened with anger. "For God's sake, the man's like a child poking a stick at a rattlesnake. He's oblivious to the realities of nature, lives in a Hollywood fantasy world. He's dangerous, Becky."

"I'll talk to him about the avalanche, explain

it's not going to happen."

"Damn right it's not gonna happen. Tell him he's a damn fool while you're at it."

Becky grinned. "I'll be sure to mention it. So what do you think? Would you suggest a quinzee or a trench? I should think a trench would be easier to make, just not so sure Cody would be comfortable in it."

Hank considered a moment. "Not comfortable, but dug out proper, he'd survive. It wouldn't be the Four Seasons, you know."

"Building a quinzee would make for a more dramatic visual."

"You sound like a producer."

"I still have to consider such things. It's my job."

"Then we'll show him how to build a quinzee," Hank said. "Have him do the work for a change."

"A fine idea," Becky said. "Plus, a hard night in a cold snow shelter might just be the kick in the rear he needs."

"Somehow," Hank said, "I doubt it'll be Cody getting kicked in the ass. He seems to think suffering is Kilpatrick's stock and trade. He'll be the one doing the overnight."

Heavy rain began raking the Bubble's windward exterior. Hank stared at the nylon wall, listening with his eyes as much his ears. "By the sound of things, the storm's arrived. When we reach subalpine tomorrow, he'll get his snow cave."

•   •   •

Tasha checked her hair in a pocket mirror. A bit tangled, but given the winds, Marshal would be none the wiser.

Cody was reclined on his bedroll, hands folded contently across his chest. "Be a dear would you and dim the lamplight on your way out. I have a big day ahead of me tomorrow, and I could use the extra sleep."

"Not so fast," Tasha said. "I need a story for Marshal. You know, in case he sees me leaving here."

"A story, right."

"I was thinking you and I were discussing changes to the upcoming itinerary."

"Whatever works," Cody said. "Go with it. Now, if you don't mind...."

Tasha's hands found her hips. "Well?"

"Well what?"

"I need details, in case Marshal asks. Have there been any changes?"

"To what?"

"To the itinerary," she said. "Haven't you been listening? I'll need to know details in case Marshal questions me. Have you made any additions or modifications?"

"Well, let's see. I added a snow cave scene."

"You're going to dig a snow cave?"

"And furnish it with a night vision camera—and Kilpatrick. Best my viewers see me hunkering down in a place of suffering. Certainly not in here. Imagine their horror if they saw where I actually resided?" He swept a hand, indicating his comfortable dome.

"Not a bad idea," Tasha said. "Are there any other changes? Anything at all?"

Cody thought. "No, not really."

"Oh, by the way, has Hank given you the coordinates to the extraction point?"

"He pointed out a ridge on the Bubble's topographical. I wasn't really paying attention."

"How about specific coordinates? He mention those?"

"You mean like longitude and latitude?"

"Yes."

"Why on Earth should I care about that? Hank knows where we're going and the extraction team knows where to pick us up. I have enough on my mind and shan't burden myself with the minutia. What's your worry, anyway? We'll get there."

Tasha regarded him with disappointment. She stood and zipped up her jacket. "No worries, just information to feed Marshal, should he ask where I've been."

"Right," Cody said. "Now, if you don't mind, I need my rest. And don't forget the lamplight."

•   •   •

When Becky emerged from her dome the following morning, she couldn't help but marvel at the landscape's dramatic transformation. Before her stretched yesterday's heathery cinquefoil and creeping wintergreen now dusted with powdery snow. Its beauty made Becky wish Gracie were here with her, healthy, to share in the experience. Before leaving for the extraction point, Becky would take advantage of the Bubble's satphone—since her own no longer received a signal—and call Gracie. It would be her only chance before striking out.

Becky smiled inwardly, glanced up and shielded her eyes against the glare of a stark white sky. She looked toward the higher distance—the day's destination. There, snow-covered spruce and fir gradually replaced lower elevation pine and aspen. Far above the treetops a red-tailed hawk turned lazy circles, its attention fixed on something below.

Stretching deeply and inhaling, Becky observed the camp, where already there had begun a flurry of activity. At the forest fringe, Tasha and Marshal were filming Kilpatrick at flank and rear angles. They had him engaged in a variety of activities. These would be stand-in shots used as needed in the studio's editing booth. Outside Cody's dome, Maloney was assembling supplies for transport up the mountain. Cody himself was nowhere to be seen. Likely he was in the Bubble gorging himself on a high-protein breakfast, despite the fact he would soon be lecturing the camera on his dire need to find food and water. Hank busied himself collapsing domes, working with proficient hands, and Becky mused that, given his experience, he could probably accomplish the feat sightless. From the look of things, the crew would be ready to move out within the hour.

Samantha approached, carrying a small white box, her face all business. "I've put together the master field kit. Inside you've got the usual: wound dressings, Elastoplast, antiseptic swabs, lancets, sun cream, and a few other essentials."

"Thank you," Becky said. "Ready for another adventure?"

"Me?" Samantha touched her chest and laughed. "Oh, I've the easy task. Sip hot chocolate, watch the wind blow, that'll be the highlight here. You, on the other hand, you have the real work. So I guess it should be me asking you that question."

"I'm as ready as I'll ever be."

"I heard about Cody's last-minute stunt dragging you along. With your daughter in the hospital, that was shameful. My sympathies."

Becky smiled her appreciation.

As they talked, Cody emerged from the Bubble dabbing the corner of his mouth with a handkerchief before shielding his eyes from the glare. "Hank! Becky! Chop, chop, front and center. I have a question I expect an answer to!"

Reluctantly, Hank dropped a bundle of tent poles, and the three gathered in the snowy meadow. Here, the chill air stirred and the smell of damp evergreen wafted from the forest fringe.

Cody's expression did little to hide his irritation. He glared at Hank. "Tasha tells me you've constructed a lean-to in the woods for this morning's departure shot."

"That's right."

"Did I not make it clear I wanted a shot of me emerging from a snow cave this morning?"

"You wanted it this morning?" Hank asked incredulously.

Cody made a sucking sound cleaning between his teeth with his tongue. "That's right, so where is it?"

"I didn't build you one."

"Why the devil not?"

"Well, seeing as the prairie received little more than a few inches last night, I went with the logical choice and built you a lean-to. You see, you can't make a quinzee without a few feet of snow. But of course given your extensive experience in the bush, you already knew that, didn't you Codwell?"

Cody flushed with embarrassment. "Oh, yes, well I guess that makes some sense."

Hank pointed to higher elevation. "The subalpine must've got plenty of snowfall last night. You'll have thick drifts up there. We'll do the quinzee tomorrow night."

"Very good, a snow cave it is, and this time no excuses. I've decided to film the experience and provide it as bonus Internet footage for my viewers. Kilpatrick will double for me and tough out a hard night."

"That's mighty thoughtful of you," Hank said.

"Yes, indeed, now if you don't mind, I've a scene to shoot." Cody turned and tramped off toward the forest.

Within minutes, the crew had gathered near the lean-to, which was a simple assemblage of aspen and spruce limbs resting over a rectangular frame. Under it, Hank had spread layers of foliage for insulation from the ground. A small fire, surmounted by an improvised tripod of stripped branches, burned near its opening. From the tripod's apex, a small cooking pot dangled over the fire and boiled with a milky porridge. A cold breeze carried its pungent scent. Becky wrinkled her nose. Hank usually had a knack for cooking up fantastic dishes, and so the revolting smell perplexed her.

Tasha was quieting the group. Under the half-light of the canopy, Cody—bundled in clothing carefully made to appear weather-beaten—readied himself on the lean-to's bed of leaves.

"Standing by for a take!" Tasha cried. "And action!"

Cody nestled into the foliage and tightened his jacket, suddenly overcome by a look of famine and fatigue. He stared ruggedly into the camera. "It's morning—day one, and I'm deep in the forest, already hungry and exhausted." He cupped his hands and blew into them for warmth. "In any survival situation, the first order of business must be to seek shelter and build a fire, so I've constructed this lean-to using foraged spruce and oak—"

"Not oak," Hank said, interrupting the shot, "spruce and aspen. Oak isn't found in these parts."

"Cut!" Tasha called out. She turned and narrowed her eyes at Hank. "I would appreciate you not interrupting the scene."

"I'm sorry," Hank said. "It's just that anyone with knowledge of these mountains and its flora would know he was full of shit. I just figured old Codwell there wouldn't want to look like an asshole on national television."

Becky stifled a grin.

Tasha said, "The procedure, if I'm not mistaken, is for you to read the script and make changes *before* filming."

"That's right," Hank said, "and I do. But I can't help it if half the things out of his mouth are off script and made up."

"I think your attitude—"

"No, no, Tasha, he's right," Cody interrupted. "Everything must be authentic. Otherwise there's sure to be some cheeky bloke who'll notice an inconsistency and turn it into an embarrassing YouTube moment."

Tasha said, "Alright then, were there any other errors we should know about?"

"Yes, as a matter of fact," Hank said. "I built the lean-to at the forest fringe, not deep inside it as Cody said."

"But the phrase 'deep in the forest' has a certain *je ne sais quoi*," Cody said. "Why wouldn't I build it deep in the forest?"

"Because less sunlight penetrates deep in the forest, and thus you have more moisture. Makes cutting wood and starting fires more difficult. Heck, it makes nearly everything you do more difficult."

"Okay, anything else?" Tasha asked impatiently.

"That's about it," Hank said. "For now."

Cody refocused, once again appearing stalwart for the camera. Tasha resumed the shot. "And action!"

"Morning of day one, and I'm at the forest fringe, hungry and exhausted. In any survival scenario, the first order of business must be to seek shelter and build a fire, so I've erected this lean-to of spruce and aspen."

Becky and Hank exchanged smiles.

Cody lifted a stick, which Hank had fashioned into a crude spoon, and dipped it into the pot. Absently he stirred. "The effort it takes to survive in the wild burns a tremendous amount of calories, so I've collected a number of wild edibles and made this highly nutritious soup." He brought the wooden spoon to his mouth, took a testing sip—and instantly recoiled. "Bloody hell," he yelled out, his face souring. "What in God's name have you concocted here, Hank?"

"Cut!" Tasha cried.

"A porridge of thistle and bitterroot, with the pith of fireweed added as a thickener. All are indigenous edibles." Hank was grinning so wide he looked to Becky like a completely different man. "It's nutritious and, as you agreed it should be, very authentic."

7

Becky said, "You might want to take it easy on Cody. You wind him up too tight this early and he's bound to snap somewhere along the way."

Hank eyed her sidelong as they walked deeper into thickets. Their breath frosted the air as they spoke. "Not to sound rude, Beck, but I'd prefer to talk about anything but Cody. The guy really sticks in my craw. I think he's a dick—if you'll excuse the language."

"I wouldn't disagree," Becky said. "I'm more worried about you getting worked up over his antics. Wouldn't want you to lose your cool and do something you'll regret later."

"You know me better than that. If you don't mind, I'd rather just focus on the walk."

"Sure, if that's what you'd like."

"What I'd like is that porterhouse I suggested yesterday." He stopped abruptly to study the trunk of a nearby spruce tree. "Now this is one I don't think

I've ever shown you before. Look here." He pointed to a mess of bark strewn among the brush at the base of the tree. Shredded and mangled, it had come from the trunk.

Becky walked a circuit around the tree, noticing that the bark had been stripped all the way around to a height of about three feet. The damage, it was clear, had been caused by an animal. What kind of animal? Becky wasn't sure, but she intended to find out.

Carefully, she sifted through the brush. Her eyes searched for a nature trail or a path along which wildlife might pass. Hank had taught her some time ago, during one of his lessons in the outdoors, that if she noticed the signs, it was always a good idea to identify nearby animals. One could never be too careful. *Stumbling blindly upon a dangerous predator never ended well for the stumbler*, he would say.

Eventually, a trail revealed itself, and Becky stooped low and crept along its path, searching for the tracks she was sure would be present. And almost immediately she stopped, perplexed by what she saw. Tracks, alright, but none she had ever seen before. Both the front and hind markings were small and pear-shaped, with the hind marking slightly larger at about three inches. Skeletal claw imprints, faint but distinct, topped the impressions. "I think you're right, Hank. This is something you've never shown me before. Don't recall it from the books either."

Hank stood over her pointing to the tracks. "Notice the thin scats linking the prints."

"Yes, what animal left it?"

"Wanna venture a guess?"

"I really don't know, but seeing what it did to that spruce tree, I'd prefer not to run into one."

"Ah, they're really not so bad. Just need to give them a wide berth."

"So what is it?"

"Here's a clue: They're animals that slow dance *very, very* carefully."

Becky thought. But the lame clue didn't help any.

"C'mon, what is it?"

"Enough already. I don't know, tell me."

"A porcupine. Get it? Slow dancing. Very, very carefully." Hank was grinning at his own corny joke.

"Awww, a porcupine? How cute," Becky said. "But why did it destroy the tree?"

"They like the cambium layer on the underside of the bark. It's like a sugary treat for them."

Becky stood up, pleased she'd learned something new.

Hank said, "You know, Beck, I've been thinking about Gracie, and I've come to the conclusion that fresh mountain air and tales around a campfire would do her a world of good. When she's feeling better, I'd like to take the two of you camping."

Becky smiled.

"But nothing like this, of course. I mean *real* camping. Somewhere pretty, with comfortable weather, by a lake with fish that jump into your frying pan. No long-distance, day-to-day hikes. Just easy living."

"Like the place you took us to a few years

back?"

"Yeah, like that."

"Gracie would be thrilled," Becky said. She squeezed Hank's hand. "I would like it, too."

Shyly, Hank turned away, searching the surrounding trees. Then he pointed to a stand of pines. "There, on the ground under the lower limbs. What do you see?"

Becky's eyes traced the line of his finger to a small grouping of wild mushrooms. She approached and knelt next to them, carefully studying the species. After a moment she said, "Well, they're growing under conifers, and their caps are small and convex, maybe two inches."

"Which rules out?"

"This time of year? Most everything, except maybe blewit, honey mushroom, and poison pie."

"Good, then which of the three is it?"

"Well, they're too small for blewit." Becky hunched down and sniffed at a mushroom. The faint odor of radish filled her nostrils. "The smell rules out honey mushrooms."

"Right."

She straightened up on her knees. "Given their smell and the fact that they're growing in rings, I'd put my money on poison pie."

"Very good, but how could you be sure?"

"Take a spore print and check the color."

"Which would be?"

"Rusty brown," Becky said, peering up at Hank for approval.

He offered her a hand and helped her to her

feet. "Beck, you're as impressive today as you were the first day we started these walks—even with Gracie in the hospital and your mind a hundred miles away."

She hugged Hank. "Thank you for saying that," she said. "Your opinion means the world to me."

Hank returned the hug before stepping back at arm's length. "So tell me, what would happen if you decided to eat some of these little beauties?" He pointed to the mushrooms.

"Nothing really—"

Hank arched an eyebrow.

"—that is, if you don't mind dizziness and vomiting." She winked.

Hank smiled and thought a moment. "Maybe we ought to pick a few to spice up Cody's next porridge."

And the two laughed before turning and heading back to camp.

8

VIKTOR PUSHED ASIDE the tent's canvas flap and passed under the eave into the morning frost. Packed together like sardines in a tin, he and his comrades had survived their first night as rich men in uncomfortable delight. The original plan had been two men to a tent, but with Sergey's unfortunate demise and the loss of his rucksack, which included the second tent and a good portion of their already limited food supply, the remaining three had been forced to make do.

Viktor filled his lungs with fresh mountain air and gazed at the low clouds that painted a dim, boltmetal sky. Last night, after retiring to the tent, there had been no snow lower than the timberline. Now, looking about, he stood in amazement at the white blanket that covered the lakeshore and opposite slopes. Ice and frost, too, had begun creeping over the water's edge. The sudden transformation gave him the sensation of having been transported elsewhere during the night.

From their camp at the margin of the forest, he walked down snow-covered scree to the edge of the lake, where Andrei stood clutching a sketchpad and working an artist's pencil. Far beyond Andrei, wind rippled the water, but nothing in its deep blue surface betrayed the secret that lay at its bottom.

As he neared, Viktor could see Andrei's sketch of the lake and the opposing mountainside. With a pencil as his only tool, he had captured the scene remarkably well, detailing the mountain's yawning folds and the lake's breaking whitecaps. Andrei was clearly a competent artist, as well as a brilliant strategist.

Viktor was first to break the silence. "We shall soon be men of means. Your plan is reaching fruition."

"I'm afraid my plan has been amended," Andrei said as he continued to work.

"Amended? In what way?"

"There will be an excursion today, a pleasure trip for Fedor."

Viktor was immediately curious. Killing was Fedor's pleasure. What did Andrei have in mind? "What sort of an excursion?"

"Do you admire my work?" Andrei asked.

"I do."

"This sketch in particular?"

"Very much so. But tell me, what is your task for Fedor?"

"Then you shall have it when I'm finished, a memory of this moment." Andrei turned from the lake, fully revealing the artwork to Viktor. You've been studying it over my shoulder, yes?"

Viktor marveled at the valley's expert rendering and nodded.

"And yet you have not seen it at all."

"Your behavior perplexes me, Andrei."

"Look closely."

Bewildered, Viktor hesitated.

"Please, my friend, look more carefully at the sketch. What does not belong?"

Once again, Viktor gazed upon it. After a long moment he frowned and pointed to a spot at the edge of the lake, angled some distance away on the opposite shore. "This here. Is it what I think?" Quickly, Viktor looked away from the sketch to study the distant lakeshore. There, ever so faintly, he saw smoke drifting skyward.

"Ah, yes. Now you see."

"A campfire." He turned back to Andrei.

"Unfortunately so."

"How long has it been there?"

"I cannot say."

"Surely, not since our arrival."

"Again, I cannot say."

Viktor looked back at Andrei. "What do you propose?"

"I should think the answer is obvious. As I've told you, an excursion for Fedor."

"It may be whoever it is, they saw nothing."

Andrei stared somberly over the lake. "Yes, but then again, it may be they saw everything."

9

I T WAS LATE afternoon, six hours into the second day of their seven-day shoot when the crew crossed a field of snow-covered talus and began climbing a wooded slope toward a distant ridge, the security of the Bubble long behind them.

The conversation with Gracie had gone worse than expected. Not because of the words Gracie spoke. She had said all the right things—that she understood why Becky couldn't be there, that she'd be brave when the doctors came for her, that she'd be a good girl for her grandmother, that she loved and missed her. It wasn't the words Gracie had spoken that anguished Becky, but the disappointment in her soft voice. Try as she did, Gracie just couldn't hide it.

For the first few hours of the hike, Becky couldn't shake the grief clutching at her heart. She had focused on the terrain ahead. Now she was removing her sunglasses to wipe the sweat from her brow and squinting against the white sky. Working in the climate-controlled offices of the studio, playing checkers with Gracie in Seattle coffeehouses, reading crime novels in bed, the weeks between shoots always softened her. And now in this, the first serious hike of the trip, she was feeling the effects. Her lower back ached from the weight of her pack, and her feet had already begun developing blisters. But as much as the weeks off softened her, the first hike always toughened her right back up. She breathed deeply, taking long careful strides, avoiding tufts of undergrowth and uneven ground. She exhaled in slow, measured breaths.

Glancing ahead, she noticed Maloney and his insane load. The poor kid, in addition to his own over-sized backpack and the two smaller knapsacks tethered and jostling at his side, he had been tasked with carrying a large case with Cody's personal belongings. Becky was highly impressed by Maloney's strength and endurance. Despite his awesome burden, he moved across the snowy slopes with speed and agility.

She quickened her pace to catch up with him. When he noticed her walking abreast he nodded politely.

"We haven't had much of a chance to talk," she said.

"You weren't missing out," he said. "Yesterday, I doubt I would've made much of a conversationalist. I was pretty sore at having been demoted to Cody's pack mule. Still can't say I'm pleased about it."

"I'm sorry. Really I am."

"And 'pack mule' are his words, not mine. Can you believe the guy?"

"I can believe him."

"He's lucky I didn't quit on the spot."

"*We're* lucky."

"Yeah, well, after this shoot, I'm going to re-consider this whole arrangement."

"After the shoot, I'll be out of the field and he'll need you. The demotion is only temporary, I'm sure."

"Hope you're right."

"And just so you know, it wasn't my decision." Becky hoped Maloney would believe her.

"That's what they tell me."

"In fact, I've been fighting for quite some time to get out of the field and produce from the studio."

"They tell me that, too," Maloney said. "Also hear you have a sick daughter. Is that right?"

"Unfortunately, yes. Gracie. She's eight."

"Mind me asking what's wrong with her?"

Becky frowned. "Nothing's wrong with her. She's ill, not criminal."

"I didn't mean it that way," Maloney said. "I'm sorry."

"Oh, damn. No, you have nothing to be sorry about. I'm just overly sensitive on the subject. I didn't mean to bare my claws."

"Sure, I understand. Hey, can I help you carry your pack? I still have a spare pinky."

Becky smiled, and she was still smiling when the group crested a sharp ridge and began their descent down a gentle slope into a long, narrow draw. At its center, snow pushed to the edges of a fast-flowing river. Rushing water hummed in the air."

Hank, leading the group, called back, "Day two

camp straight ahead!"

Tasha hollered to Marshal, "Let's stop in about a hundred feet and shoot Cody's approach. When we reach the bank, I want to set up ASAP for the river crossing. No wasting time people."

"Hey, hon," Marshal said. "What do you say a little breather first?"

Tasha regarded him critically. "Did I marry a man or a wuss? Suck it up, we don't have the time. I don't want to lose the light."

"Not even for a minute?"

"You don't see Cody complaining, do you?"

Becky looked at Cody who, free of a backpack or load of any kind, was practically gliding along the snow, munching a granola bar and humming *Strawberry Fields Forever.*

Marshal didn't bother answering Tasha. He walked staring at the ground.

Minutes later, they stopped and unloaded their equipment.

"Why we stopping here?" Maloney asked Becky.

"To film Cody's entry scene."

Maloney looked puzzled.

Becky said, "Basically, here's how it works: Hank will feed Cody technical information about the river valley, which Cody will then embellish and repeat on camera to warn viewers of the danger he's about to face—in this case crossing the rapids."

Maloney looked in the middle distance at the churning river. "He's going to cross that?"

"Actually, no," Becky said. "That'll be Kilpatrick's job. Here, come with me, you'll understand."

Becky and Maloney broke from the group and walked a hypotenuse toward the river, heading upstream.

"How is it Hank knows the terrain so well, anyway?" Maloney asked. "He from these parts?"

"No, he's native Alaskan," Becky said. "It works like this: after the production company decides on a new episode environment, they send Hank out into the field with a list of event parameters. For this trip, top brass wanted mountainous terrain that would provide adventure shots, such as crossing river rapids and exploring abandoned mines. And so on."

"Hank has already been out here?"

"Yes, two weeks ago before the weather turned. If you ask him about it, he'll probably just grunt that it was all a pain in the ass. But don't let that fool you. Fact is Hank's a free spirit, and ever since his wife passed away, he prefers being out here alone, away from it all."

"I can respect that."

Soon enough, they reached the river, where crystal water roiled over massive rocks, turning from azure to a frothy white. Fine spray hung in the air. They turned and followed the bank upstream.

At length Becky said, "Tricuspid Atresia."

"I beg your pardon?"

"Tricuspid Atresia, it's a congenital heart defect. You asked earlier what ailed Gracie."

Maloney's look became dispirited. "It sounds serious."

"It is. When she was born, Gracie came into the world blue, from a lack of oxygen. My baby couldn't breathe. That's what the defect does, it constricts blood flow to the lungs making it nearly impossible to get sufficient air."

"Is she okay now?"

"She just finished another surgery—and hopefully her last. Her prognosis is good. Mine, on the other hand, not so much."

"What do you mean?"

"Well, aside from her first procedure, I've never been there for her. She has never woken from a surgery to hear the sound of my voice, or to feel the touch of my hand. What kind of mother does that to her child?"

"In my book, a damn good one."

Becky glanced at him in confusion.

"What I mean is medical bills aren't cheap, so you need a job. How else would Gracie get the care she needs? Children may not understand the economics, but they understand love, and somewhere in Gracie's heart, she understands the sacrifice you've made."

Becky stopped astride Maloney and squeezed his forearm. "You're a kind man," she said. "This production's lucky to have you."

Maloney thanked her with a smile.

"I'm glad we had a chance to talk."

For a short distance they continued hiking in amicable silence, until finally rounding a bend in the river. Here, slow-moving water fell over an escarpment before churning and transforming into rapids.

"This is it," Becky said.

Maloney looked bewildered.

"…Where Cody will cross the river."

"I don't understand. Won't people notice the difference in the moving water? Here it's quiet and lazy. Downstream it's screaming like a banshee."

Becky smiled. "Ah, but you forget movie magic."

"So educate me."

The two followed the riverbank upstream, well past the escarpment. Becky said, "As we speak, Hank has already set up a dome and built a fire. He's probably now scavenging in the woods for rafting materials. After some instruction, Cody will be filmed fashioning the materials into a raft, which Kilpatrick, doubling as Cody, will then use to cross the river."

"In this water? The man will freeze to death!"

"Thus the fire and dome, to quickly get Kilpatrick out of the cold and into dry clothing."

"And Cody? What about him?"

"Oh, he'll just dampen his hair and huddle by the fire, pretending he's restoring body heat, feeding the camera a bunch of false bravado."

Maloney laughed critically. "Yeah, he will, won't he?"

"That's what he does."

"What about you and me? Why are we here?"

"The others will be along soon, then we'll film the cheat shots."

"Okay, I'm beginning to see."

"We'll bob the waterproof pole cam in and out of the river to capture video of Cody at the surface, pulling the raft ashore. Marshal will be sure to get a lot of good face shots. With plenty of splashing and vigorous camera movement, we'll create the illusion of rapids."

"Genius."

"We'll do something similar with a splash bag over the Betacam. Shoot from different angles and edit it all together until we have verisimilitude. And voilá, Cody just crossed the rapids, risking life and limb for the entertainment of the audience."

"Yeah, presto change-o. Got to love reality television."

10

ROGER GRUBB SAT on the trunk of a fallen tree and warmed his hands by the campfire. He gazed out beyond the lake at the whitened mountainside, unable to believe his crappy luck. He'd invested more money in camera and sound equipment than he'd ever invested before, hiked deeper into the mountains than he'd ever hiked before, and lanced more goddamn blisters than he'd ever lanced before, and for what?

Snow.

Thick, powdery, *unexpected* snow.

Discouraged, Roger lifted his camera and snapped a few shots of the snow-flecked spruce that covered the rising slopes of the opposite shore. No question the snow cover was pretty, but he wasn't here for pretty snow. He was here for pretty birds, and most birds didn't like snow. They hated it. It kept them migrating south. Sure, he could find some finches or crossbills, maybe record a little of their trilling, which wouldn't be much with snow restricting their activity. And anyway, his focus this season was on migratory species. So unless the weather cleared and this snow melted within a day or two, he'd have to put off work until next year.

As he stewed, movement over the lake caught his eye. There, a flock of tundra swan came gliding majestically over the rippling water and, with wings beating in a flurry, came to rest peacefully on the surface. Roger lifted his camera, zoomed in, focused, and saw a scene of immense beauty.

With wingspans of nearly seven feet, these were the largest birds in the Canadian Rockies, larger even than the bald eagle.

The camera chattered as he snapped rapidly, following the gorgeous creatures in their respite on the lake.

"And here I thought I was alone in these woods."

The deep voice came from behind Roger and was so sudden and unexpected Roger tweaked his back jerking around in surprise.

"My, how easily you startle."

The voice was heavily accented, Russian maybe, and Roger saw that it belonged to a towering, thick-limbed man with a meaty face. He stood at the forest fringe, his eyes darker than the fir trees silhouetting him.

"Holy crap," Roger said. "Where did you come from, mister?" All thoughts of the tundra swan were lost.

"I saw the smoke from your fire."

Roger was nonplussed. He had hiked a good

ten miles deeper into no man's land than even the most diehard backpackers would dare venture. And now here he was face-to-face with another living soul. Christ, where did a man have to go to get away from it all?

The stranger crossed the snow to the camp's clearing. His sudden presence had rattled Roger so completely he wasn't sure what to say. He decided to be obliging. "Would you like some coffee," he asked. "It's cowboy style, but it does the trick."

"I would not."

The studious way in which the man's dark eyes scanned the camp gave Roger the creeps. He shifted uncomfortably on the tree trunk. "If not my hospitality, then what is it you want?"

The stranger's eyes continued searching.

"If you don't mind me asking," Roger quickly added.

"I see you have a camera. Are you a photographer?"

"A birder, actually."

"A birder?"

"I watch birds. Photograph them, record their songs. A birder."

"What an odd thing to do."

Roger chuckled nervously. "Hey, to each his own."

"And you're without company?"

The barrage of questions only heightened Roger's sense of unease. Casually he stood. It was better he was on his feet in case there was trouble. "Hell of a storm last night, eh? Those low-pressure systems are a real bitch."

"How long have you been camped here?" the man asked.

"Arrived this morning from higher elevation," Roger said. He could hear the nervousness in his own voice, and he thought of grizzlies and of cougars, and their ability to smell fear. He hoped this gorilla hadn't a similar sense. "Season's ended early and I'm heading home. Time to put together this field guide I'm working on. It's not Audubon quality mind you, just something for a coffee table."

The stranger leaned in front of Roger's tent and glanced inside.

"I'm sorry, we haven't traded introductions. I'm Roger, and your name is?" Roger extended a hand, which went unshaken.

"I am Fedor and I, too, must apologize," the man said grimly.

"Oh, for startling me?"

A crooked smile. "No, for what I must do."

Roger tensed. There was something chilling in the tenor of the man's voice, as much his words. Roger's throat swelled. He found it difficult to swallow. "What do you mean? Is that some kind of a threat?"

The man reached into his jacket pocket, a move that unnerved Roger to the point of action. He glanced up the slope toward the edge of the forest, twenty feet away. An ardent hiker, he was in damn good shape and figured he could make a dash into the trees and get away from this guy.

As the man's hand emerged from his pocket,

Roger could see the black handle of a gun. Fear gripped him, and his flight instinct took hold. In a sudden burst, he barreled forward toward the forest, screaming from the adrenaline rush, crushing against the stranger's shoulder as he passed.

Glancing back, Roger saw the gun drop to the ground. He turned back to the forest and pushed ahead, reaching the trees, then beyond. Here the light was muted and the snow thicker, gathering in drifts around the arrowhead-shaped firs.

He paused to choose a direction. Through fogged breath, he glanced upslope. In the snow, the incline would slow him down, maybe enough for this psychopath to recover the gun and get a shot at him. He dashed right, opting instead to follow the slope's contour. A *pop* sounded and something burned past his ear. A chunk of bark burst out from an adjacent tree. Because of the suppressed report, it took Roger a moment to realize he'd been shot at—and nearly hit!

Now there was no question, the man intended to kill him. Roger's panic intensified. He raced deeper into the forest and soon ducked to his left where the spacing of the trees began to narrow. Snow crunched under his boots, and he stopped long enough to turn back and curse the deep tracks he was leaving behind. They were like a neon sign pointing his direction. The sound of movement downslope made him resume his run. Breathing wildly he fought to come up with a plan. How could he hide his tracks? How could he possibly escape?

Then, as he scrambled up a shrub-choked

embankment, looking back for signs of his pursuer, the answer came to him. The gorge. Yes, the gorge! He had come upon it before reaching the lake and stopped to photograph a rough-legged hawk he'd seen feeding on carrion. Running, he could reach it in maybe ten minutes. The gorge was long and narrow and lined heavily with black spruce, but more importantly, its edges were free of snow, having been driven off the sides by steady winds. There, he would leave no tracks.

Roger sprinted faster, angling in the direction of the gorge, expelling his breath in misty clouds. He soon passed a fallen tree with a fractured trunk and remembered it from earlier, on his hike from the gorge to the lake. He felt a growing confidence. He could make it there. He could escape.

He topped a craggy rise and noticed a sprinkling of black spruce intermixed among the fir trees. Excellent, he was getting closer. From here, all he had to do was descend to the gorge—but carefully. The deep fissure was hidden by the forest fringe and would appear suddenly.

Roger descended, half running, half sidestepping as he traversed the downward slope. The snow thinned and his feet began to dislodge rocks. He peered back and saw that his tracks were disappearing. His confidence rose. Ahead the snow ended and the black spruce multiplied. Roger knew the gorge was just on the other side of the trees. He would reach it, then follow it west deeper into the mountains. His pursuer would likely head east, thinking Roger would turn in the direction of the foothills and small towns.

When Roger emerged from the trees, he beheld the gorge, its edge roughly ten feet from his position. He followed its length until he was well enough away from where he'd emerged from the forest and then he ducked behind the trunk of a tree. He crouched onto the ground's covering of frozen moss, staring upslope through tangled tree limbs. He listened and heard boots scraping against stone, followed by the clatter of sliding rocks. The son-of-a-bitch was at the top of the rise, maybe fifty feet away. With great care, Roger continued creeping west along the treeline, his eyes fixed back upon the forest's edge.

Moments later the big man emerged, gun in hand.

Roger stopped, knelt behind a thicket of ferns, and waited.

The crazed brute looked left, then right. Then he studied the ground for signs of Roger's trail. He glanced back up bewildered. After a few seconds he turned left and headed east in the opposite direction, just as Roger had anticipated.

Wind swept through the gorge and chilled his sweat-dampened skin. His teeth chattered, but still he felt an immense relief. Shivering, he slowly began to back up, covertly watching the man until he was no longer in sight.

Damn, that was a close call, Roger thought. But now he felt emboldened. All he had to do was put some distance between him and this gorilla. He was deep in the middle of nowhere, and once he was away from this gorge, escaping would be a cinch.

With a nervous grin, Roger stood triumphantly erect, turned, and then froze in shock.

In front of him was a second man, tall, dark-haired, with a thin smile. He held his empty hands in front of him, as if to tell Roger he was a friend.

Instinctively, Roger backed away, but was stopped by the gorge's precipice. "I don't know what it is you guys want, but if it's money you're after, I don't have any."

"Relax," the man said, "we have no desire for your money, and we're not going to hurt you." His accent, too, was Russian, but his tone was soothing.

"Bullshit, your buddy shot at me."

"An egregious mistake, you understand. It won't happen again. Let me assure you, we will not hurt you."

"You won't?"

"No, of course not." His smile deepened, further reassuring Roger. "My name is Andrei, and it seems there's been a misunderstanding."

"A misunderstanding?"

"Indeed, last night someone snuck into our camp and stole some of our provisions. We thought it might be you."

"No, no, it wasn't me!" Roger exhaled a nervous breath. "I'm not a thief, I'm a birder. I'd never do anything like that. Yeah, this has all just been a big misunderstanding."

"Of course. I rummaged through your tent and saw you had nothing that belonged to us. Mistake confirmed. I'm glad we caught up with you to apologize and explain our embarrassment."

Still, he spoke softly and Roger felt an immense relief.

"We regret what has transpired and wish to make things right. Again, our apologies."

Roger could feel his hands shaking from the fading adrenaline rush. Yes, this whole thing had been a huge mix-up. He laughed.

Andrei extended an open, friendly hand.

Roger accepted the gesture and shook it vigorously.

Andrei nodded to the gorge behind Roger. "You'd best step away. It's a devilish drop."

And that was no exaggeration. Roger stole a glance behind him. At least two hundred feet straight down. Sure, this had all been just a big misunderstanding.

As Roger turned back, Andrei lunged forward with a front kick. A heavy blow struck Roger in the solar plexus, and he stumbled back a step to the edge of the precipice. His arms windmilled as he fought to keep his balance.

Andrei stepped closer, his smile deepening, and bludgeoned Roger with a kick to the chest. For a brief moment, Roger saw in Andrei's eyes what could only be described as delight, then toppled helplessly over the side of the gorge. His arms flailed and his hands snatched at the air.

And unlike the birds he watched, Roger was falling helplessly, listening to the echoes of his own screams as they resounded from the canyon walls.

Sick weightlessness foretold his imminent doom.

Then came a warm, numbing impact.
And then darkness.

11

"YOUR HANDLING OF the quarry was sloppy and inefficient," Andrei told Fedor. "His escape would have jeopardized everything."

Fedor shrugged. "Had you not killed him, the elements surely would have. Anyway, what did he know of us?"

"He knew that we exist. That was enough."

Fedor considered this. Though Andrei was difficult to please, he had always proven himself one of the organization's more effective designers. It was best, Fedor decided, not to argue the point. "I shall work harder to improve my efficiency."

"A very good answer." Andrei gave Fedor a hardy slap on the back. "Let us strike camp and proceed with phase two!"

Andrei showed confidence. Maybe too much confidence, Fedor thought. With Sergey dead, and much of their food supply resting at the bottom of the lake, Fedor was less certain about their future. They had searched the photographer's camp for supplies, but found only a few cans of beans and tools with which to fish the lake. Sooner or later food would become a problem.

While Viktor disassembled the tent, Andrei busied himself turning a compass and studying a map.

"What will we do about food?" Fedor said. "Most of what we brought was with Sergey."

Andrei peered up from the map. "Steel your resolve and you'll find it manageable."

"Endure without? That is your answer?"

"We shall divide what is left and forage for the rest. If my calculations are correct, the railway is a two- maybe three-day journey to the east. And at most we will wait another two for a passing freight train."

"But that is five days," Fedor complained. "I cannot survive such a period without food."

"We will make do, Fedor. Consider the fine restaurants you'll soon frequent. That should satiate your hunger." Andrei turned back to his map. "Now, not another word. Assist Viktor with camp and take care to eliminate all signs of our presence."

An hour later, packed and ready to travel, the three Russians struck out from the frozen lakeshore, not a sign remaining that their camp had ever existed.

12

ALONE IN A meadow, Hank knocked the dottle from his pipe and appraised the second wave of weather amassing over the western range. A short time ago, after filming had wrapped, the cloud cover yielded to blue skies—a typical clearing trend this time of year. But already a second, more powerful storm was brewing.

Among tufts of snow-kissed foxtail a cold breeze blew. Hank loaded a pinch of tobacco into the pipe's bowl, keeping an eye on the distant squall line. There, thunderheads roiled and arced with electricity. By his estimation, the new storm would arrive sometime in the early morning hours. And it was going to be a whopper.

Hank lit his pipe and observed the smoke to gauge the strength of the wind, then took a long drag from the bit. The spicy-sweet tobacco pleased his palate.

Enjoying his solitude, he was disappointed to see Cody approaching from camp, marching through the snow like a man bent on an answer.

"Follow the smell of tobacco," Cody said as he neared, "and there you'll find Hank Guthry."

Hank narrowed his eyes. "What can I do you for, Codwell?"

Cody stopped and leaned smugly against a tree. "You're aware that habit will put you in an early grave?"

"So will swimming against an avalanche, you doofus."

"An avalanche, hah, touché!"

"That ain't why you're here, is it? To talk to me about your cockamamie avalanche idea? Because if it is, my decision is already made. You can turn and march yourself back from where you came. And anyway your explosives were left at base camp."

"No, that's not the purpose of my visit. Concerning the avalanche, I've come to agree with your assessment. It would simply be too dangerous. And as you point out, we haven't the charges. We'd be hard-pressed to trigger one without them."

"Glad you wised up."

"I've come about the old mine."

Hank puffed on his pipe. "What about it?"

"You told me it was by the river. I've been searching, yet unable to find it?"

"I told you it was *near* the river. You haven't found it because it's half a mile away, off an old mining road, through woods and thickets." Hank nodded north across the river. "What's your rush anyway? I'll take you all there in the morning."

Cody tented his hands at his mouth. "North,

you say, on the eastern or western side of the river?"

"West, our side," Hank said. "Why? You're not thinking about hiking there now, are you?"

"No, no, of course not."

"Good, because darkness is coming, and with it creatures of the night. I'd rather you not be traipsing through the bush and caught unawares."

"Indeed. Anyway, tomorrow will be fine."

"Since we're on the subject of the mine," Hank said, "I want you to be aware of a few things, so you don't go and do anything foolish."

Cody sighed his irritation.

"Understand we'll be exploring a dark hole in the earth, a hole unseen by human eyes for over a century. It won't be a ride at Disneyland."

"Really, you don't give me enough credit. I've been making these trips for some time now."

"Even so, you need to remember the mines in these mountains have been subjected to years of extreme weather, some made into dens by dangerous animals. You've got blind shafts, rotting timbers, unstable walls, and any number of other hazards that'll kill a man dead. When we arrive tomorrow, I'll need you to heed my advice, how I give it and when I give it."

Cody's stare became distant, and he smiled at some personal thought. Hank wasn't sure he was getting through to him. "Do you understand me?"

Cody blinked out of his distraction and said, "Yes, yes, of course, heed your advice. Very good, Hank. Don't think me rude, but it's been a taxing day and I'm knackered. Think I'll retire."

With that, Cody turned and hurried back across the meadow. But there was something in his determined gait, something in the way he spoke those last words that disturbed Hank. Cody never agreed with a directive: to do so was to show humility. It made Hank suspicious.

He puffed at his pipe, savoring the tobacco and enjoying the smell as it mingled with the fresh alpine air. He wasn't sure what Cody was up to, but whatever the hell it was, Hank decided, he would be sure to keep a closer eye on him.

•   •   •

I need you to heed my advice, how I give it and when I give it. Cody mentally repeated Hank's imperative as he dimmed the light in his dome. Clearly, the man suffered from a God complex. Having lived in the backcountry for so many years, he had come to think himself its master, and by extension everyone and everything in it. But the fact was he was nothing but a surly tyrant, and his King of the Wild attitude didn't impress Cody in the least.

What did Hank Guthry know about the *real* world? About the world of Hollywood entertainment, about producing a successful, highly acclaimed television show?

Nothing. Absolutely nothing.

And by contrast, Cody knew everything. Last season, he had topped thirty-six million viewers nationwide. And the reason for his profound success was clear: he possessed superior vision and timing.

Cody had his finger on the pulse of his genre and knew what it took to keep one step ahead of the cable and network competition.

Now, *The Survivalist* was at its season finale, and Cody understood it was time for something big, something dramatic.

On these facts Cody meditated deep into the night, until he was certain the others had fallen asleep. Then slowly, carefully, he slipped into his parka, grabbed the knapsack he had packed earlier, and ran down a mental checklist of the tools he would likely need for the job. When he felt satisfied that he had not forgotten anything, he carefully unzipped the door to his dome. A chill wind buffeted his face as he peeked outside for the all clear. By the faint light of the stars, he could see the clearing within the circle of domes, dark and still. He stepped out gripping the small pack—so as not to rattle any of its contents—then zipped his dome closed and crept from the clearing.

The stars arcing across the sky were amazing, each a brilliant seed shining with fierce intensity. A flash in the distance turned Cody toward the west, where some miles away a blackened sky extinguished the stars. Another flash and he could see the storm itself, moving in the direction of camp. He heard faint thunder and realized the front was yet some distance away, far enough certainly for him to complete his task and return.

He headed north along the western bank of the river. The snowpack under his feet left soft impressions, but he knew the storm would soon hide any traces of his presence. In the morning, the crew would be none the wiser. Cody searched the forest fringe for signs of an old road, and after putting some distance between himself and camp, he pulled a flashlight from his pack and turned it on, being careful to keep the beam from lancing back toward the domes.

Soon he came upon a thinning in the forest. He paused and inspected the area, concluding by the absence of large, older trees that a trail once existed here. Stunted trees of some sort and blankets of shrubbery had reclaimed the area, but the trail's presence was unmistakable.

Here, Cody entered the forest. A gentle wind whistled mournfully through branches. Beyond the glow of his flashlight, the plants became inky shapes, twisted and contorted like grotesque apparitions. The scene made him shudder. He hadn't accounted for the creepiness brought about by night. And reality set in. He was miles from civilization, and this was a harsh, brutal world. He recalled Hank's earlier warning: *Darkness is coming, and with it creatures of the night.* His imagination began to free itself. He fought mentally to vanquish thoughts of wild animals and hidden deadfalls, but to no avail.

The wind picked up force and rustled trees. Or was the rustling the result of some predatory beast stalking him, nearing him, readying an attack? Cody felt his flesh crawl. He took a deep breath and scolded himself for his cowardice. This was nothing but a damned forest, a tangle of limbs and leaves. They could not hurt him. He had an objective, and he would accomplish it for the good of the show.

Yes, the show!

He pushed forward, firming his resolve and forcing himself to consider the task's original purpose. Hank had been a serious wanker for objecting to the avalanche scene, and after some consideration, Cody realized it would be best not to argue with the man. He surrendered the charges, as Hank had demanded, but later had surreptitiously recovered them from the Bubble's storage locker. If Hank was unwilling to help precipitate an avalanche, Cody would simply do it himself. When the time was right, he would send Hank off on some fool's errand, then stage and film the scene before his return. Sure, Hank would later learn of the deception, no doubt Becky would blab to him every last detail, but with filming complete he would have no recourse. What's done is done. No turning back the clock. Cody relished the idea of defying the all-mighty Hank Guthry.

But first there was the matter of this mine scene to contend with. And it, too, would be a key event in the finale. The idea had come to Cody during an interview with some bloke from *Esquire*. What if, he had thought, during the filming of the mine exploration a crew member suffered a mishap and sustained a semi-serious injury? And what if, Cody had mused, what if *he* were the one to rescue and aid said crew member? Well, the intensity of the mine scene would surely increase tenfold, and Cody no doubt would come off to viewers as a heroic figure. The idea was a stroke of genius. Over the remaining few days of the shoot, Cody would be filmed leading the injured crew member to the safety of the extraction point for airlift back to base camp, where much needed medical attention awaited. None of Cody's cable and network competitors had yet captured such an event. No doubt because of the unreasonably stringent safety measures studios were forced to implement these days. The mine mishap, along with the subsequent avalanche scene, would without question boost ratings to unprecedented levels. Cody bristled with excitement.

Focusing on matters of import had carried Cody through the woods and into a sloped clearing. He played the light over the snow-covered ground, where he discovered parallel ties that ran to the base of a hill. Peeking through the snow and affixed to the timbers were iron tracks rusted brown by years of exposure. Cody traced the light along the tracks to the base of the hill. There, they disappeared into a dark, timber-framed maw.

Finding the mine hadn't been too difficult after all, and Cody decided to interpret it as a sign he was meant to proceed as planned. His heart knocking rapidly in his chest, he stepped forward scanning the light over the ground, so as not to misstep upon the fractured railway ties. In the near distance to his right, Cody could make out a tall, wooden-framed structure. Rectangular, it stood roughly ten feet wide and rose twenty feet high with two thick crossbeams at the top and center. Rusted iron shafts ran its length through holes in the crossbeams. It was an immense construct reminiscent of a medieval torture device.

Puzzled as to its nature, Cody angled his light askew, where he could see knee-high mounds of rock and gravel with snow settled between their gaps. Upon observing this, he suddenly understood the implement's function. Some weeks before, during preparation for the finale, he had wanted to plan for all contingencies, so in the hope that he might capture the perfect scene, he had researched these abandoned mines. Amazingly, tens of thousands of them, most from the days of the Gold Rush and the Klondike, riddled the mountainsides, undiscovered. In his research, Cody had learned of a device called a stamp mill. Its function, essentially, was to crush larger pieces of ore removed from the mine. In this way, the gold was more easily extracted from the encased rock. What had looked to Cody like a torture device, he now understood, was really just a century-old press mill. He made a mental note to point it out to Tasha. It would certainly make good window dressing for the entry scene.

He turned back to the tracks and slowly followed, pausing at the threshold of the mine. A chill breeze panted from the dark opening. No doubt tomorrow, under the muted light of the storm, this, too, would make excellent imagery.

Cody hesitated at the threshold, unable to bring himself to step forward. It was as if some unseen force acted against him, rooting him fast. Then the wind rattled the brush and startled him into action. Breathing deeply, he stepped through the timber-framed opening only to learn that until now he'd never truly experienced absolute darkness. More than simply the lack of starlight or city-glow, this was a darkness born by the complete and utter absence of light. It was as if the very walls of the mine acted to dispel the beam cast forth by his flashlight. The moving air of the mineshaft continued its regular pulse, and the faint scent of wood rot lingered in the air.

Gradually, Cody began circling the beam down the low narrow tunnel and proceeded into the gloom, following the railway tracks as they continued along the jagged earth. Timbers shored the walls and ceiling at ten-foot intervals. Against the walls, diagonal crossbeams acted as support between each rib. Cody stopped and unsheathed a utility knife from his waist. He forced the blade into a nearby timber, testing multiple spots in the wood. In some locations, the blade sunk easily with a crunch; in others, the wood resisted firmly. Rot had set in, but the thick timbers for the most part remained solid. This, Cody thought, was perfect for his plan. He would need the shoring to prove solid enough to justify exploring the mine, yet weak enough in places to explain away a sudden, unfortunate mishap.

Ahead, the rails ended at a T-junction. Long iron spikes with looped ends protruded from each of the support's vertical timbers. Recalling his research, Cody immediately recognized them as miner's candlesticks. Candles were wedged into the loops at the ends of the spikes, providing much-needed illumination for the workers.

At the junction, Cody peered to his left. As good a direction as any to explore. He stepped under the timbered crossbeam and suddenly froze. The mine's temperature was comfortable enough, well above the icy cold of the outdoors, but what Cody saw here instantly chilled his blood. High in the bleakness overhead, an organic mass of some sort clung to the low ceiling, undulating ever so slightly. It was a moment before Cody realized he was staring at a colony of bats. Hundreds of them. Maybe a thousand. They hung like living stalactites, silent and brooding. Cody, without conscious thought, crept back a step, then two, and as he receded from the tunnel, his flesh crawling, he tried to think what he knew about these creatures. Were they dangerous? Did they carry rabies? Might they attack? He had more questions than answers and was three steps into the opposite tunnel before he realized he was moving. Abruptly he stopped, spun on his heel, and jerked the flashlight up toward the ceiling, searching for more bats. But ahead, the tunnel was bare of the little devils. Cody sighed relief.

Exploring the left tunnel was out of the question. Tomorrow, perhaps, he would send Maloney there in hopes the dimwitted Irishman would disturb the roost and send the bats corkscrewing from the mine like a hellish swarm. Since a time-lapse would be set up, the film crew would serendipitously capture the spectacle on tape.

Cody studied the tunnel ahead. He tugged off his gloves and advanced, dragging his fingers absently along the wall between the timbered ribbings. The cold, scratchy stone had numbed his fingertips by the time he came to a bend in the tunnel. He slowed, once again examining the ceiling for bats. To his relief, there were none.

Lowering the beam of light, he looked ahead. The tunnel ran straight and deep into the mountainside. The miner's, presumably, had been following a large vein of gold-bearing ore, for at irregular intervals thin boards lay bridging sunken shafts. Cody's heartbeat quickened as he realized he had discovered opportunity. Hurrying to the first covering, he shrugged off his backpack and dropped to his knees before a series of eight or ten boards. Inches apart, each was about a foot wide and as thick as his thumb. The key, Cody thought, was to find a shaft of the appropriate depth. Too deep and the fall might be fatal. Too shallow and the fall would elicit more laughs than gasps.

Slivers splintered away from the boards as he slid them aside. Angling his flashlight over the lip of the pit, he peered down into the shaft. Gloom continued beyond the beam's limit. He plucked up a stone from the ground and dropped it, counting three seconds between the time the stone entered the gloom and struck the ground.

Far too deep.

A fall that would precipitate an injury—a broken ankle, some lacerated flesh perhaps—was what was needed. Certainly not death. The liability could prove costly.

Next he tested the strength of the boards and, satisfied they would hold his weight, arranged them back into a bridge and carefully crossed. They bent and creaked under his weight, but held fast. Ahead he saw many more shafts, each covered in a similar fashion. He forged ahead, determined.

Finding a shaft the appropriate depth—twenty feet by Cody's estimation—was the work of half an hour. He knelt, removed a small saw, and went to work on all but two select boards. By the glow of the flashlight, he positioned the blade's teeth at the center of each board's underbelly and began to saw, being mindful not to cut too deep. Halfway through would do the trick. A deep cut and years of slow decay, Cody suspected, would compromise the boards sufficiently to collapse them under the weight of a man. He worked hard and continuously, dampening his thermals from the sweat of his labor, until at last he finished and replaced each of the planks. All total, there was a dozen that stretched six feet wall-to-wall over the shaft. But the genius of his plan was in leaving two boards intact. In this way, Cody would be able to lead the unsuspecting crew member over the pit, without fear of himself falling victim to it. He double-checked the solid boards: the first board—two from the right wall; the second board—four from the right wall. This particular shaft, he knew, was the fifth shaft along the right tunnel. Fifth shaft, second and fourth board.

Five-two-four, five-two-four, five-two-four, he repeated, over and over again.

And he was still repeating the sequence an hour later when, amidst the first flurries of the coming storm, he crept back into camp and slipped unnoticed into his dome.

13

"WHAT'S FIVE, TWO, four," the soft voice was saying as Cody emerged groggily from his sleep.

"What? Who's there?" Cody blurted out and sat up with a start from his sleeping bag, throwing off a satin night mask.

"Relax, it's me, Tasha," the voice said.

Cody shook the cobwebs from his brain and slowly his faculties returned. So, too, did memories of last night.

"What's five, two, four? You've been repeating it in your sleep."

Cody rubbed his face vigorously, then blinked at Tasha. "How long have you been standing there?"

"Long enough to hear you repeating those odd numbers. What do they mean?"

"I haven't a clue what you're talking about," Cody lied.

"Fine," Tasha said. "Anyway, you've overslept. Hurry and dress. There was serious snowfall last night, but there's been a break in the weather. Hank says if we want to reach the mine with minimal discomfort, now is the best time to do it."

Cody unbundled himself from the blankets in his bag. Even through his thermals, the dome air chilled his skin. It hurried him into action. He quickly layered on clothing, zipped up his parka, and grabbed for his sunglasses and gloves. "Last night I had an idea, a stroke of brilliance, really," he said to Tasha as he finished dressing.

"Let's hear it."

"Understand, it's not anything original, but it's employed in our genre so infrequently that I thought it would make a great addition to the season finale, a sort of bonus episode afterward."

Tasha unzipped the dome and pulled aside the door to hurry him out. "What is it?"

"The making of," Cody said enthusiastically, before shrinking back from the frozen air. "Blimey, that's cold!"

"That's nature," Tasha said as-a-matter-of-factly. "You mean the making of the finale?"

"Yes."

"You want to film the crew filming you?"

"Indeed. I figured why not give those who work so hard on this production a little face time, as well." Cody smiled inwardly at his deception. In reality he couldn't care less about giving any of the crew credit for their work. It was what he paid them to do. What was important was capturing on film whomever he ultimately selected as his cameraman for the mine scene. The first cameraman would become the unfortunate, the second would continue filming. In this way, his heroic attempt at rescue would forever be immortalized on film.

"Not a bad idea," Tasha said. She ducked from the dome, and Cody followed. Outside, he noticed that a second, much deeper layer of snow had fallen. The gray cloud cover had settled just above the treetops, pressing down on the clearing like a burial shroud. Camp had already been struck, and his was the final dome to be collapsed.

"Logistically," Tasha asked, "how would you like it done?"

"I was thinking Becky could film on a handheld. She would follow you and the others as you busy yourselves with your various duties. Simple enough. We'll do voiceover in the studio."

"Sure," Tasha said. "I'll discuss it with Becky."

Maloney walked past Cody and disappeared inside the dome to collect Cody's personal things. Hank waited nearby for the Irish pack mule to finish, likely so he could break down the dome. The rest of the crew milled about with their packs on, ready to move out.

"Promptness, very good everybody," Cody called out to spirit them up. "This is precisely what I had in mind when I urged you to give it your best!" He had hoped for smiles, and perhaps a cheer or two, but was met instead with irritable glares.

"They've been ready for the better part of an hour," he heard Hank say. "They're waiting on you, Codwell."

Tasha stood next to Becky chatting, presumably to discuss Cody's idea. Hank worked quickly to collapse and store the dome, then met with the gathered crew and made an announcement, "A reminder, everyone. We're not the only ones who've climbed from the lower forests to a higher elevation."

"We're not?" Maloney asked, glancing around as if to spot other hikers.

"This time of year, bears do the same thing. Black bears and grizzlies. They ascend here to gorge themselves on food and fatten-up for their coming hibernation. It's important we all remain aware. If you have a sighting, or even just see signs, let me know so we can take the appropriate precautions."

"Which would be?" Maloney asked nervously, peering into the dark woods.

"Avoidance," Hank said. "Let me reassure you, we'll have no problems, so long as we're aware and don't surprise any of them."

"But if I do surprise one, a grizzly I mean?" Maloney asked.

"Do as I say and you won't."

"Yeah, but if I do?"

"If you do?" Hank's look was somber. "May the good Lord be with you."

•　　•　　•

The morning landscape en route to the mine was an image vastly different from the haunting one Cody had experienced the night before. There was a beauty to the muted forest, and the clean air filling his lungs heightened his sense of anticipation.

Towering trees heavy with fresh snow flanked the trail's stunted variety. Periodically along the way, the Irishman, with his bulky load, would brush aside limbs, dislodging powder upon the heads of the crew. It wasn't long before he was walking alone.

Becky trailed, operating a handheld camera and frequently switching the targets of her focus.

At length, they reached the mine's clearing.

"Here we are," Hank called out. "Take it all in, folks."

Cody emerged from the forest, doing his best to imitate the wonder he saw on the others' faces. "Yes, it's quite lovely, in a rustic, nineteenth-century sort of way."

Gaping at the monstrous stamp mill, Tasha lowered her camera. "This is going to make a fantastic visual."

"So where's the entrance to this mine?" Cody asked.

"Just over there." Tasha indicated by pointing. "I wonder how safe it is inside?"

Hank said, "That depends upon each of us. We could all leave here with a fond memory, or just as easily kill ourselves dropping into a blind shaft. Which one depends entirely on each of you and your respect for the mine."

Maloney's eyes were narrowed on the entrance. "Hank, you mentioned bears. Think any of them could be holed up in there for the winter?"

"Probably all sorts of critters in there, but bears? Unlikely. Denning in mines and caves isn't nearly as common as around fallen trees and strewn boulders, where they tend to burrow simple shelters underneath. Grizzlies prefer steep slopes, and usually hunker in a bit deeper than black bears. I've never actually seen one in a cave, except when I was a boy watching *The Yogi Bear Show.*"

Relief softened Maloney's expression. He began exploring the clearing with a more comfortable gait.

"Here's how we'll proceed, people!" Tasha called out. "Marshal, set up a stationary here at the forest fringe. I want a time-lapse of the whole clearing, from now till dawn. Use a wide-angle and frame the entrance at center. Then ready the infrared for the inside sequence. Modify Becky's handheld while you're at it. And Maloney, you watch Marshal to see how it's done. Kilpatrick, I need you to Cody-up and get ready for the mine."

As everyone prepared, Cody removed a field mirror and make-up kit from his pack and began preparing his face. His hands shook from nervous excitement as he ran styling gel through his hair and gave it a good tousle. This was it, he thought, the scene that would make or break the finale.

On the trail here, he'd decided to use Marshal as the unfortunate. And why not? Marshal was an incessant whiner, always pleading with Tasha for one thing or another. He was the perfect type to assume the role of victim and would adopt it naturally.

After Cody rescued Marshal from the mineshaft, the direction of the episode would take a new, more powerful direction. The remainder of the show would focus on Cody stabilizing the poor sod and leading him back to base camp for urgent medical attention. To hell with pushing higher and deeper into the mountains.

In his excitement, Cody nearly missed seeing Hank approach the entrance to the mine. Cody stuffed his supplies back into his pack and hurried across the snowfield to intercept him.

"What're you up to, Hank?"

Hank was examining the timbered frame of the entrance. "Inspecting things before you head inside to film."

"What do you say we shoot this scene raw, surprises and all?" Cody said in a manner he hoped wouldn't sound too suspicious.

"I don't think that would be a good idea. No telling what sort of shape the mine's in."

"Yes, but without an avalanche scene this may end up being the show's climax. I'd prefer to experience what this whore has to offer me fresh, without the prior knowledge you typically provide. My reactions will thus be more natural, more authentic."

Hank rubbed his beard. "I'm not sure that's such a good idea. Could be dangerous."

"Let us hope so." Cody slapped Hank on the shoulder. "Anyway, I'll be in the lead. Any obstacles, I'll be the first to face them. And I intend to keep all my parts intact."

"I'm not so sure—"

"Look," Cody said. "It's no secret what you think of my survival skills. And partly I'm responsible for that impression. But I have some ability, and I'm no coward. Please, give me a chance to change your opinion."

There was silence. Hank's face showed he was struggling with the decision.

Cody added, "I'll be damned if I let anything happen to my crew. First sign of something I can't handle and we'll turn and make our way back."

After a long moment he said, "Alright, Codwell. Impress the hell out of me. And remember, you lead the way. Marshal and Becky follow at all times. If anything gives you pause—anything at all—err on the side of caution and get yourselves back here."

Cody smiled. "I wouldn't have it any other way."

•　　•　　•

Becky readied the handheld camera fitted with infrared.

Hank took her aside. "Keep a close eye on Cody in there. He's unpredictable."

"It'll be fine," she said. "You know the routine: thirty minutes of dark, creepy footage with Cody pretending to be something he's not, then we'll be out of there."

"Even so, you watch him closely."

Becky touched Hank's forearm and smiled. She appreciated his concern. "I'll be back in a bit."

At the mine's entrance, Marshal balanced a portable Sony on his right shoulder. Tasha gave him a handheld halogen. "I covered it with a red gel. It'll give you faint light and a good IR boost."

"Great, how about a kiss, hon?"

"This is a big shot. Don't screw it up." She

turned and walked back to the tripod, leaving his puckered lips untouched.

Cody, Marshal, and Becky gathered at the opening to the mine.

Cody said, "I'll be performing the lead exploration. You follow. And make sure to mind my instructions."

"Where's that air coming from?" Marshal asked. He nodded at the entrance, indicating its regular exhalations.

Becky said, "According to Hank back when these mines were tunneled, one of the first things dug out were ventilation shafts, to feed in fresh air. They cut through the rock to the slopes above."

"Alright, people," Tasha called out from the forest's margin. "We still have a long hike ahead of us. Let's get rolling."

The group turned toward the dark opening and Becky began to film. She lagged a few feet behind Marshal, who in turn followed and filmed Cody at a comfortable distance.

The three entered and moved cautiously.

Dim light from outside bled hazily into the tunnel, but as they penetrated farther, it soon disappeared altogether, and the darkness began to feel overwhelming. It was deeper, more enveloping than she had expected. The only light now came from the soft red glow of the halogen. She peered into her viewfinder, saw the tunnel light up spectrally.

Cody wasted no time beginning his theatrics, his face an eerie contrast of ghostly light and shadow. "In addition to fierce weather and deadly predators, explorers of these mountains have additional obstacles to face. I'm here in a nineteenth-century gold mine, long abandoned and suffering from decades of neglect and decay. Let's explore it together, shall we? You from the warmth and safety of your home, me up close and deadly personal." His face became grim and he pivoted in a crouch and began stalking down the tunnel.

Marshal and Becky followed. The mine's chill breath seemed to come at regular intervals. Through her boots, Becky could feel the jagged, uneven rock of the tunnel floor. Her soles scraped as she moved. She imagined stumbling to the ground. Such a blunder would likely lacerate her hands and knees. The thought made her move with extra caution.

With each step, Cody's hands reached out, as if warding off some unseen evil. "Rock is an effective insulator, and so throughout the year, temperatures in these mines vary by only a few degrees. Currently, it's about forty-two degrees Fahrenheit. Though you may think it cold, this is quite pleasant compared to the bitterness outside."

Becky was careful to keep Marshal in the frame as he shifted positions looking for the best angle from which to film Cody, who suddenly stopped at an intersection.

"As we progress deeper into these tunnels, they'll begin to split away, then split again, and yet again. You see, the miners of ages past hunted eagerly for veins of gold, picking and digging with unrelenting determination. And the result was this, an insane complex of shafts—some horizontal, others vertical. Now, one wrong step could send me plummeting hundreds of feet to my untimely demise."

The atmosphere here was powerful, Becky thought, and Cody's words, together with a current of chill air, sent a shiver of dread down her spine. It was an effect he had never instilled in her before. She had to hand it to him, his monologue was effective. This would undoubtedly be a high point in the finale. Cody turned and looked both ways down the deep, looming intersection, then quickly turned right and proceeded ahead. Marshal and Becky followed.

Soon they came upon a series of parallel boards that crossed the tunnel floor from wall to wall. Cody stopped to study them. After a moment, he turned to the camera. "These boards conceal shafts sunken deep into the mountain. Their depths are uncertain, some perhaps twenty feet, others perhaps much farther. I would prefer not to measure them the hard way." He smiled and his teeth flashed bright in the infrared.

There was no telling the condition of the planks. Becky wondered how he intended to cross.

From the lip of the boards, he gave each a testing step. They creaked ever so quietly. "These boards are about six feet long. Normally, I would leap across, but my crew carrying the cameras would never make the jump. For their safety, I'll have to first determine the wood's integrity. If sufficiently strong, we'll cross the planks together."

He took another probing step. His courage surprised Becky. Odd how he hadn't brought Kilpatrick along for this sort of work.

Cody stepped to the center—a deeper creak. Then another step, and yet another, and in an instant he was safely across the bridge.

Becky and Marshal exchanged glances.

"Come," Cody said. "Follow exactly how you saw me do it. The boards are old, but fortunately rot hasn't compromised their strength."

Marshal imitated Cody's actions and quickly crossed.

Becky stepped onto the bridge as the gentle breath of the mine brushed her skin. With careful steps, she too gained the other side. There was no telling the depth of the shaft she had just traversed. The uncertainty quickened her heartbeat.

The group continued ahead until soon they reached another bridge and repeated the process. And again, Becky enjoyed the thrill of it all.

Farther into the mine the darkness seemed to intensify, a condition Becky thought impossible. The tunnel walls around Cody narrowed. But because the length of the supporting timbers remained relatively fixed, Becky knew this was just an illusion created by the deeper darkness.

The group crossed a third bridge, then a fourth. The crossings were almost becoming routine. Yet still they thrilled her. The tunnel seemed to stretch on forever.

At a fifth bridge, Cody peered inquisitively behind them. "I wonder just how far we've come," he said. "Marshal, turn the red-light behind you, would you please? Let's see if we have a visual of the intersection."

They had penetrated to such a great depth that Becky thought it an odd question. How could they possibly see so far behind them when at most they could see ten feet ahead?

Still, Marshal obeyed and swung the halogen around to glow the tunnel red behind them. Becky glanced back and, of course, had been right. In both directions, the distance of visibility was the same—maybe ten feet.

The creak of boards turned Becky back to Cody, who was already waiting on the other side of the bridge. "Alright, let's move on," he said. "Much still to explore."

"Where did you cross?" Marshal asked.

Cody pointed. "There at the center."

At the edge of the boards, Marshal lifted his right foot and took a first step. Then a strange movement caught Becky's attention, a crawling sensation on the ceiling above Cody. She narrowed her eyes to better resolve the source of the movement.

And what she saw shivered her flesh.

There, and extending deeper into the gloom, a grotesque legion of bats hung suspended from the rock, just inches from Cody's head. Dark and leathery, their subtle shifting created the impression of a single living and breathing mass.

Becky whispered across the bridge to Cody, "Whatever you do, don't turn around."

Marshal stopped, but continued filming.

Cody said, "What are you talking about, Becky?"

"Don't ask questions. Just slowly and quietly

come back."

Fright in Becky's voice must have alerted Cody to the danger, for he pivoted suddenly and gaped up at the ceiling. The creatures shifted above him, inches from his face. His hands flew up as a shield, and he screamed with an intensity that roused the colony into chaos.

At once, the bats dislodged themselves, forming into a sickening cloud of black. Some darted against Cody, who backed away, lowering his face and slapping furiously at his head.

And still Marshal filmed.

A bat clung to the rear of Cody's neck, startling him back a step. His boot caught the lip of a board and he went tumbling onto the center of the bridge.

Becky watched in horror as his weight and momentum carried him crashing through the boards, which split with a cracking burst.

Falling, screaming, Cody disappeared into the void.

•   •   •

Hank sat on his pack and savored his pipe's tobacco, considering their next move. It was unlikely, he thought, that the break in weather would hold until they made camp later in the evening. Still, he hoped for a few good hours of travel.

From across the clearing, he watched Maloney and Kilpatrick engage in friendly conversation. They were both solid fellows, and he was pleased to have them along. Maloney was a bit green, but one day he would make a fine field producer.

Hank was admiring the smoke from his pipe as it drifted in curls skyward when a scream from somewhere deep in the mine ended his meditation. He jumped up erect.

Then there came another scream, a man's scream.

Hank plunged his pipe into the snow and bolted for the entrance. Sidelong, he noticed Maloney and Kilpatrick hustling there, as well, eyes wide with concern.

A cry for help was quick to follow. A female's. *Becky!*

As Hank neared the mine, a tumultuous noise, like a riot of slapping leather, rang out from the darkness. At the entrance, Hank dove for the snow when he saw emerging from the grayish maw a hellish stream of bats.

14

THE SWARM OF birds flittering and corkscrewing through the treetops had nearly reached him before Viktor realized he was looking at bats.

The three Russians crouched over the forest floor as the creatures darted overhead in a panic.

"Bats. They should be overwintering," Andrei said. "Something ahead must have disturbed them."

Stepping forward to lead his comrades, Viktor pushed past snow-covered tree limbs and moved in the direction from which the creatures had scattered.

•　　•　　•

Instinctively, Becky dropped her handheld and dove toward the yawning shaft. She hit the ground flat. The force of impact expelled her breath. Her bare palms scraped against the rock as she reached out toward the edge. But Cody had already disappeared below. Becky swallowed and peered over the lip, expecting the worst.

Marshal stood over her, angling the camera down into the void. The faint glow of the red halogen illuminated only a portion of the shaft's depth, maybe ten feet. But it was enough. There, four feet below, against the far wall of the shaft, Cody swayed from a long iron spike that protruded from the rock. Between his ragged breaths, Becky could hear him sobbing. The fact he hadn't been killed brought her some calm.

"Cody, listen to me," she said. "I'm going to get you out of there. Don't struggle. There's no telling how secure you are."

"Don't leave me," he said, his voice high-pitched and defeated.

"I'm not going to leave you."

"Please don't leave me," he repeated, as if in a daze.

Becky stood, turned, and called down the black tunnel, "Help! Hank! Anybody!" Her voice reverberated from the walls.

She pivoted back to Cody. Suspended from the opposite wall of the shaft, he would be impossible to reach from her side, so she backed up a few steps and bolted forward. At the edge of the pit she launched herself into the air and over, landing with a squishy skid that nearly sent her sliding onto her backside. Surprised by the lack of friction, she turned, looked to the ground, and saw faintly a field of guano.

Without hesitation, she flattened herself onto the slimy ground. The strong smell of ammonia forced her to breathe through her mouth. She stretched over the edge of the shaft and reached for Cody.

He continued to sob. "Please don't leave me, Becky, for the love of God, please."

Becky realized the trauma of falling had destroyed his resolve, and she knew she had to comfort him if she were to elicit his help saving his own life.

"Cody, listen to me. It's Becky, your friend. I'm not going to leave you. With your help, I'm going to get you out of there. Do you understand me?"

Cody swayed, sobbing.

"Tell me you understand."

A convulsive breath, and then a faint, "Yes, yes, I understand."

"Good, I need you to carefully extend your arm and reach up to me with your hand. A spike snagged your jacket, but it may not have the strength to hold you for long."

"Oh, God, don't leave me."

"I'm not going to leave you. I'm going to help you."

Becky could sense Marshal's presence, still filming on the other side of the shaft. The fumes of guano stung her throat as she breathed more deeply.

"Extend me your hand, so that we can hold on to each other. I won't have the strength or the leverage to pull you up, but I can ease the burden on the spike and help ensure it won't fail. Hank's on his way. We'll pull you out together. You'll be just fine."

Cody extended his arms. His fingertips were about two feet down.

She stretched farther over the edge, extending

her hand, but before she could reach his, she heard a terrible scraping sound. The spike dislodged slightly and Cody dropped a foot before jerking to a stop. Fragments of rock trickled down, disappearing into the darkness.

The sudden shift had frightened Cody, and he began flailing his arms. "I'm going to fall. Help me!"

Becky stretched farther. She could feel her center of balance shifting dangerously toward the pit, where beyond the feeble light it continued downward to an unknown depth. She stretched more and their fingertips touched, but it wasn't enough to secure a grip.

She heard Hank's and the others' voices before she saw the glow of their flashlights.

"For chrissake, Marshal," Hank's voice echoed out, "why aren't you helping her?"

"I film, no matter what happens," he called back in answer. "That's Cody's rule."

Becky stretched to impossible limits. The fibrous muscles in her shoulder felt as if they were tearing from the effort. Then she heard the beating of boots and glimpsed a large form gliding across the shaft. It hit the ground beside her, and from the deepness of the grunt, she knew it was Hank.

"Where is he?" she heard his voice behind her now. "Let me see if I can get to him."

But his effort had come too late. With a long, sickening scrape, the iron spike dislodged and Cody plummeted.

It was reaction more than thought that made Becky lunge over the edge and grab Cody's wrist. She could feel his hand grip hers in return, and together they fell.

Then Becky felt an awesome tightness around her ankles and she jerked to a stop. Her shoulder contorted in pain as Cody's weight distended her arm, forcing her to cry out with clenched teeth.

"Maloney, Kilpatrick, Hank pleaded, hurry over here and help me."

Now, she and Cody managed to grab hold with their other hand, which distributed his weight and eased the pain in her shoulder. Still, she felt her strength beginning to falter.

Heavy footfalls clapped against the ground above her. "We got you, Hank!" Becky heard Maloney say. There came a heaving bellow, and she began to rise, her thighs and belly scraping the lip of the pit as she was hauled over. Kilpatrick was now beside her, stretching with longer, more powerful arms. Reaching down, he grasped Cody's hands. Becky felt the relief of a tremendous weight, and seconds later, she was being hefted up and out of the shaft. Hank eased her onto the ground. Together, Maloney and Kilpatrick pulled up Cody, who quickly huddled himself against the mine wall and buried his face in his hands.

15

GATHERED IN A circle, the crew stood outside the entrance of the mine. As they talked, Maloney busied himself cleaning the guano from their jackets while Kilpatrick carefully cleaned the lacerations on Becky's palms with antiseptic wipes. The alcohol, though it stung the cuts, was a welcome change of smell.

"What in the hell happened in there?" Hank demanded to know. He glared at Cody.

Marshal raised his arms. "Hey, I was just doing my job." Then he stared at Cody with a look of derision. "Talk to the survivalist here, he'll tell you. I'm going to take a piss." He stalked off and disappeared into the trees.

Marshal's jibe at Cody seemed to have an awakening effect, for his brow furrowed and his nostrils flared. He raised his chin and cleared his throat. "I'll tell you what happened. It was Becky, she ruined everything."

To Becky, Cody's unexpected accusation had

the effect of a slap in the face. She stood in stunned disbelief.

Maloney and Kilpatrick appeared uncomfortable, as if sensing the beginning of a difficult conversation.

"Becky, I'll go for some gauze and medical tape," Kilpatrick said. "Your palms are going to be sore, but the cuts don't look too bad." He hurried away.

Maloney awkwardly followed.

"How was it Becky's fault?" Hank asked Cody. "Aren't you the one who fell in a shaft?"

"Indeed, but the blame can be placed squarely upon Becky. First, I was well aware of the bats above me. Had she not called out a warning—an act woefully ill-advised—they surely would not have been startled, in which case we could have quietly proceeded with our exploration, unmolested."

Becky couldn't speak.

"Second, my fall into the shaft was certainly unexpected, but once so challenged, I saw it as an opportunity to demonstrate extreme survival tactics. Her half-hearted attempt to 'rescue' me only foiled my own efforts."

At this, Becky found her voice. "Why are you saying this?"

"Because it's true."

"But you begged me not to leave you."

"Rubbish, you misunderstood, apparently. I was urging you not to panic or run for help. I had the situation well under control. I expected you to remain filming. Instead, you dropped the camera—broke it, in fact—and inserted yourself into a scene in which you had no business."

Despite the chill mountain air, Becky felt herself flush with anger. "So this is the thanks I get?"

"Now that the handheld is damaged, how do you expect to film the crew? My brilliant 'making of' idea is now in the tank. All because of you."

Hank interrupted. "She says she was trying to save your life."

"Please, she can barely manage her own."

"You arrogant, ungrateful shit. I never should have come here in the first place."

"Indeed, I never should have demanded it. My confidence in you was grossly misplaced. If I could do it over, I'd leave you behind to tend to your decrepit offspring."

Cody's insult of Gracie hit Becky with the force of a hammer. Enraged, she balled her hand into a fist and suddenly lashed out. Her knuckles struck Cody square in the nose. She felt the cartilage pop, then stepped back, shocked at what she had just done.

Cody cried out and fell ass first into the snow, his hands cupped to his nose. A trickle of blood escaped down his chin. It was a long moment before the shock passed, then he peered up through watery eyes and screamed, "Becky, you're fired!"

●　　●　　●

Fedor could hear the activity beyond the trees, distinct voices arguing. Unlike the lone naturalist he'd encountered at the lake, a larger group would pose greater difficulties. The challenge enticed him.

He whispered to Andrei, "Maybe we should entertain ourselves." He touched his pocketed pistol.

"First, I'd much rather learn who we have found here. It's possible they have transport, which might hasten our departure."

Andrei's idea was sound. A quicker departure meant Fedor would dine sooner on hearty meals. He nodded agreement and the three men crept forward through the trees, sinking their boots quietly into the snow. The voices soon became louder.

Ahead, a clearing loomed, and from between the trees, Fedor could see people hustling about in brisk activity, both men and women, a few with cameras. The group appeared to be some sort of film crew. The fact that they were not armed hunters pleased him. "Their packs are surely filled with provisions," he whispered. "I'd imagine plenty of food. Our meager rations—"

Abruptly to their right, the limbs of two spruce trees parted and a man emerged, zipping up his trousers. His gaping stare widened Fedor's grin.

"Holy shit," the man said. "Who the hell are you guys?"

Andrei stepped forward. "Oh, thank God we found someone." Desperation tinged his voice.

Following his lead Viktor, too, did his best to feign relief. "Yes, you couldn't have come at a better time."

Fedor spoke no words, just grinned.

•　　•　　•

"So it's just the three of you?" Hank asked. He had built a campfire around which he, Becky and the strangers stood. Becky thought she sensed some skepticism in Hank's voice.

"That's right," said the handsome one, who had introduced himself as Andrei.

"And you say you were just hiking?"

"Yes, much farther afield than we had anticipated, I'm afraid."

"You're not Canadian, obviously."

"No, of course not. My friends and I come from Russia, Moscow originally. We're on work visas, engineers in Edmonton."

Becky glanced at Andrei's heavily built friend. He stood silently, almost anxiously. He wasn't her image of an engineer.

Andrei said, "Our plan was to explore the heart of these mountains. We've heard much about the Rockies. Perhaps our curiosity got the better of us."

"A nature trip," added the other hiker. He had blue eyes, perhaps the deepest blue Becky had ever seen. "I am Viktor," he said. "And again, allow me to express my gratitude for your help."

"A nature trip, huh?" Hank said.

"Yes," Andrei said. "I have an affinity for art and the outdoors. Made some wonderful sketches before the storm struck." He removed a sketchpad from his rucksack and handed it to Hank. "Please, enjoy the fruits of my passion."

Hank turned some of the pages, stopped at

one sketch in particular. "Not bad," he said. "I see here you're headed east."

"Yes, how did you know?"

"This here lake you sketched is some miles to the west of us. It's where we're headed." Hank studied the illustration. It was good, real good. Someone who knew better might say professional. He didn't have the eye to tell for sure. He gave back the sketchpad.

"The lake's lovely," Andrei said. "But I never expected to see so much snow so quickly. The storms are what turned us around. That and a loss of most of our provisions sent us into a panic."

"Getting lost out here will do that to folks," Hank said.

"You say you're a film crew?"

"They are," Becky said, indicating the rest of the group. "I've been fired. I'm now just an observer."

"Nonsense," came Cody's voice from behind her. He stepped up, tugged off his gloves, and leaned into the fire, rubbing his hands. "Why would I fire my best field producer?"

"Because I 'ruined everything,' remember?"

"Oh, Becky, I was upset. Never meant a word of it. Of course I behaved ungentlemanly and I do apologize, more so for my barbaric reference to your lovely Gracie. The pop you gave me...well I deserved it."

Cody's humility surprised Becky. He wasn't the type to ever apologize. "Thank you for that, but just the same, I'd prefer to move on and pursue other avenues."

"Becky, please, I just apologized. Anyway, I promise you that this is the last time you'll ever be required in the field."

"That's what you said the last time."

"But I mean it this time. No excuses. As God, Hank, and these gentlemen as my witnesses, You'll never have to set foot in the outdoors again. Unless, that is, you choose to. Please, Becky, this is the finale."

"And the next one is the season premiere, which you'll claim is even more important, and the cycle will continue."

Hank said, "Don't be rash, Beck. Remember you have Gracie to think about. Anyway, we'll lead these fellows back to base camp and call for an emergency transport. You can give it some thought on your way back."

"Not so fast," Cody objected. "What reason would we have to scrap the production?"

Hank looked baffled. "These men are lost and nearly out of supplies. What would you expect us to do? Send them on their way?"

"Why not simply move forward? The journey to the extraction site is only a day longer than if we were to concede failure and return to base camp. And the transport helicopter can certainly fit three more."

"Yes, but a day is a day, and moving forward is moving higher into the mountains and deeper into the snow, a more difficult undertaking with three unexpected mouths to feed. Under those circumstances a day means a lot."

Cody looked at the Russians pleadingly. "Gentlemen, are you injured in any way?"

"No, thankfully not," Andrei said.

"Are you dehydrated or suffering malnutrition?"

"No, haven't been without supplies long enough."

"You see, Hank, they haven't yet suffered the ill-effects of becoming lost. We found them just in time, and now in your care, with your trapping skills, we should have no difficulties feeding them. If anything, with three more strong men, our equipment burden will be greatly reduced. Look at this one here." Cody pointed to Fedor. "Why, I'll bet he can carry more than Maloney. I mean, who would have thought it possible?"

Hank rubbed his beard, brooding over the option.

"Oh, come now, do the calculus. The good of moving forward far exceeds that of returning to base camp. Hank? What say you?"

"Of course, we're grateful we came upon you," Andrei said, "but we wouldn't want to interrupt your production. If your intention was to rendezvous at a point deeper in the mountains, then by all means continue. We'll simply accompany you on your journey."

Cody beamed, his swollen red nose contrasting sharply with his rack of white teeth. "See, Hank? Even Andrei here says we should move forward."

There was a long moment of silence as Hank continued deliberating. The wind began to gust with greater force. The chill it carried deepened. The new front was pushing closer.

Finally, Hank said, "Alright, we'll move forward, but I want your assurance, Cody, that you'll quit arguing and defer to any opinions I have concerning our safety."

"Agreed," Cody said, almost before Hank finished his words.

"We've spent more time here than anticipated," Becky said. "Think we'll make our destination before the weather hits?"

"No, I don't think we can," Hank said. "And the approaching squall is going to be fierce. Comparatively speaking, things thus far have been sunshine in the park. I think it best we just hunker down here for the night and try making up for lost time in the morning."

"Very good, old boy," Cody said. "That'll work splendidly, as I would like to discuss with Becky ways in which we might salvage the mine scene. Nothing dangerous, of course."

Becky thought of Cody's insufferable attitude, then of the potential difficulties finding another job. And then she thought of Gracie. After a moment of consideration she said, "Alright Cody, we'll put our heads together. But I'm holding you to your promise. Until Gracie's healthy—and that may be some time— I'm producing from the studio."

Cody flashed his teeth. "I wouldn't have it any other way."

Hank said, "Okay, see what you two can come up with, but run it by me before anyone goes back into that mine. Afterwards, Codwell, I'll show you how to build a quinzee shelter. You wanted to sleep in a snow cave, right? That's good because it's going to be your bedroom tonight. Not Kilpatrick's."

There was some hesitation before Cody begrudged a smile and said, "Alright, Hank, I suppose I deserve that one."

16

CAMP HAD LONG been established and night fallen. While Fedor slept alone in the small tent, Andrei and Viktor reclined comfortably in Cody's. The dome's walls whipped and shuddered as gale winds struck from the west. Still, Viktor felt a level of comfort that far exceeded the previous night: a small generator hummed, powering a lamp. A propane heater warmed the air. It confused Viktor that a man who claimed to be a survival expert reveled in so many personal luxuries. He shrugged, looked at Andrei. "It seems the bearded man is the only one with knowledge of their destination."

"Yes. Hank. So we must maintain the ruse for as long as possible. Travel to the extraction will be much easier if they go willingly."

"We could force the coordinates out of him."

"Too risky," Andrei said. "He appears to be a man of great resolve."

"The woman is his weakness."

"Yes, but again, we cannot risk it."

"And what of Fedor?"

"What of him?"

"He will not be pleased."

"He is *myshtsa*. He needn't be pleased, or burdened with details. We've had this discussion."

Viktor fell silent.

Wind-driven snow lashed harder at the dome. Andrei paused to listen to the violence. "So it's settled. We'll allow them to lead us to their destination, after which time a tragedy will befall them."

Viktor nodded assent.

"The three of us will then commandeer the aircraft and plot a course to a remote location near the U.S. border, northern Montana I should think. From there, provisioned, we'll make our way into the States and emerge in some backwater American community."

Viktor reclined against his pack. His hands folded at his chest, he stared into the dome's shuddering walls. "And we shall live the remainder of our lives as very rich men."

●　　　●　　　●

In absolute darkness, Becky huddled in her sleeping bag. Nearby, Hank did the same. The temperature outside had dropped far below zero.

Of all nights for a snow shelter, Becky thought, this one was the worst. Cody, no doubt, was awake and miserable in his tiny tomb, a camera his only company.

But still, Becky had to give him some credit.

He followed Hank's directions for building the shelter to the very last detail and smiled all the while he worked, likely because Becky had come up with (and executed) a brilliant plan for salvaging the mine scene.

Making Cody look the hero had been as simple as locating a shallow shaft, then collecting and driving into one of its walls more of those iron spikes. Cody had called them miners' candlesticks, but he could just as easily have called them angelsticks seeing as one had saved him from a devastating fall.

Afterward, Marshal captured a face-shot of Cody grimacing up from the shaft, hanging with both hands from one of the lower spikes as if he had caught himself and stopped his fall. In reality, he was standing at the bottom of a fifteen-foot shaft, but with the faint red light of the camera, only his face and extended arms were visible from the lip of the pit.

Finally, Kilpatrick replaced him and, with a lowered head, muscled his way back up the spikes. In the studio, all of the footage—from Cody's actual fall into the pit to Kilpatrick's staged climb back out of it—would be edited into one harrowing scene minus, of course, Cody's pleading and sobbing. He would look every bit the intrepid survivalist. Becky smiled inwardly, pleased with how she had managed it all.

"Do you buy their story?" Hank's deep, disembodied voice interrupted her thoughts.

"What do you mean?"

"I mean the Russians. Do you believe their story?"

Becky thought the question odd. People went out hiking in the mountains all the time, often unprepared, only to get turned around and lost in unexpected weather. These three were lucky to be found. What wasn't to believe?

"You're skeptical?" Becky said.

"The big guy, what's his name?"

"Fedor."

"Right, Fedor." Hank spoke the name suspiciously. "He looks like no engineer I've ever seen."

"I agree with you, but come on, that's your reason for being suspicious? On television Cody passes as a survivalist. Looks can be deceiving."

"It's not just that. If they're engineers, not outdoorsmen, it's unlikely they would have made it this far from civilization without showing more signs of wear. I mean their clothes, their untanned skin, their stubbled faces, it just doesn't feel right."

"Oh, Hank, I think this trip—Cody in particular—has gotten to you."

In the darkness, he sighed. "Yeah, you might be right. It's probably nothing. Anyway, in a few more days this trip will be over. I won't have to worry about the Russians *or* Cody."

His words made Becky think about being home with Gracie, and she smiled. "Yes, in a few days it'll all be a thing of the past."

A long amicable silence followed before Hank once again spoke, this time more heartfelt. "You know, Beck, seeing as this is your last trip in the field, it's got me thinking, maybe it's time I hang up my hat."

Becky turned her head and looked into the blackness toward his voice.

"I don't belong out here. Not selling myself like this, I don't. The woods and me, we have a special relationship, one that wasn't meant to be shared with cameras and spoiled rich kids."

"What are you saying?"

"I'm saying this is going to be my last trip. I'm done with it all. I have enough saved, I'm just going to retire. I mean, not from the outdoors, of course, just from all this."

"You know I'll support you, no matter what you do."

"And I appreciate it."

The subject slowly turned to idle conversation.

Outside the storm intensified. Becky closed her eyes and listened to the swaying trees and their bending branches. It made her long for home and the false security of her bedcovers. "Anyway, if you do retire," she said, returning to the topic of his confession, "it'll give us time to do some of that fair-weather camping you were talking about."

Now there was joy in Hank's voice. "Yes, you bet it will."

17

IN THE MINE'S CLEARING, snow had accumulated to a depth of nearly three feet. In places, small mangled tree limbs—victims of the night's storm—poked from beneath the fresh blanket. A large campfire blazed at the clearing's center. Encircling it, the crew and the three Russians stood in the shadows of the eastern peaks with tins of hot oatmeal and coffee. Their breath frosted the air as they chatted.

The gray shadows made Becky remove her sunglasses as she inserted herself into the circle next to Andrei, who was facing the stamp mill with an open sketchpad. Furiously he worked an artist's pencil. Becky glimpsed the sketch, which turned out to be truly amazing.

"It's uncanny how you captured the age of the timbers, all in black and white, no less. You've been doing this a long time, haven't you?"

He smiled. "Since I was very young."

"I'd imagine your talent comes in handy as an engineer."

Andrei stopped his work and studied Becky's face. "You've a lovely profile, Rebecca. May I call you that?"

Becky felt herself blush. "I don't see why not."

"I would be honored if you would allow me to sketch your portrait sometime, perhaps during camp this evening?"

Before Becky could accept his offer with the appropriate feigned reluctance, Cody and his swollen nose squeezed in next to her. His face was heavily stubbled and aglow from the fire. "Good morning, Becky. I trust your night was a pleasant one?"

"I'd say so, compared to your night in the quinzee."

Cody shivered as answer, then said, "May I have a word with you in private?"

She turned back to Andrei, "If you'll excuse me."

"Of course," he said and continued his sketch of the mill.

Cody tugged her away from the fire. "The snow cave really wasn't all that bad. My body heat warmed it considerably. The bloke who invented the thing was a genius."

"But still, not what you're used to."

"Oh, Becky, the luxuries in which you perceive I indulge are not for my comfort. They are to keep me functioning in top form. I can't very well succumb to the elements while in the middle of a shoot now, can I?"

"Oh no, we would never want that," she said. "So what is it you pulled me away for? To discuss a new plan?"

Cody grinned. "Am I that predictable?"

"You are," Becky said. "Yesterday after the mine debacle, you transformed instantly from an ogre to a decent man, and it just so happened to coincide with the appearance of Andrei and his buddies."

"Indeed. What do you think about changing the focus of the finale from survival tactics to rescue operation?"

"The Russians you mean?"

"Yes. Of course survival techniques will continue to drive the show, but in the context of me leading these poor fellows to the safety of our extraction team. Along the way, I'll forage, trap, build them shelters, you get the idea."

"All in an effort to ease their suffering in this wilderness hell, I presume?"

"Precisely."

Becky shrugged. "Since they're tagging along, I already assumed as much. With four days of travel we haven't enough food to feed everyone, so I guess all those things you mention will be necessary anyway."

"Yes, yes, and in voiceover, I'll play up their plight at becoming lost, hint at their desperation for rescue. Whatever footage Tasha and Marshal manage to capture, we'll edit out any smiles or cheerful conversations. Focus upon the more grim."

"You asked to talk away from the group. Can I assume you want this done subtly?"

"Of course, I wouldn't want our guests to feel like actors and adopt actors' mentalities. It might affect their natural behavior. They may very well put on brave faces for the camera. We can't have that."

Hank emerged from the forest, his sunglasses, beard, and Mariner's cap conspiring to make him faceless. He cradled a pyramid of long, supple tree limbs between the crooks of his arms, dropped them onto a pile he had begun building earlier in the morning. He rolled his shoulders and stretched before calling out to the crew, "Gather round, everyone. Before we head out this morning, you'll each be making a pair of snowshoes."

"Snowshoes, wonderful!" Cody said. He turned and called out to Tasha, "Let's film this!"

"I'm on it."

Hank said to Cody, "Get your crew and come with me. I left a few saplings attached for you to cut off and explain to your audience."

Cody beamed. "Tasha, Marshal, follow Hank and me."

Hank said, "Maloney, why don't you and our new friends here collect some sharp rocks and strip the bark from these limbs the best you can. They'll bind better naked."

"Sure thing," Maloney said.

•   •   •

It was the work of two hours for Cody to explain to the camera the procedure for making improvised snow shows, and for each crewmember to construct a pair.

By late morning, the group was sledging over

deep snow on their way to the day's destination: timberline on the eastern slope of the opposing range.

To the dismay of the Russians, Cody remained close in the lead, at times warning them to watch their steps or stopping to offer them moral and motivational support.

More than once, Hank noticed the three men exchanging irritated glances and chatting amongst themselves in Russian, presumably about Cody's curious, overprotective behavior.

Marshal remained behind the knot, filming all the while.

Hank focused ahead, where the jagged ridgeline loomed high above them. The cries of an eagle echoed from somewhere off its rocky slopes, and wind from the summit carried down the scent of fir trees. As they ascended, each step more difficult than the last, Hank's eyes searched higher elevations for avalanche tracks. All the signs were present: fresh unsettled snow, bare stretches of ground that reached high into the mountains, and steep, leeward slopes.

Together, they all spelled avalanche. And it made Hank nervous.

As he followed the group, searching for danger spots, he turned his attention to the Russians. The more he thought about them, the more he felt uncomfortable. This morning, having watched Andrei and Viktor expertly weave tree limbs into makeshift snowshoes, Hank's distrust had grown. Though, apparently, they were just engineers, their hands had manipulated the wood with a familiarity that made him think they had done it before—survival training, in the military, maybe.

Hank called for the group to stop. He pointed. "Cody, you see there that stretch of treeless slope?"

Cody looked ahead. "Yes."

"Further upslope you'll notice the ground rises convex. With that snow accumulation there, this is a bad place for us to ascend. We'll need to cross over one at a time to those trees there and continue around this area."

"Right, I concur." He studied the landscape, nodding sagely as if he knew what the hell Hank was looking at.

Hank said, "Would you like to explain all that to the camera before we cross?"

"Indeed I would."

"After I cross," Hank said, "you can retrace my path with Marshal filming you."

"With you out of the shot, of course?"

"Of course."

"I'm curious," Cody asked. "Will similar conditions be present farther upslope in the mountains?"

"You betcha," Hank said. "In fact, conditions for a slide will be more ripe. Best everyone know what to look for and keep an eye out. Never can be too careful."

Cody smiled, produced a pocket mirror and checked his face. He tousled his hair and sucked at his teeth before calling for Tasha and Marshal to stage the shot.

His monologue was quick and dramatic. Afterward, he turned to the Russians and spoke over the rising wind in a volume that would ensure capture by Marshal's microphone. "Andrei, given your group's compromised condition and gross inexperience in the wild, I think it best each of you follow my path carefully. You mustn't stray from it in the least. Heed my warnings and I shall lead you all safely across."

Fedor's eyes narrowed and he made a move toward Cody. Andrei stepped between them, smiling. "Your concern for our welfare is admirable, my friend. Lead the way."

With everyone assembled, Hank carefully crossed the treeless terrain, then turned to observe the others one at a time sledging their way along in his wake. Thirty minutes later, the group had reassembled where the forest continued its rise upslope. On the other side of the ridge, the mountain would dip into a gorgeous valley studded with trees and dominated by a large lake. The same lake, Hank knew from having seen Andrei's sketch, where the Russians had camped some nights prior.

The group shifted higher through the fir trees, the air sweet with the scent of evergreen. Towering in spirals, the firs did little to protect the ground from snow accumulation. Here and there, barrel-shaped cones lay nestled in the snow.

The day progressed, and the incline steepened. Hank fell into step next to Becky to give her assistance. She smiled when he shouldered next to her, and in silence the group labored onward and upward, stopping only occasionally for Cody to demonstrate survival tactics.

The afternoon lengthened, and as twilight neared, the temperature fell. With each passing minute, the frost from their breath thickened. More than once Hank caught Becky by the elbow as she faltered from weariness.

Soon they crested a tree-lined ridge and stopped high above the distant valley, each member huffing from exertion. Here, Hank watched their faces and smiled. He knew this was the moment their effort would pay dividends. Becky laced her arm through his and gazed out over the valley.

"My Lord," she said. "It's lovely."

Hank inhaled deeply and took in the sight, as well. It was a wide panorama of natural beauty. From their position on the ridge, the snowy, fir-studded slope descended sharply into an oval-shaped valley. A lake, like a giant blue teardrop, lay cradled in its bosom, ice creeping from its shore halfway to its center. Beyond the lake, the high central range of the Rockies marked the valley's western edge, and thick dark clouds crowded over its peaks. By nightfall, Hank knew, the snow-laden clouds would be over the valley, dropping more precipitation upon an already heavy layer of snow.

Marshal was filming quietly when Cody broke the silence. "I'd like everyone to back away, if you would. Marshal, you'll film me and my friends here as we re-approach the ridge. We'll hike there—" he pointed to a bald granite shelf "—where the drop into the valley is steepest. I'm going to caution them to stay clear of its edge while they behold Mother Nature's beauty. Make sure to go tight on my face when

I warn them about the precipice."

"And when you're done," Hank said, "we need to pick our way down while we still have enough light to do so safely. You'll all take up residence on the northern shore, then tomorrow, after striking camp, you'll continue skirting the lake west till you reach the slopes. There, you'll continue the climb till day's end about halfway up the mountainside. I'll describe to you some natural markers so you won't get lost."

Becky smiled. "I don't understand," she said, tightening her grip around Hank's arm. "You speak as though we'll be doing this without you."

Hank gazed at her somberly. "That's because you will be. After reaching the valley floor, we'll be parting ways."

18

A FROZEN WIND swept up from the valley, chilling Becky deeply. "What do you mean we'll be parting ways?" she asked Hank.

"When we reach the lake, you and the crew will follow the instructions I just gave. I'll be heading south."

Andrei said, "Do you think splitting up is a good idea? Alone, a man is more vulnerable. Perhaps we should stick together."

"I'll remind you, I'm not the one who got lost in the bush," Hank said sharply.

Becky watched the Russians trade nervous glances.

"Anyway, you needn't worry about me. I'll be meeting back up with you tomorrow night at your camp midway up the mountainside. We have three extra mouths to feed. If I'm going to sustain this group comfortably, I need to find some protein. And that ain't gonna happen unless I do some trapping."

Maloney asked, "Why not stick with us and

trap near camp?"

Becky said, "Because animals shy away from people, and a group like this will drive most of them into hiding."

"That's right," Hank said. "Remember, their senses aren't our senses. We're scarcely aware of their presence. But for a mile around us, every critter that can see, hear and smell knows we're intruding. By myself, some distance away from the group, I'll have much better luck trapping. I'll hunker down overnight in that tent Fedor slept in, then check my snares for groceries in the morning."

"I see," Maloney said.

"Anyway, you shouldn't have any problems, just so long as none of you go and do anything stupid. Let your gut guide you."

Andrei smiled. "Yes, your explanation makes perfect sense now. My apologies for objecting uninformed."

"Then it's settled," Becky said, relieved to learn Hank's departure would only be temporary. "Tasha, Marshal, let's get this shot staged, then afterward we'll tackle the descent into the valley."

•   •   •

With their improvised snowshoes, the group descended using the cautious technique of sidestepping at an angle to the slope, so that their path resembled a series of switchbacks. In so doing, their footholds became surer, their speed more controlled.

Cody, with dramatic flair, offered plenty of encouragement to the Russians, while Marshal filmed behind them. By the time the group reached the lake and set camp, the sun had crowned the western peaks, rolling out long shadows over the lake's icy waters.

Another magnificent view and Becky once again thought of Gracie. How she wished her daughter to be at her side right now, to share in the dichotomous beauty and savagery of nature. It would have been a special bonding experience.

Becky looked to the south, in the direction Hank had departed. She had been following his course along the lakeshore, but now he had disappeared into the distant firs of the southern slopes.

Angry voices turned her head toward camp. Near the fire, Maloney and Fedor had begun arguing. Becky hurried toward them.

"You Americans," Fedor growled, "all so protective of your space." He spoke the word 'Americans' as if it were a pejorative.

"It don't matter where you're from. You don't go rummaging through a man's things without his permission."

"I hunger. Why do you chirp like a little bird over a protein bar?"

"I'll show you a little bird."

"Please, stop!" Becky called out, nearing the fire. But her plea was ignored.

In that instant, Fedor lashed out with a fist and struck Maloney squarely in the throat.

Maloney tumbled back clutching his neck and

gasping for air. Then quickly he recovered, lowered his shoulder, and bull rushed Fedor, driving the stout Russian backward.

The two men tumbled through the fire, into the snow, and onto their backsides. Orange embers mushroomed aloft and blossomed into the wind.

Fedor mounted Maloney with a quick maneuver and cocked back his fist to strike.

Horrified, Becky threw her hands to her mouth.

But before Fedor could deliver the blow, Andrei was behind him. He clutched the powerful man's forearm and pulled him away from Maloney. "You'll stop this! Immediately. We are not animals."

Kilpatrick inserted himself between the two men, who had scrambled to their feet, chests heaving. Their rapid breathing clouded the air. The smell of ash hung heavy. Kilpatrick rested a hand on Maloney's shoulder. "It's okay, buddy. Cool down."

"You see that? The son-of-a-bitch was digging through my pack."

Becky said, "Let's everybody just take a deep breath."

Fedor grinned. In the glow of the campfire, his face appeared bestial.

Andrei said, "It would be wise not to fight. Nature already tests us. Why complicate our condition?"

"He better not go digging through my pack again." Maloney's jaw tightened. "I'll tell you that much."

"I can assure you, it will not happen a second time, my friend."

Fedor, his eyes menacing, was now staring at the crew, each in turn. There was a quiet rage about him. A moment of fear prickled Becky's spine.

"You should retire for the evening," Andrei told him. "Clearly, the environment has unsettled you."

Fedor finished his threatening appraisal before walking to a dome and disappearing inside.

•   •   •

Hank finished arranging the last of his deadfalls. Because night had settled so quickly, he'd started by baiting and setting snares along game trails, using the dim light of dusk to work. Deadfalls were much easier to manage by flashlight, and so he had saved them for last.

Standing to his feet, he pulled his gloves back onto his frozen hands and headed for the southern shore of the lake. He had lied to Becky about the reason for his departure—at least partially. True, the group needed additional sustenance now that there was a dwindling food supply and three extra mouths to feed. But what he had not told her was the other more significant reason he'd parted from the group.

Since running into the Russians, Hank had been nagged by a growing suspicion. Much of what they told him, while technically reasonable, didn't ring true. In addition to the concerns he had aired to Becky, there was also the problem of Andrei's sketch of the lake.

Hank picked his way down a snowy, rock-studded slope and emerged from the forest near the shore. The wind was stronger here, gusting from the west. Trees swayed. Limbs scratched limbs. Hank stared far across the lake at a glowing smudge that was the crew's campfire. Most likely they had all retired for the night.

Hank recollected Andrei's sketch. Something in it had bothered him. He decided to hike a good distance from his traps before erecting his tent and hunkering down for the night. In the morning he would return, collect whatever bounty the good Lord offered, then look into the matter that disturbed him.

19

When Becky emerged from her dome the next morning, the smell of wood ash remained faint in the air. Snow had once again fallen, adding to the already thick ground layer. And here, where the group's presence between the eastern and western peaks shielded their camp from the rising sun, an immense shadow smothered them. The great pall, coupled with last night's attack on Maloney depressed her spirits.

"Good morning, Rebecca." The voice was Andrei's. He was emerging from the forest with his sketchpad.

"I see you've been hard at work," she said, nodding to the sketchpad and ascending a snowy rise to greet him. "Find any good subjects?"

"Yes, the woods offered much, but I settled upon a sad, yet lovely scene. Last night's wind felled a young fir tree. Here, see for yourself. I would love your opinion." He extended her the pad.

She took it and studied the illustration. The

tree, lying uprooted and fractured at its center, had been sketched in striking detail. Once again, she thought, he had produced an image of transcendent beauty.

"Do you like it?"

She peered up at him. He was a pleasant looking man with sincerity in his eyes. "Do I like it? Of course. I love it. It's wonderful."

He smiled. "Then my efforts have been rewarded. I am pleased."

"You're different than your friend Fedor," Becky said admittedly. "After last night, after seeing his awful behavior…I'm sorry to say, but he frightens me."

For a moment Andrei was quiet, as if considering an explanation. "The stress of the environment has had a negative effect upon him. Made him a different person. You shouldn't be concerned. He'll not harm you."

"Yes, but—"

"On the previous page," Andrei quickly added, indicating the sketchpad, "you'll find another of my favorites."

Her curiosity piqued, she turned the page. The image she saw immediately shocked her.

"I must apologize," Andrei said, observing her surprise.

Becky was staring down at the sketch of a beautiful woman. "This is me," she said.

"Yes, in profile. After helping establish camp yesterday evening you stood gazing toward the south. You seemed so deep in thought, pensive really. For some time, you didn't stir, not a muscle. I couldn't help but wonder your thoughts. I saw it as an opportunity. I should have asked your permission, of course, but feared losing the moment. If I overstepped, I apologize."

"No no, don't apologize."

"If you feel I have violated your privacy...."

"Not at all," Becky said. "It's just that I've never seen myself as a work of art before."

"Oh but you are, Rebecca. You're very beautiful, like the valley that surrounds you."

Becky felt a sudden flutter in her breast. She couldn't help but smile. She found Andrei charming, and it had been some time since a man moved her with such kind words. Feeling herself begin to flush, she returned the sketchpad and turned away, starting back for camp. "I see the others are striking their domes and getting ready for a long day," she said. "I guess we should do the same."

•   •   •

With the snow cleared at the base of a fir tree, Hank sat smoking his pipe and watching in the distance as the group marched west along the lakeshore. Cody led the Russians, now and again stopping to point at something in the snow. Exactly what in Sam Hill he thought he was identifying, Hank had no idea. But at one point, the intrepid idiot even picked something up, gave an explanation to the Russians, then rubbed whatever the hell it was against his cheeks and forehead. Marshal filmed diligently.

Hank just chuckled and shook his head.

He glanced down at the string of meat by his side: two squirrels and a good-sized woodrat. Seasoned properly and roasted over an open flame, they would make a decent meal. In addition to this, he had nearly trapped a snowshoe hare. *Nearly.* Its tracks had told the story: The critter had come close to the deadfall to investigate, thought better of the bait, and escaped without ever touching the trigger. Hank pined over the loss. It would have been a treat for him and Becky.

He looked back and watched the group recede further into the distance. And soon they disappeared altogether. He would intercept them at a later time.

Finishing a second plug of tobacco, he whacked the dottle from his pipe, stood to his feet and headed west along the lakeshore.

His focus of attention narrowed back on Andrei's sketch of the lake. What bothered Hank wasn't the drawing itself, as much as something he'd seen in it—a campfire.

When first they met at the mine, Andrei said they'd been turned around and lost for a few days, but just the morning before, they'd been here at the lake. Now in Hank's estimation, that left only three possibilities: the first, Andrei had simply taken the liberty of adding a nonexistent campfire to his sketch. If that was the case, fine, so be it. It would offer Hank a little relief.

But the other two possibilities nagged at him.

If the campfire was the Russian's own, and

they truly were lost and low on provisions, why make the effort to hike all the way to the opposite shore just to sketch it? And if the campfire belonged to someone else, why not go and ask whoever had built it for some help?

The first two possibilities simply made these men losers. But the third one made them liars.

And Hank needed to know which one they were.

He continued to pick his way over the snow-covered scree and soon reached a bend in the lake where it curved north. Ahead, something red and snow-covered perked him right up. As he neared, he could see the remains of a collapsed tent. Scattered around it and frozen in the snow were meal tins and a pot for brewing coffee.

So the campfire had been real, not just an addition to Andrei's sketch. But who had made it? The Russians? Why not take some of this stuff with them? Hank cleared away snow from the collapsed tent and examined it. The frame was bent and twisted beyond usefulness, which might explain why it was left behind. But the tins, why not take the tins? They were perfectly good, and out here in the backcountry they were a convenient tool to have.

The logic didn't sit well with Hank. And somewhere inside his mind, a mental alarm sounded.

He looked to where the valley floor rose steeply into the western mountains. A forest of fir trees concealed Becky and the others, who were likely picking along at a reasonable pace. Hank drew a long, deep breath.

He wanted to know more about who had been here and what had happened, so he knelt and searched for signs of activity, but the snow had covered any and all clues. Standing, he removed his Mariners cap, scratched his head, then repositioned the cap. He turned, looked away from the abandoned camp toward the forest fringe and studied the apron of trees. There, he saw something interesting.

He climbed his way to the margin, stopped, and absently tugged at his beard. The past few days, the winds had been blowing from the west, and patterns of limb damage should bear that out.

But at the closest point from the forest to camp, a series of trees leading deeper into the woods had subtle breakages from north to south, as if someone had been in a hurry, forcing themselves in a direction at a right angle to the heavy winds.

Hank touched a thin, fractured branch. Then he found another, and still another. These breaks, he was sure, had not been caused by the wind.

Following the subtle signs, he searched deeper into the woods until he came upon a massive fir. There, he stopped. At about head high, he noticed damage to the bark, damage of the sort he wasn't used to seeing. It was too high for most animals to reach, and those that could—such as bear—would have left other markings, like claw gouges.

Hank peered closer at the damage. There seemed to be a small hole. He unsheathed his knife and probed the inside with its tip. Then he hit something hard. He dug the blade deep into the wood to pry out whatever was inside. A glint of gray caught his eye, followed by a cylindrical shape. He worked quickly to dig out the object. A slug fell into the palm of his glove.

For a time, Hank stared down at it, unwilling to admit that this was proof of anything. The reasons for a slug being there were many, he told himself. Whoever it was that fired it might have been scaring off a predator, or simply target shooting.

Still, none of this made him feel better about the Russians, who were no doubt hiding something, and Beck being with them right now didn't please Hank any either. But surely she'd be fine till tonight, when he could meet back up with them.

But what would he do then?

Forming a plan was almost instant. Tonight, after reaching the others, he would show Cody how to skin and gut the meat, then as everyone watched the filming, he'd pull Becky aside and air his concerns. Together, discreetly, they would inform the others. The next morning, after striking out for the peaks, he'd find some excuse to lead the Russians away from the crew long enough for everyone to turn in another direction. After giving them time to distance themselves, he would ditch the scoundrels and meet up with everyone at a predetermined location. Cody wouldn't like losing his unwitting extras, of course, but Hank would just have to put his foot down.

Afterwards, he and the crew would hightail it back to base camp and use the satphone to call in a rescue party to pick up the Russians. They could explain themselves to authorities. If it turned out Hank had overreacted and misjudged their character, well fine, he'd apologize over a beer, no harm done. If, on the other hand, these were men of rotten character, well then his precautions would turn out justified. Either way everyone would make it out of the mountains safely.

Satisfied with this idea, Hank began his hike back.

When he reached the shoreline, he skirted it west until it began its arc northward. The sun had finally topped the eastern ridge and, with the sky temporarily clearing, sunlight glistened from the ice-covered lake. A deep azure, its surface was quiet and unmoving, and it wasn't long before Hank started his move away from the shore and up the western slope. But as he took his first step, a glimmer from the lake caught the corner of his eye.

He turned toward the water and approached to investigate. At its edge, now frozen over, a reflective mass protruded—a ball of clear plastic that was covering something dark and solid. Nearing it, he could see that whatever it was, it had become wedged and frozen in the surface ice.

Hank reached the point where he couldn't advance any farther, and at six feet from shore, the plastic mass was still well out of reach. He could try treading lightly over the ice, but this early in the freezing process, he doubted it would support him.

He slogged up to the forest to scavenge for storm-torn tree limbs. He found two, one thin and over six feet long, the other much shorter, more solid. The first he would use as a fishing pole of sorts, the second as a club.

Back at the lake, he stripped and sharpened the longer branch. As he worked, thick clouds replaced clear skies, and a creeping mist materialized over the lake. The air turned bitterly cold.

He finished preparing the branch, then carefully prodded out to the plastic until he managed to pierce it. He laid the long limb on the ground and braced it with a foot. Raising the thicker limb, he clubbed the ice, and as he suspected, it gave easily, shattering into a web.

A few more strikes and the ice surrounding the plastic separated completely. Hank tossed away the club, reached for the branch, and hefted it high, keeping it level to prevent the plastic from slipping off and back into the drink. Whatever was inside had become waterlogged and frozen, giving it serious weight. Grunting, Hank swung the branch over the shore and lowered it to the ground, jerked away and discarded the sharpened branch.

And there he stood staring at the thing. What first filled him with a sense of foreboding was not that the mass was the size and shape of a human head. Nor was it the ever-so-faint stench emanating from the thing. No, what first unsettled him was the sight of black hair under the plastic.

Unnerved, Hank knelt beside the grisly mass and slowly reached out and rolled it over. Through the plastic a man's bloated face revealed itself, gray and flesh-torn. Hank startled back onto his haunches.

For a time, he sat rigid, gaping down at the

horror.

Then, ever so gradually, the shock began to abate and his faculties returned. When he could reason again, he dismissed the possibility of another coincidence. First, running into the Russians, then finding the deserted camp and bullet hole. And now this! It took Hank but a second to decide these men were more than just no-good liars. These men were murderers.

Despite the cold, sweat slicked his forehead. He yanked off his cap and wiped his brow, then turned toward the western slope and searched into the distant trees. *My God, Becky.*

20

ECKY LABORED UP the snowy incline, slogging ahead of Maloney and Kilpatrick. The three followed the film crew. Cody maintained his heroic lead of the Russians, never once failing to caution them against some imaginary danger. Dutifully, Marshal filmed, now and again getting scolded by his wife for taking a lazy angle on a shot.

The early afternoon clearing had passed, and now a slate of gray clouds pressed down upon them. Snow-blanketed meadows grew less frequent, and Becky noticed that conifers were becoming sparse and more stunted—an indication they were nearing the timberline.

"There?" Kilpatrick called out, pointing ahead. "That looks like the landmark Hank described."

Becky traced his sight to a towering rock shelf in the distance. "It certainly does."

"Problem is," he added, now less enthusiastically, "the slopes to either side of it are plugged up by drifts. How we supposed to get around it?"

Becky stopped and assessed the shelf. Kilpatrick was right. Heavy snowdrifts walled the passes around it. This close to the summit, westerly winds had driven sleet and snow over the ridge and deposited it here on the leeward side. Hank had told the group they would reach this point and could skirt the shelf and continue beyond, where the terrain temporarily leveled. There, camp would be possible, and they should await his arrival later this evening.

Becky continued studying the terrain on both sides of the shelf, searching for an alternate route. To her left, as far as she could see, the slope rose nearly vertical, an angle impossible to climb without serious mountaineering equipment. To her right, the same problem persisted. Short of backtracking down the mountain and climbing another face, there was no way around.

Ahead, the others had stopped, too, having presumably seen the barrier and drawn the same conclusion.

Tasha turned to Becky. "What are we supposed to do now?"

"Yeah, we can't camp here," Marshal said. "The snow is too thick and there's nowhere level to build a fire or pitch a dome."

Tasha scowled at him. "Isn't that what I just said?"

Marshal shrugged. "Not exactly, hon."

Becky considered their options. They could hunker down and wait here for Hank, or they could hike back down the mountainside and stop at a meadow they had passed two hours earlier. The problem with the first option was that by the time Hank reached them, it would be dark and still impossible to set camp. With option two, Hank would eventually come across them on his way up, and she could explain her decision to stray from the schedule. Really, no other option presented itself. The second delayed them reaching the extraction point, but the first was just plain foolish.

"We go back down," Becky said. "Two hours back, we passed a meadow. We'll return to it and camp there until Hank arrives. He'll see us and explain how to proceed."

Cody descended toward her awkwardly in his snowshoes. "Becky, a word please!"

"What is it?"

"You're not seriously asking us to hike ground we already covered, are you?"

"Yes, in fact, I am. Can't you see the problem?"

"What you call a problem, I call an opportunity."

"Cody, look, this isn't the time."

"No, please, hear me out," he said. "We have plenty of rope. Why not just climb it?"

Becky looked again at the rock shelf. Its height was unsettling. At its base, jagged rocks that had spalled from the face lay in a field, half-hidden by the snow.

Cody said, "It's my understanding Kilpatrick has some free-hand climbing experience. If he can manage his way to the top with a rope, he could tie it off and assist the others in a safer, more controlled ascent."

Becky glanced at Kilpatrick, who was gazing up at the monolith with a mixture of awe and concern.

Cody said, "What do you say, ol' Killy? Wanna give it a whirl?"

Kilpatrick's face gathered in an expression of doubt. "I don't know. Looks pretty formidable."

"But you are a climber. Are you not?"

"I am, but not what you would call hardcore, and I've only climbed in fair weather. Anyway, my contract with the network states explicitly that I shall not be required to climb any vertical surfaces in excess of twenty feet without what I deem to be the necessary equipment. As far as I'm concerned, something like this requires climbing rope, pitons, and a harness. All we got is rope."

"We don't have the other things," Cody said, "because Hank's route didn't call for any serious vertical ascents."

"Maybe so," Kilpatrick said, "but whatever the reason, we still don't have all the proper equipment."

"See there?" Becky said. "He'd rather not, and his contract backs him. Okay everyone gather your packs. We're heading down to the meadow."

"Not so fast," Cody said.

Inwardly, Becky cringed. She had hoped by giving a decisive command, she could avoid a prolonged argument.

Cody steepled his fingers at his chin before saying in a more theatrical tone, "Earlier in this expedition, many of you suggested that I was being unfair to Mr. Kilpatrick, that at times I ask too much of him."

Heads nodded.

"Well, I've come to the conclusion that you were all absolutely correct."

Becky started to object, but was quickly taken aback by Cody's admission. "Well, I'm glad to hear you've—"

"Which is why from this point forward, I am prepared to offer Mr. Kilpatrick a generous bonus on the performance of any stunt that exceeds his contractual obligations, and which I deem extraordinary in nature. Such as this."

Becky said, "Wait a second. Are you really going to bribe him to risk his life?"

"It's not a bribe; it's a contract renegotiation. Verbally binding."

"That's ridiculous."

"Wait a second," Kilpatrick said. "Exactly what kind of a bonus are we talking about?"

Cody smiled. "I should think ten thousand dollars per extraordinary stunt is a fair sum."

Kilpatrick's wide eyes blinked, and Becky could see him now considering the climb. He trudged to the base of the monolith, carefully avoiding protruding rocks, and began a careful examination.

Becky turned on Cody and narrowed her eyes. "That was an awful thing to do."

"I'm sorry, I don't see it that way," Cody said. "Exactly how is instituting a performance-based bonus an awful thing?"

"You know damn good and well. Dangle money in front of a man, especially one with a baby on the way, and you're sure to get him to take risks he would otherwise never consider."

"Becky, you don't give him enough credit."

"You tell him right now your idea was a mistake. Rescind your offer. Tell him it's far too dangerous."

"I'll do no such thing." Cody waved his hand and turned away. His eyes were on Kilpatrick as the stuntman approached the group.

Cody was all smiles. "So, how does she look?"

"Well, about one-third of the way up on the left side, the cliff spalled off a massive piece of rock, leaving behind a U-shaped cleft that runs to the top, deep enough for me to squeeze into. If I can manage the first twenty feet freehand, the last forty or so inside the cleft would be a simple wall-walk to the top."

"Are we looking at the same cliff face?" Becky asked. "A fall from that height would land you on those jagged rocks."

"There are enough handholds that'll make the beginning of the climb possible," Kilpatrick said. "Becky, really, others make this sort of climb all the time. I think I can do it."

"As you said yourself, in fair weather." She turned an earnest expression. "Please, reconsider."

Viktor said, "Forgive my intrusion, but if it's of any consequence, Andrei and I have some experience in these matters. Prior to becoming engineers, we were both in the Russian military. Belaying and repelling are a few of the skills in which we are trained. After Mr. Kilpatrick reaches the top, should he choose to make the climb, Andrei and I could ascend the rope and give assistance pulling up the others."

"Then it's settled," Cody announced, glancing disapprovingly at Becky. "To the top we go!"

•   •   •

Cody stared steely-eyed into the camera. "If there's one thing I've learned over my years navigating the treacherous backcountry, it's that I must always expect the unexpected."

Kilpatrick watched as the crew filmed the opening of the climb scene at the base of the monolith. Still, the massive wall of stone garnered most of his attention. While the idea of a huge bonus excited him, he knew the climb would not be without risks.

He glanced back to the filming.

"In an effort to reach the peak," Cody continued, "I've encountered an obstacle of immense proportion. The fierce weather has unloaded obscene amounts of snow in the form of impassible drifts. And so it seems if I wish to proceed, I've little choice but to tackle this behemoth before me."

Kilpatrick watched Marshal carefully back away and raise the camera, attempting to capture the dramatic impact of the cliff face.

"After inspecting the quality of rock, I've concluded that with its cracks and natural imperfections, my fingers and boots should find sufficient purchase to make the ascent possible."

Kilpatrick began flexing his fingers to limber them up. He wished for hand chalk.

Cody's expression to the camera turned grave.

"Free climbing is not without its risks, however. If you look here," he indicated the base of the cliff, "you'll see that over the centuries, large pieces of jagged rock have fractured from the face, littering the earth before it. One mishap, one careless mistake, and I risk plunging onto these monstrosities. That, ladies and gentlemen, you wouldn't want to see."

Cody turned to the rock face, stripped down to his underlayers, and reached for a handhold. Then with a confident spring he hefted himself up and found purchase for one boot, then the other.

"Cut!" Tasha called out. Cody dropped two feet to the ground and hurried on his parka and gloves.

•   •   •

Kilpatrick's fingertips ached from the frozen stone as he neared the cleft twenty-five feet above the field of fractured rock. For flexibility, and to match Cody's dress, he had stripped down to his underlayers, and now, consequently, the weather was beginning to hinder his efforts. But another five feet, he knew, and he'd reach the narrow cleft, where he could squeeze between the rock and use his legs and arms in a reverse vise maneuver to wall-walk to the top.

Kilpatrick's breath frosted the stone inches in front of his face. He surveyed the subtle textures of the wall and reached carefully for another handhold, then shifted his position another foot higher and repeated the process until he had reached the cleft and ascended a few feet into it.

Now, with two firm footholds, he quickly reached for opposite sides of the narrow kerf and pressed firmly against them. Next, he exerted enough pressure to wedge himself, then kicked out his feet so that they firmly gripped the walls. Spread-eagle, he glanced down. Thirty feet below him, he could see Marshal filming his progress, balanced precariously over the litter of split rocks. Somewhere, from a much greater distance, Tasha was likely doing the same, capturing his progress from another angle. The group stood quietly, watching.

"All is good!" Kilpatrick called down to ease their fears.

Cody hollered up, "Head turned away, if you please Mr. Kilpatrick. I'd like to keep the number of cutaways to a minimum."

Kilpatrick turned his face to the inside of the cleft. The rock felt like ice against his palms. They began to burn. The sooner he reached the top, he knew, the sooner he could get his gloves back on, so he attacked the climb with renewed vigor. First, he used his legs to push himself higher, then his arms to wedge himself secure. He repeated the process in an alternating rhythm, and began ascending rapidly.

Maybe too rapidly.

Nearing the top, thirty feet higher, as he repositioned his hands, he felt a boot slip against the rock, followed by the sudden, frightening pull of gravity. Panic wrenched his gut, and he found himself sliding downward.

He didn't feel himself scream as much as he heard it reverberating in the cleft. In response, his hands dug against the rock, and he could feel his flesh tearing away from his fingertips. Still, like a brake, he forced his palms harder into the stone, and before his downward momentum reached a critical point, his boots caught against a natural gap in the rock.

He halted with a jerk.

And in this moment of calm, his mind whirled. The sounds of the crew calling out to him were indistinct. Rapidly his lungs took in cold air, and after a moment, his senses returned. He assessed his position. He had slid down maybe ten feet, but he was still only twenty from the top. His arms and shoulders ached, and although he could see his hands had left behind streaks of blood, he felt nothing but a numbing freeze. Far below him, he saw the others gaping up in horror. Becky's hands covered her mouth, and even Cody had paled. Marshal continued to film.

Finding his voice, Kilpatrick called down, "I'm okay, nothing to worry about." But he knew he had just defied death and might as easily be lying over the rocks below.

Carefully and calmly, he continued his wall-walk to the top, opting this time for caution over speed and enduring the numbing sting against his hands. After climbing over the lip of the cleft, he rolled onto his back, looked up into the somber gray clouds and exhaled a heavy breath.

Hey, that was ten grand, he thought. Ten grand sure would buy a lot of diapers.

21

Hank pushed his body harder up the steep slope. The western peaks loomed starkly above him. His quads ached from the effort, but the pain barely registered as his mind raced with thoughts of Becky and the others. While he climbed, a question repeatedly nagged him.

Who were these men?

Clearly, they were more than just hikers or nature enthusiasts. And why had they sought help in the first place? They hadn't shown any real signs of distress. None of it made much sense to Hank. But what he was certain of was that these bastards were brutal killers.

Hank worried about Becky, how she was fairing, and cursed himself for not trusting his gut. He had sensed the Russians were bad men, right from the get-go, but had left her with them anyway to confirm his suspicions. It was a boneheaded move. He never should have done it. If anything happened to her, he'd never forgive himself. He forced his pace faster, accepting the pain as penance for having been such a fool.

Soon, he leveled into a small meadow fringed with fir-choked woods. Ahead, he could see heavy animal tracks in the snow, tracks that bisected the meadow and disappeared into the trees. He knelt and studied them. In deep snow, it wasn't the details of the imprint that gave away the animal. There usually were none. It was the width and depth. And at a diameter of twelve inches and a depth of eighteen, this one was unmistakable—grizzly. A male. Hank estimated the animal at about six or seven hundred pounds.

A beast fattened for hibernation.

The two-foot spacing between both the front and hind paws confirmed it.

He lifted his head and scanned the woods. At this time of year, bears were searching for a suitable den in which to hibernate, and grizzlies sought theirs high on sub-alpine slopes and meadows. Places much like this one.

Hank looked back at the tracks. They were fresh, which meant the animal was somewhere nearby. He removed the frozen meat from his pack and strung it at his side. If he encountered this Goliath up-close and personal, and if it decided to take an ornery interest in him, he wanted to be able to discard the carcasses quickly.

He turned his attention back to his primary concern—Becky and the crew. The fact he wasn't with them sickened him. He lumbered on through the meadow and was soon climbing another steep slope. The sun, backlighting a heavy cloud layer, dipped near the peaks. Soon, the glare of the white mountainside softened into gray. The wind began to mount, gusting steadily over the ridge, raking the trees. Its freeze grew more intense. Hank lowered his head and pushed on.

•   •   •

Maloney adjusted his tethering and stared up the rock face. He decided that when he returned to the city he'd pursue other options as a producer, something a little less vertical. Talking about these forays into the wild was one thing. Experiencing them firsthand was something else altogether. This weather sucked shit. And now here he was next in line to be hauled up a towering precipice on a rope that couldn't have been more than half an inch thick.

Maloney breathed deeply of the cold air and took some comfort in knowing that he was in good hands. Though Fedor was clearly a thief and an asshole, his buddies Andrei and Viktor weren't so bad. In fact, they seemed to be stand-up guys.

After Kilpatrick's harrowing climb, he had secured the rope to a tree, allowing Andrei and Viktor to pull themselves to the top. Maloney had watched in admiration as they ascended impressively up the rope using some sort of technique whereby they entwined one leg around the rope and used their other foot as a sort of brake. In fact, at points along their climb, they had even been able to stop for a minute or two to relax their arms. Clearly, they had practiced this many times before.

Fedor, on the other hand, he had to be hauled up like a side of beef. And now finally, with the equipment and the others safely at the top, it was Maloney's turn to feel the nagging tug of the rope. In spasmodic jerks, he ascended, two feet at a time. He looked toward the white heavens. Wind streamed over the rock face, numbing his nose and cheeks.

Another tug against his lats, another two feet. He glanced down. The distance to the rocks dizzied him, so he turned his sight back skyward and imagined himself standing on firm ground.

Another sharp tug, another two feet.

He swayed against the cliff face. Now thirty feet from the top he could now see a pair of large, black gloves as they worked in rhythm to draw in more rope. Judging by the size of the hands, Maloney figured they were Fedor's, a fact that didn't sit well with him. He didn't want any reason to have to thank the son-of-a-bitch. In fact, he wouldn't. He would make a point instead to give a nod to his two buddies, who were undoubtedly assisting.

Soon, Maloney was near enough to the top where he could see Fedor rocking forward and backward as he and the others pulled. Briefly their eyes locked, and Fedor smirked. Then he called out behind him something in Russian and movement stopped. The wind was stronger here, making Maloney's eyes water. Tears froze against his face.

He saw he was only a foot or two from the top. Why the hell had they stopped pulling?

He dangled precariously.

Then Fedor appeared and called down to him, "The rope is beginning to fray against the edge. Give me your hand as a precaution."

Being close to the edge himself, Maloney couldn't see any damage to the rope. What was he talking about?

Fedor extended a hand. Maloney stretched for it, but rather than locking a firm grip, Fedor stopped short and took hold of the rope. The smirk changed to an expression both smug and sinister. His dark eyes were unsettling.

At that instant, Fedor turned up his other hand, revealing the razor edge of a black steel blade, and in a single swift motion, he slipped it under the rope and sliced.

Panic-filled, Maloney cried out and snatched for a hold against the wall. Sheer, it offered none. He stretched up to slap away the blade, but it was too far out of reach.

"Help," he cried out to the others.

His plea was answered by Fedor's own. "Yes, help, the rope is fraying! Quickly, somebody!" And with this deception came the final slash of the blade.

Maloney watched in terror as the last of the nylon braids severed. Hate and anger drew his eyes like magnets back to Fedor's. The Russian smiled menacingly.

And then Maloney was plummeting, aware of the frozen wind as it rushed up like a hurricane behind him. Weightlessness sent an electric sensation rippling through his stomach, and it seemed to him that his screams emanated from somewhere outside of his body. The crushing blow to his skull came painlessly.

22

THE CRY WAS a man's, and it came from somewhere upslope beyond the woods. Momentarily, the cry's echo lingered, causing fresh worry to rear up in the pit of Hank's gut. A gray twilight offered only fading illumination, but he knew he was getting close. He pushed through the trees, over uneven ground, across steep banks of snow.

Ahead, the rock face where he'd chosen to meet the others loomed above the stunted firs. Hank could see figures amassed atop it. Among them, Becky. Her hands covered her mouth as she gazed downward from the precipice.

Then, in Hank's mind, the numbers added up: a man's cry, the crew gaping over the rock face. A sense of tragedy stabbed at his nerves. As much as he wanted to believe it a coincidence, he knew it wasn't. Someone had gone over the edge, someone had fallen. His hope was that it wasn't one of the crew.

He trudged forward up the incline. The trees

began to thin before him, and soon he could see a rope dangling the length of the rock face. At its base, Kilpatrick was kneeling by a body. From its size and the color of the clothes, Hank knew it was Maloney. His measured steps turned to a run, causing the improvised snowshoes to break off his feet. His boots plunged deep into the snow as he ran. Sweat heated his thermals, and he felt himself burning inside. He stumbled, corrected himself, then continued running.

He heard Marshal call his name from atop the precipice, then the group pointed toward the ground. Kilpatrick stood to his feet and turned as Hank neared. His face was a mask of grief.

Hank stopped. His rapid breathing produced cottony clouds. Kilpatrick's grim expression told the tale, and Hank knew Maloney was dead.

He looked down and knelt at the broken body as it lay splayed over jagged rocks. Blood pooled in the snow behind the poor kid's cratered skull. His eyes gazed lifelessly toward the heavens.

Hank removed a glove, reached down, and with his fingertips gently closed Maloney's eyes. "My God, what happened here?"

Kilpatrick explained best he knew.

"Why were you climbing the thing in the first place?"

"The slopes on both sides are plugged with heavy drifts. They're impassible."

Hank shook his head. "Damn. You should have backtracked to level ground and pitched camp at lower elevation."

"Yes, we should have," Kilpatrick admitted.

"That was Becky's suggestion, too. Cody overruled her."

Hank stood and glanced up the precipice, where the faces of the crew stared down in stunned silence. Becky's hands still covered her mouth. Hank called up, "I want everyone to back away from the edge. If you haven't already built a fire and set camp, I want you to do that now."

He waited for everyone to comply, then peered at Kilpatrick and spoke in a hushed voice. "I have news that makes me think this was no accident."

Kilpatrick stared back at him bewildered. "Not an accident? What are you talking about?"

"What I'm talking about is the reason I left the group."

"To go trapping?"

"That, yes, but also because I had my suspicions about these Russians, and I wanted to check out a thing or two. What I found was this." Hank produced the slug he'd dug from the tree. "Found it near the lake where our friends were camping."

Kilpatrick stared at it. "But couldn't there be other—"

"—explanations? Sure there could be, but after I found this slug, I fished from the lake the head of a corpse, gift wrapped in a plastic bag. That's no coincidence."

Kilpatrick stood speechless. His eyes showed concern.

"These men are not who they say they are, I'm sure of it. And I've no doubt they're dangerous." He indicated Maloney's body. "Now a good kid has paid the price."

When Kilpatrick found his voice he said, "We're miles from nowhere, with no communication, what are we going to do? Tell me you have a plan?"

Hank's stare was intense. "You bet I do. Listen very carefully."

23

BECKY'S TREMBLING HANDS made pitching her dome difficult. As she worked frantically, so too did her mind. Against her better judgment, she had given in to Cody and accepted his dangerous proposal.

And because of this, Maloney was dead.

Deep down inside, she knew she was to blame. As the field producer, she had final say in the matter, but rather than champion safety and the welfare of the crew, she had caved to Cody and his ludicrous plan.

Her welling tears chilled so quickly her eyes stung. She swiped them away and continued assembling the tent poles. Angry with herself, she wanted nothing more to do with this production. In every way imaginable the job was a curse, and in that moment she resolved to resign from the show the moment she returned to Seattle. Where medical bills were concerned, she would just have to make do, somehow, someway.

Through a momentary lull in the wind, she could hear Cody nearby questioning Marshal, who was himself busy erecting a dome.

Cody's tone was business. "Yes, I too wish it had never happened. That's not my point. All I'm asking is how much of it do you think you captured on camera?"

"None of it. I was up here and had no angle." Marshal shook his head. "Jesus Christ, what's this obsession over your stupid-ass show, anyway? A man is dead. Can't you give it a rest?"

Cody said, "There'll be questions, an investigation. Our insurers will demand to know if negligence was at play here. I'm merely pointing out that had the tragedy been recorded, the question of liability could more easily be settled."

Becky dropped her tent poles and turned on Cody. "How could you be concerned about such things right now? Have you no conscience? Maloney is dead, and you and I are to blame."

"Careful with your words, Becky. Neither of us is to blame. It was a horrible accident. Nothing more. It was wholly unpreventable."

"Unpreventable!"

"Yes, and for your own sake, and the sake of your daughter, you would do well to remember that, especially when talking with investigators, who'll surely be speaking with you."

Becky turned away disgusted with Cody and finished assembling her dome.

From the edge of the precipice, Andrei was calling down to Hank and Kilpatrick to ready themselves, and after double-checking the rope for weaknesses, the three Russians began hauling them up, one at a time.

Finally, her dome complete, Becky ducked inside, crawled into her sleeping bag, and wept.

•   •   •

Outside Becky's dome the wind thrashed, which was why she mistook the rapping at her door for worsening weather, but when she heard Hank call to her, she bolted up straight and used the sleeve of her thermals to dry her eyes.

"Come in." She could hear the defeat in her own voice.

Hank unzipped the dome and slipped inside. The deepening twilight darkened his form.

"How you feeling, Beck?"

His deep voice was welcoming, but still, she was unable to look him in the eyes. "I'm glad you've returned. I was worried about you."

"I'm fine. And you'll be fine, too."

She peered up, her anger with herself freshly renewed. "I don't deserve to be fine. Maloney's not fine. The poor man is dead. And I'm the reason for it. Had I simply stood up to Cody, had I the courage to say no—"

"Maloney would still be dead." Hank's face was grim. "What happened to that kid isn't your fault. Kilpatrick explained to me your attempt to reason with Cody. You knew better, but Kilpatrick was blinded by the prospect of a bonus, and Hobbs, his own ambition."

"Yes, but what do you mean Maloney would still be dead?"

There came a drawn silence while Hank appeared to wrestle with some sort of internal conflict.

"Hank, what did you mean?"

"I meant what happened to Maloney was no accident."

"What are you saying? Of course it was an accident."

"Becky, it wasn't an accident. He was murdered."

The mention of murder threw a terrifying silence over the dome. Becky's mind reeled in a state of confusion.

"What I'm gonna tell you is going to make your hair stand on end, but you need to promise me you'll be strong. From this point forward all you need to worry about is yourself and getting back to base camp."

"Hank, you're scaring me."

"Promise me, Beck. Promise me you'll steel yourself against what I'm about to tell you, against what's to come."

Becky edged up close to Hank. "What happened to you out there?"

Hank gripped her shoulders. "I had doubts about these Russians. You knew that. Part of the reason I broke away from the crew was to confirm my suspicions."

"Confirm your suspicions? Hank, I don't understand."

"Andrei's sketch of the lake. It showed a camp-fire that struck me as odd. That and their lack of distress made me need to know. And what I discovered confirmed the worst."

Becky tensed. "What did you find?"

"I've already made Kilpatrick aware. I have a plan for all of us. Come morning, we'll be doing things differently. Cody's no longer running the show. He's now one of us, an equal. He'll cooperate or he'll get left behind. No more *Survivalist*. The show's over. We've got to get back to base camp. We've got to call for help."

Becky stopped Hank with a firm grip on his forearm and stared hard into his eyes. "I'll do what you say. I promise you that. But you need to tell me everything. What did you find out there, Hank?"

The wind lashed fiercely against the nylon dome. In the dimness of the fading twilight, Hank cupped Becky's hands and began to explain.

24

MORNING ABOVE timberline was a whiteout. Fresh snow had fallen copiously, further smothering the barren, treeless landscape. Against the starkness a white sky blended seamlessly with the ridge, and it was difficult to discern where one ended and the other began.

Becky's head hummed from the fatigue of a sleepless night. But still, her mind focused on the plan. Hank had described his discoveries in gruesome detail, and Becky could do little but agree with his conclusion. Too much of a coincidence meant no coincidence at all. Andrei and the others surely had something to do with the abandoned camp and, even worse, the horror Hank had fished from the lake.

And it shocked Becky.

Andrei seemed such a kind, gentle man. An artist. She wanted to believe it was his companions, Fedor particularly, who had committed these awful acts, but reason and objective thinking convinced her otherwise. Andrei must have knowingly played a part.

How could he have not?

Now, the crew had assembled at Becky's request for what she claimed to be a crew meeting aimed at discussing Maloney's death and the fate of the current production. Hank kept an eye on the Russians, drinking coffee with them around the campfire, somberly discussing the recent tragedy.

"Before we begin," Becky told the crew, "I need to make certain each of you are clear about something extremely important."

Cody said, "Yes, certainly, Maloney was a good man. We all agree. But what's done is done, and we must press on. We must complete the production in his honor. It's what he would have wanted. I'm sure of it. The finale, of course, will be dedicated in his memory, and the credits will reflect as much in a memorial blurb."

"Shut up," Becky said. "Not another word from you. You're an awful human being and a sorry excuse for a man. Had I the courage to stand against you yesterday, Maloney would be standing with us today."

Cody's mouth fell agape. Becky's words were enough to momentarily silence him.

She continued, "What I'm about to tell everyone is going to hit hard, but you must listen, you must mind my words carefully, and most of all you must heed my advice to the letter. Anything less could mean your death."

At this pronouncement, all extraneous movement by the crew stopped, and each stood wide-eyed, except Kilpatrick, who shook his head knowingly, appearing ready to back her up if need be.

"From this point forward, the production is over."

"Now wait just a minute, Becky," Cody said.

"The lady told you to shut your mouth," Kilpatrick said. "Speak again and I'll personally feed you a mouthful of your own teeth."

Unused to threats from Kilpatrick, Cody recoiled.

Becky continued, "No doubt we're all stunned by what happened to Maloney. Myself, I'm sickened by it. But yesterday, Hank revealed something to me that needs to be shared with everyone. These men, Andrei and the others, they're not who they claim to be. In fact, they're bad men. They're killers."

The word *killers* aroused the crew. Excitedly, they all spoke at once, words of confusion.

"What do you mean they're killers?" Marshal said. "What makes you think that? Maloney's accident?"

"This sounds like paranoia," Tasha said. "Look, Becky, we're all saddened by what happened yesterday, and ultimately we'll all have to deal with it in our own way, but to conclude murder is extreme."

"Becky's referring to more than just Maloney," Kilpatrick said somberly. "There's something else."

Tasha listened.

The crew huddled close and Becky explained the events Hank had described to her. When she finished, nobody stirred. Their faces registered a mixture of shock and disbelief.

It was Cody who spoke first. "If this is all true,

Becky, what is it you propose we do? I mean, against ruthless killers what *can* we do?"

"We can separate," she said. "Remove ourselves from the threat."

Marshal said, "But if they've done what Hank says they've done, they won't just let us walk away." Fear raised his voice an octave. "My God, they'll kill us, too."

"You're embarrassing yourself," Tasha said. "Behave like a man."

"But he's right," Cody said. "Don't you see? They're going to kill us." He looked over Becky's shoulder in the direction of the Russians, then cast a panicked glance toward the trees.

It looked to Becky as if he intended to bolt. "Relax, Cody. Stay put. We can't let on that we know anything. As I said, we have a plan."

"Separate, that's your big plan? You yourself said Hank dug a bullet from a tree. They have guns. They'll shoot us. No, no, I can't die in this hellhole. I have too much still to accomplish. My career, my—"

"Calm down," Kilpatrick said. "Piss yourself and you'll tip them off for sure."

"After we strike camp," Becky said, "Hank plans to lead them off to collect firewood and wild edibles, while we set up for a shoot just below the treeline."

"A shoot?" Cody said. "Now? How can you expect me to perform under these circumstances?"

"You dumb-ass," Kilpatrick said. "It's not really a shoot. The show's over. It's an excuse to separate ourselves. You need to start using your head before you get us all killed."

Becky lowered her hands as if to ask for calm. "Look, we can't afford to start arguing with each other. We're all under pressure right now, and we need to be more tolerant of each other." She looked at Cody. "At the same time, we need to be careful how we act around these men. In an hour or two, it won't matter. We'll be working our way back down the mountain toward base camp."

Marshal was looking in the direction of the precipice. "Am I the only one who sees a problem here? How are we going to scale back down that thing? It was a problem just getting up it."

"We have rope," Becky said, "and Kilpatrick understands enough principles of mountaineering. He'll lower us down, one at a time, then rappel himself."

"With all our gear, seriously? It'll take us nearly as long to get down as it did to get up. By that time, the Russians will have returned."

"We won't be taking all our gear," Becky said, "just survival essentials. Cameras and related equipment stay."

"And Hank? What about him?"

"Hank plans to lead the Russians a good distance away, then lose them in the bush. He'll meet back up with us at base camp, sooner if he can find us."

"Yes," Cody said, this time more optimistically. "That might actually work."

"It will work," Becky said, "but we need to get moving now. Any last questions?"

The crew glanced at one another silently.

"Good. Remember, be yourselves until Hank leads them away. We're setting up for another shoot. That's all we're doing."

The group nodded their understanding, then broke away and went to work.

25

CODY FUMBLED WITH the frame of his dome, having never actually taken the bloody thing apart himself. Nearby, he could hear Andrei and his two mates speaking together sotto voce, their belongings packed and ready at their feet. Cody called out to them with a bright smile. Given his skill as an actor, he was certain his countenance would air the appropriate amiability. "I ever tell you gentlemen the healthy respect I have for you and your brethren in the Motherland?" He flashed a toothy grin. "Indeed, I once fancied this girl from St. Petersburg. A real stunner. Had the loveliest dimples you ever saw. Not a bad bosom either. Yes, you Russians, a genuine people, you are."

The three men exchanged glances before Andrei broke away from them to join Cody. "Looks like you're having some difficulty there." He nodded to indicate the dome. "Allow me to assist you."

"See, that's precisely what I'm talking about. You Russians are stand-up people."

Andrei knelt and began expertly collapsing the parts Cody couldn't manage. "You must be devastated at the loss of your friend. You have my condolences."

"Thank you, thank you sincerely. Yes, Maloney was a good fellow. A dear friend. This has been quite a tragedy for me, you understand." There came a flash of lightning and the rumble of thunder, and Cody looked quickly upslope. A few hundred yards past tusklike rocks and scattered krummholz, the mountaintop loomed. The storm front beyond it was churning the color of ash. Lightning arced, while frozen wind and sleet crested the ridgeline and rolled downslope.

"That should do it for you," Andrei said, seemingly oblivious to the hellish weather. He stood and brushed off his gloves. "This morning you seem a little distracted, my friend, not like yourself? Is there something the matter? Something more than the death of Maloney?"

Cody stiffened. Had he let down his façade? He would use the weather as an excuse. "Yes, a storm is on the move. Travel is going to be brutal today."

"Ah, but brutality is a fact of nature, is it not? Look around you, we're in the midst of it. You, the survivalist, will have little fear meeting it head-on."

Hank's deep voice called out over the now tumultuous winds. "I'd like everyone to gather around the fire!"

And for Cody, Hank's interruption couldn't have come at a better time. With unusual haste, he and the crew assembled.

Hank began, "We haven't much time before the front's upon us, so I'm going to make this short and sweet, people. What happened yesterday was tragic, but here and now is not the place to dwell on it. You do and you'll only lose focus. I'm calling for a renewed sense of safety. Each step you take, each action you perform must be done with the utmost care. This by far will be the worst weather we've experienced yet, so I want everyone to be prepared."

Nods from the crew.

"I figure we have about an hour, maybe less, so here's what we're going to do: Becky, Tasha, you gals take care of business, set up for the opening shot, whatever it is you got planned."

Becky said, "A segment on the perils of the alpine zone, something to segue into the day's travel. We'll be working somewhere beyond those stunted firs."

His accented voice tinged with surprise, Andrei said. "You plan to continue production?"

"Yes, of course," Becky said.

"I had assumed under such tragic circumstances, filming would be—"

"—put on hold?" Becky said.

"Yes."

"That's understandable, but tragedy or not, we're still in the thick of things and have to reach the extraction point, whether we film or not. Best not waste the travel time. We're here, we have the equipment, so we film. There'll be time to grieve later."

"Okay, very good," Hank said. "Andrei, your friends and I will—"

"That's right!" Cody interjected. "That's precisely what we'll be doing, and nothing more, just filming a segue. I mean, it's routine. We do shots like it all the time. And Hank, since it'll only bore our friends, perhaps you can find something else for them to do?" He smiled, knowing his impromptu lines had been brilliant and would add marvelously to the authenticity of their ruse. Hank and the crew must have been quite impressed, as well, for their expressions were one of amazement.

"As I was saying," Hank quickly added, "you three fellows will come with me for some scavenging. We'll augment the game I caught with a supply of wild edibles. After this storm moves over us, we may not have another opportunity. Any questions? No? Then let's move."

Cody continued, "And in case our friends here are interested, let me point out the location where the crew will be shooting. Becky was far too general. Andrei, Viktor, Fedor, my friends, if you look there beyond that cluster of trees, you'll see that—"

"Cody, we haven't the time for this," Becky interjected. "As Hank pointed out, the storm is moving fast. Okay everyone, let's get going."

The crew began to disperse.

"One moment, everyone," Andrei said, halting the crew in their tracks.

"I should think it more prudent if we all remain together. Hank, surely if we half-ration what we already have, we should have little difficulty making the extraction point. Collecting edibles seems unnecessary."

Hank's eyes narrowed. "I don't remember any-one electing you decision-maker, best you leave the bushcraft to me. I think I know best."

"Then it's settled," Becky said. "Let's get start-ed."

"One more thing, if you please," came Andrei's cool reply.

Cody could feel the tension between Andrei and Hank building, and it worried him. "Look, An-drei, I've told you how much I respect you and your mates, right? I mean hey, I could see us chumming around together when all this is said and done. Why don't you just—"

"Man, shut up," Kilpatrick said.

There came a momentary pause.

Then Cody exploded in a plea, "I'm begging you gentlemen, let us do our filming. I mean it's only filming, that's all we're going to do, nothing more, re-ally."

Fedor laughed heartily. "Why is it this one cries like a small child? Has he been touched with fever?"

Cody smiled, his upper lip twitching nervous-ly. "Ha, Fedor that's funny. A child, yes. But hey, what's a little jibe between friends, right?"

Andrei said, "Hank, I think it best we remain together. All of us. You yourself mentioned predatory animals. There is safety in numbers."

"You see, Becky," Cody blurted out, unable to stop the words, "I knew this wouldn't work." His lip maintained its quiver. His eyes darted nervously be-tween the Russians. The tone of his voice was infantile. "Please, we don't know who you are or what you've done. Just leave us alone, not a word about you will be spoken to the authorities. On that I can assure you."

•　　•　　•

Becky found herself dumbfounded by Cody's sudden breakdown. The man had no courage. She looked at the faces of the crew. Everyone watched in amazement. Everyone that is, except Hank, who had been watching the Russians with an assessing eye.

And when Fedor, quick as a snake, tugged off a glove and jerked a pistol from his waistband, Hank was ready and sprang.

26

IT LOOKED TO Becky as if Hank would surely be shot, but he was quick and determined and drove into Fedor with the fury of a bull, wresting the Russian's arm erect. The pistol, now threatening the sky, fired a muffled shot.

The slope upon which they stood favored Hank, who had the higher ground. And while Fedor was powerfully built, he was unable to fight both gravity and the strength of a hardened outdoorsman. A few staggered steps backward and the momentum of their struggle sent both tumbling to the ground. Fedor's gun flung from his grip and disappeared somewhere in the powdery snow. Fedor landed on his back, Hank atop him in a mounted position.

At the same time, Andrei and Viktor reacted.

So, too, did Kilpatrick and Marshal. An all-out melee ensued.

Kilpatrick rushed Andrei.

Marshal, holding a camera, threw it at Viktor and followed with a flurry of wild swings and curses.

Cody, on the other hand, turned and high-tailed it toward the safety of the krummholz.

For a moment Becky was paralyzed by fear, but then instinct seized hold, and she acted.

A quick look was enough for her to see Hank raising and lowering his fists like a hammer against Fedor's head. Blood streamed from the brute's face, and the snow around him crimsoned.

So she rushed to the aid of Marshal, whom she felt least capable to fight. There, teaming up with him, she clawed savagely at Viktor's eyes. Deftly, he dodged before spinning suddenly and striking Becky with the back of his hand. The blow hit her squarely on the jaw, sending her crashing into the snow. She expected pain but registered only numbness.

Desperation quickly cleared her mind and rallied her to her feet. She saw Viktor clinch Marshal behind the head and pull him forward, kneeing him viciously in the solar plexus. Marshal doubled over gasping for breath.

Hank now gained his feet and was searching frantically for the pistol. Unsuccessful, he turned and bound toward Becky.

She leaped to her feet and pivoted in time to see Andrei, who had knocked Kilpatrick to the ground, remove his own pistol and level it at the defenseless man.

Hank pleaded, "No, don't shoot!"

But his call went unheeded.

Becky screamed in horror as Andrei's finger tightened against the trigger. A quick squeeze, a muffled shot, and Kilpatrick, who had attempted to gain his feet, jerked his head. A sick purple hole appeared between his eyes, and the poor man crumbled into the snow.

"You son-of-a-bitch!" Becky screamed, rushing at Andrei, and before he could redirect the pistol, Becky balled her fist and swung wildly at it. Her knuckles struck steel, and the pistol went arcing through the gusty air in the direction of Tasha, who had been watching the melee from afar. The weapon fell into the snow at her feet.

"Grab it!" Becky heard Hank shout to her.

And quickly Tasha acted. She knelt and snatched up the pistol, pointed it into the fray.

This brought everyone to a sudden stop.

And for a long moment, chests heaved and the air fogged before them.

Becky felt an immense relief and rubbed at her swollen jaw. Instinctively, she sought protection near Hank and Marshal.

Marshal cheered Tasha, "Attagirl, honey."

Viktor and Andrei slowly moved abreast, their eyes fixed intently upon Tasha.

"Don't either of you sonsabitches move another muscle," Hank commanded. "Tasha, either of them so much as twitch and you shoot to kill."

Becky turned and looked toward Fedor. He was beginning to recover, sitting up in the deep red snow. His face was a mass of swollen flesh.

Hank started for Tasha to claim the gun. "Great job. Let me take that."

And what Becky saw next turned her blood cold as the sleeting wind.

27

A^{S H}ANK APPROACHED Tasha, she turned to him. And the gun turned with her.

"Be careful where you point that thing," Hank said. "Train it back on them fellows there." He continued slogging toward her.

Tasha didn't stir. Her eyes narrowed down the barrel. "I would say," she began speaking emotionlessly, "that I am pointing it at precisely the person I intend to. Don't come any closer, Mr. Guthry."

Hank stopped dead in his tracks.

The next words from Tasha's mouth were in a language Hank recognized as Russian.

Andrei responded in kind, and Tasha smiled.

Viktor pulled a pistol from under his coat, and Hank knew he and the others were suddenly in a world of trouble.

Marshal said, "Tasha, what the hell are you doing, hon?"

"Shut up, you sorry excuse for a man."

"I—I don't understand. What's going on?"

She ignored his question, and when Andrei reached her, she surrendered the gun and kissed him lightly on both cheeks.

Andrei said, "It has been too long, my dear. My apologies for not expressing my thrill of seeing you. But of course the façade you understand."

From a safe distance, Viktor held his gun on the group. "Tasha, a pleasure to meet you again," he said, his eyes never straying from his targets.

Fedor, his tumid face showing bewilderment, had found and recovered his own gun and was now rejoining the group. He reached Hank and pressed the barrel to his head.

"No," Becky cried. Her hands flung out pleadingly.

Fedor's knuckles whitened around the grip, his baleful eyes gleaming with sick delight.

Andrei said, "Stay your weapon, Fedor. Hank's services are still required."

His animal eyes glowering, Fedor's compliance was not immediate. His finger remained poised over the trigger. He stared at Andrei and barked in Russian, his tone revealing anger and disappointment. Andrei answered him tersely and the two held their gaze. Tense seconds passed before Fedor finally looked away and lowered the gun.

Andrei said, "Now is your chance to redeem your earlier failure. Find Cody and put a bullet in his head. You needn't show restraint."

Tasha looked at Andrei disapprovingly. "Must you?"

"I'm sorry, my dear, but it's necessary."

"But I did so enjoy his private company."

"Like a mare with her stallion, I suppose?"

A guilty smile was Tasha's answer.

"I'm afraid he is now a liability."

"Very well," she said. "He may have been an embarrassment, but physically he possessed such alluring qualities. I shall miss his touch."

Marshal said, "Tasha, what's going on here?" His voice was shrilling. "How do you know these guys, and what do you mean you'll miss Cody's touch?"

Tasha turned to her husband, her eyes narrowing with irritation. "Marshal, have I ever told you I find the sound of your voice grating and unbearable?"

"I don't get it. Please, Tasha, hun, help me understand. How do you know these guys? What's all this you're saying? For chrissake, we're married!"

"Indeed we are. Thank you for the American citizenship. It has proven most useful. And now that I'm reunited with family...." She looked and smiled lovingly at Andrei.

"Are you telling me that, that—" Marshal's face contorted in disbelief.

"Don't act so surprised. You didn't think I married you for your charm, did you?"

"But, but I love you, you're my wife."

"Oh yes," she said, "*that* I must remedy. Brother, may I?" She indicated the gun.

Andrei complied without hesitation.

"Marshal, my dear thorn-in-the-side, you were useful for a time, but no longer, I'm afraid. Consider this a divorce."

"No, Tasha, don't do it!" Hank took a step forward, his hands waving.

Tasha turned the pistol on Marshal and fired three rounds in rapid succession.

Becky gasped and turned away.

Hank could see the shock on Marshal's face, even before the slugs punched into his chest and he dropped to his knees, gaping down at his reddening parka. "I—I don't understand..." He hiccupped a stream of blood and his eyes, now glassy orbs, rolled unseeing into his head. He toppled face down into the snow.

Tasha turned up a mirthless smile. "Till death do us part... far simpler than retaining an attorney."

Fedor emitted a sick, guttural chuckle. The murder had lifted his spirits.

Hank's mind reeled from this cruel predicament in which he and Becky now found themselves. He could feel his jaw stiffening, his blood boiling. "Let me just say the whole lot of you are murderous sonsabitches, and I hope each of you burn in hell for what you've done."

"Look around," Andrei said. "We're already in hell, but alas, soon our suffering will be over. Everyone's. Including your own. I am not an unreasonable man. Cooperate, and I give you my assurance, both you and Rebecca will remain unharmed."

"We need to move forward," Viktor urged, "the weather is worsening."

And he was right about the weather, Hank realized. Having been focused on the fight, he scarcely noticed the winds mounting. Now, gusts were driving denser sheets of sleet over the ridge and down the slope. The stunted conifers and rocky terrain helped shield the group from the brunt of it, but snow was accumulating fast, and soon cresting the ridge would be difficult, if not downright impossible.

Andrei called out, "Fedor, get moving on Cody. You haven't much time. Tasha, I want you to destroy the camera equipment. Throw it all into the fire. Burn it well. Viktor, collect weapons—I know Hank carries a knife and axe—then supervise him and Rebecca while they jettison all extraneous equipment. It's no longer needed. All food is to be stored in one location—Fedor's backpack would be best. No doubt, he'll protect the contents with his life. Hank, if you please, I would like the topographical map Tasha tells me you possess."

Hank's smile was a revealing one. "Sure thing. If you hike back down to the lake and take a dip, you may have the good fortune of finding it wrapped to a rock at the bottom."

"You discarded it?"

"You're a smart fellow. Don't believe me? You can check my person. But I had a feeling before leaving the lake it might not be a good thing having a map that shows from which peak we'll be extracted. You know, just in case I was right about you guys."

Andrei was nodding and studying Hank. "Tell me, at what point did you know?"

"I suspected early on, but confirmed my suspicions after fishing a man's head out of the lake, which I knew wasn't the result of a predator. Animals aren't in the habit of bagging leftovers."

"Ah, the pilot," Andrei said. "He was a brave soul. Personally, I regretted having to kill him."

Becky stepped forward, her face as sober as a judge. Hank could see a silent storm brewing inside her, and he hoped she wouldn't do anything foolish.

Over the whistle of tumultuous winds she said, "Our running into you was obviously a calculated meeting." She glanced at Tasha. "You must have a goal of some sort. Why else cause all this mayhem? What is it you want from us?"

"Indeed, we do work to an end, but none of it need concern you, Rebecca."

"My life concerns me you bastard. And here I thought you were a decent man, only to find out you're nothing but a goddamn psychopath. How could I have misjudged you so badly?"

"Becky," Hank said, cautioning her.

"Again, our intentions needn't concern you, with the exception of one thing."

"Which is?"

"Which is guiding us beyond the next valley to the extraction point. Hank, I'm afraid, is the only one among us who knows the precise location, and his talents will come in quite handy. And you Rebecca, I'm sparing you simply because I enjoy your company."

Becky's steely stare intensified. It was obvious to Hank she wanted to kill him.

Tasha asked, "What of these bodies?"

Andrei waved a dismissive hand. "Soon they'll be covered deep in snow, and come first thaw animals searching for meat will be pleasantly surprised."

Hank lowered his head, sickened by Andrei's callousness.

"If there's nothing else, let us proceed."

"There is one thing," Becky said.

"You have my undivided attention."

"Life is precious, but you treat it as something inconsequential. Because of you, three men are dead. That's three mothers who will never see their sons again. Ever."

"A fact of which I'm well aware."

"And sometime soon, a baby boy will be born without a father—also because of you. Until the day you die, which I hope will be soon, I want you to remember that."

"I shall remember, Rebecca. But it'll not concern me, not in the least. Men die every day, and the world is filled with fatherless children."

Hank interrupted, "You really want to have this conversation right now?" He lifted an arm and pointed against the start of sleeting winds. "As it stands, we're on the leeward side of that ridge. We don't cross it and get below treeline in the next few hours, we don't cross it at all. Drifts will make it impossible."

Andrei looked critically toward the summit. "I'm inclined to agree. Let us discard the excess and leave at once."

28

CODY DIDN'T THINK he could manage another step. His heart knocked rapidly in his chest. His breath came in spasmodic gasps. His clothing had become soaked with perspiration. If he remembered one thing Hank had said about survival in the frozen backcountry, it was that unless you had a fire—or the means to quickly build one—never ever, under any circumstance, sweat yourself wet. And now here was Cody, breathless, terrified, and under his parka, wet as a baby seal.

He searched behind him for any sign of pursuit. He saw nothing, nor did he hear anything. Of course that meant nothing. Given the painful shrill of the wind, even if the Russians were hot on his heels, they could be whistling *Korobushka* and he still wouldn't be able to hear them.

Cody shivered. He sniffled, and then his hands flew to his head, where he felt his frozen hair. Having stopped to assess his predicament, the chill had alerted him to his missing toque. Bloody hell! He must have lost it somewhere along the way. In his panicked flight, he never felt it come off!

His ears ached. His teeth chattered. Panic seized him. He paced circles between a stand of conifers. He was a dead man walking, plain and simple. If he returned now, Andrei and the other two nutters would undoubtedly kill him. He recalled how Fedor had yanked out his gun, so eager to fire, bloodlust in his eyes. The rest of the crew was certainly dead now. Cody would be dead soon, too, but not by a madman's bullet, but rather by nature's ruthless indifference. Cold and confused he stopped pacing, slumped onto his haunches between two trees and, began to cry.

●   ●   ●

Hank set about doing as he was told. So, too, did Becky. Viktor maintained vigil over them both.

Broodingly Hank worked. How he planned to get Becky out of this mess hadn't yet come to him, but on that problem he would keep his mind focused. He began to jettison all non-essentials from the packs. Food he set aside for Fedor to carry. Becky did likewise. It was only when Hank began discarding Cody's personal supplies did he make the discovery that he thought might actually give them a chance.

Peering into a small metallic case, Hank spied the explosives he had earlier confiscated, four charges tucked neatly under a miscellany of useless junk. Leave it to Cody to do something so sneaky and underhanded. Boy, the kid sure was an idiot. But in this instance, Hank was relieved. The charges would be useful. There were too many for him to carry inconspicuously, but one, he believed, could be tucked discreetly under his parka.

But not yet, Viktor's stare was unyielding.

Hank closed the case and found an excuse to shoulder up to Becky. His back to Viktor, he made like he was busy and said to her, "Found something, I'll explain to you later. Once you see me kneel at Cody's case over there, distract Viktor."

Hank was pleased Becky knew enough not to ask for an explanation. It would only draw attention. She said, "Gotcha," then set about searching Kilpatrick's belongings.

A moment later Hank went back to the case.

When he did, Becky stood, snatched up some nearby equipment, and marched toward Viktor. She approached from an angle that forced him to turn askew. "Andrei didn't clearly define 'essential' equipment," she said. "Are we packing Cody's heater and propane cylinders or aren't we?"

Sidelong, Hank watched her performance, even as his hands went quietly to work.

Viktor considered her question.

She added, "Fact is they're not essential for anything but Cody's convenience."

"We travel for purpose, not for convenience," was his monotone response. His blue eyes stared piercingly. "Fire and domes will suffice for warmth. Leave them."

Becky dropped the equipment in the snow at his feet, wheeled around and marched back to complete her chores.

Hank closed Cody's case, tossed it afar into the brush, and moved on to another backpack.

•   •   •

Fedor pulled his swollen face from the snow, probed the ridge of his brow, which he knew was broken, and cursed himself for letting the American get the better of him. Having begun following Cody's tracks, Fedor had stopped to ice his face, then repeated the process at five-minute intervals. This was the fifth such treatment, which meant he had been pursuing the coward for nearly half an hour.

And all he had to show for it was Cody's knitted cap found snagged to a tree limb. The problem had been following the tracks. Sleet and heavy snow were covering them, and Fedor was uncertain how to proceed. How could he both find and kill this sniveling fool and return in time to cross the ridge with the others?

By his figuring he couldn't. Finding Cody would take more time than was wise to spend, and so Fedor took one last look ahead through the slashing sleet and turned back, cap in hand, convinced that the Brit was now dead or would soon die from exposure anyway. After all, Fedor mused, Cody was no survivalist.

•   •   •

Out of tears, Cody had ceased sobbing

minutes earlier. He shivered violently and stared at the snow accumulating in gentle drifts around the trees—and around himself! If he didn't move soon, he would be buried alive. He hefted to his feet, then just as quickly dropped back onto his rump. He was a dead man, he reminded himself. Why not just freeze to death here? It was as good a place as any. Feeling sleepy, he drew his arms into his chest, and rocked. His mind began to drift. Vague scenes of episodes past began filtering through his consciousness. He saw himself trekking through the brutal sands of the Sahara, braving the cruel heat and searching intrepidly for water. So, too, did he witness himself hacking heroically through the jungles of the Amazon, blazing a trail with his machete, beads of sweat and humidity dripping from his face. Soon the scene faded and he could see himself once again.

But this time, the images unsettled his ethereal self. Here, he wasn't heroic in the least. Here, he lay in a heap, deathly still, couched on a bed of snow in a frozen wasteland. As he neared himself, his visage began to resolve itself, and what he saw terrified him. His face had shriveled and iced, pain and anguish frozen upon it.

Horror snapped Cody out of his delirium, and his eyes flew open. In a supreme force of will, he brought himself back to reality and fought away the sleepiness that ensconced him. He fought away the unexpected warmth settling over his body. He fought away the voice in his head that consoled him and gave him permission to give up. He fought as he had never fought before.

"No!" he screamed, and staggered to his feet.

And his courage was rewarded with an idea!

He had everything he needed to survive! Not here, but back at camp. With the crew likely dead, the three Russians couldn't possibly travel with the supplies of eight men and women. It would be impractical, impossible even. They would have to leave much of it behind. All Cody needed to do, he realized now in a moment of brilliant clarity, was to return, spy from a distance, and after they departed, collect the things he would need to survive.

With renewed vigor, Cody Hobbs lowered his face against the merciless wind and struck out back for camp.

29

WHEN FEDOR RETURNED half an hour later, tossed Cody's woolen cap on the ground at Andrei's feet and announced, "*The Survivalist* has been cancelled!" Becky lowered her head regretfully and spoke a silent prayer, as she had done for the others.

Cody, by no means, had been an honorable or courageous man. In fact, at times he had been downright despicable, but Becky never wished for him the kind of end he had now suffered.

She took a deep, calming breath, inhaled the snow-laden air swirling down from the summit, and finished readying herself for the brutal weather that had descended upon them. She pulled the open-face balaclava down around her head and gave it a quick smoothing, then snugged on her toque and sunglasses. The Russians, she saw, had done the same, having stolen the deceased men's extreme weather gear.

Then wordlessly, Becky and Hank marched forth from the littered campsite, sledging carefully over the deep, powdery snow. In single file, their captors followed. Behind them, sheltered by a riot of large stones, cameras crackled in a blazing fire. And, at the leeward base of a craggy rock, three men lay in deathly slumber.

The distance to the crest, Becky estimated, was roughly a thousand feet. Had this been a stroll in the park, a few minutes would have sufficed to reach it. But this would not be a stroll in the park. It would be a struggle over the world's most inhospitable terrain; it would be a supreme test of will and endurance; and with these killers in step behind her, it would be for Becky the most arduous task she ever faced.

Her mind set about formulating a plan, a means by which she and Hank might escape, or better yet, incapacitate the Russians altogether. For such men, she would offer no fair play. Vengefully, Becky brooded.

High ahead, the already indistinct ridgeline disappeared as the daylight darkened into a pall of gray mist. Snow flurried about them. The treeless, boulder-strewn slope rose at a steep thirty-degree angle. Surefooted, Hank and Becky switchbacked sluggishly up the mountainside, their shoulders lowered into the stinging wind. Progress was in inches.

Becky felt a small degree of comfort when through it all, Hank leaned into to her and said over the din of the storm, "Don't you worry, Beck, somehow, someway, I'm gonna get you safely through this. That's a promise you can take to the bank!"

•   •   •

Because of the uniqueness of the terrain, mainly the extended precipice to his left, finding his way back to camp through the blinding snow had been a manageable task for Cody. What had not been so simple was keeping his body functioning. At several points during the march, he had become severely fatigued, dizzy in fact, having at one point even succumbed to another strange vision, mistaking wind and swaying trees for music and dancing girls. But make it back he had done. He was the survivalist, after all, and survive he would.

Huddled low near the camp's weakening fire and shielded from the wind by a bulwark of massive stones, Cody extended his hands and rubbed them vigorously over the blessed flames. Heaped in the fire was a melted mass of plastic and glowing metal. The stench of burnt electronics mingled with the fresh air. Still he shivered, but at least now he was comforted by the knowledge he would survive. Presumably, the three Russians had left for the ridge; although with the nasty weather pressing upon the mountaintop, Cody couldn't actually see them. Still, he knew they were up there somewhere, moving away from him.

But he wasn't out of the woods yet. Under ordinary circumstances, he would have mused over his pun. But as it stood he just looked about. Through the flurry of snow, he could see a litter of supplies strewn haphazardly, even the vague outline of a disassembled dome. He would collect enough essentials to get him back down the mountain and to base camp. Yes, indeed, he was going to survive!

The cold stung his ears, his lips, his swollen nose. Every inch of exposed flesh ignited ablaze. The pain reminded him that he needed his severe weather gear, a balaclava and new toque. Reluctantly he moved from the warmth of the dying fire to the mess of supplies, where he began to scavenge. A small effort was enough to locate his clothing. He brushed away snow from trousers and sweaters, turtlenecks and thermals. Next he collected a dome—and oh my, what was this? His heart leapt for joy when he spotted his heater, a propane cylinder, too! The fools had left them! Their logic mystified him. He had found no food—they had taken that—but running the heater would provide gratifying warmth. He could even heat large stones for inside his sleeping bag and melt snow for drinking water! He gathered everything up, then set about finding a location to erect the dome. He would have to wait out the storm before proceeding down to sub-alpine in the morning.

He glanced about for the perfect spot. Through undulating, snow-laden flurries he spotted a large crag near a cluster of stunted firs. It would make the best location. In fact, it had been his very spot the night before. But as he approached it, he was surprised by what he saw at its base. Pure carnage. Three bodies lay morbidly displayed, partially covered in snow. They were the corpses of Maloney, Marshal, and Kilpatrick. The sight of it revolted Cody. He turned away.

At first, the discrepancy in the body count did

not register with him. It was only after he began lamenting the loss of Tasha and her sublime figure did he realize he had not actually seen her body. Quickly, he went about searching for it—Hank's and Becky's, too. But unable to find a single one, he trudged back to the equipment and began a search for their belongings. When he discovered much of it missing, understanding settled over him. The three had survived. But how? Did they escape as did he, or were they forced along as captives of the Russians?

The brutal, arctic conditions purged his thoughts and pained him into action. He began the grim task of moving the bodies, followed by the novelty of pitching his own dome.

30

I T WAS EARLY in the afternoon when the first pangs of hunger rumbled through Becky's stomach. Though fortunate to have eaten breakfast, she now looked to her next meal with uncertainty. She ignored the discomfort and forged ahead, focused on the climb. Through the lashing snow, she was unable to see the summit, but sensed that it loomed somewhere near. Hank still led the group, moving carefully and steadily. Becky wondered what he was thinking. Knowing Hank, his mind was likely building up and tearing down scenarios for escape. Just as Becky had been doing.

Then abruptly a scream, muffled by the howling winds, sounded from behind her. Becky turned in time to see Tasha tumbling downslope. Helplessly, she twisted and somersaulted in a trail of mushrooming snow before the dense sleet swallowed her form completely, and her pain-filled cries became lost in the din.

Becky remained still, free of the instinct to

help. Hank, too, observed, but nothing more.

Andrei, however, wasted no time. "Kill them if they move," he instructed his partners and jettisoned his backpack. In long loping strides he zigzagged down the incline, disappearing quickly into the swirling snow. And just as quickly, Viktor ungloved a hand and brandished his pistol, a warning to Hank and Becky to remain still.

Everyone watched and waited.

Becky peered expectantly into the canvass of white, listening against the savage winds.

And only after some time did Andrei's and Tasha's forms begin to resolve themselves, at first as indistinct shadow, then as individuals plodding abreast. Tasha struggled to climb, helped at the waist by Andrei. Vaguely, Becky could see that she now favored her right arm, crooking it against her chest, using her left hand to support it.

Their progress was slow. Minutes were needed for them to regain the group, at which time Andrei announced Tasha had broken her arm, and that the group would set camp at the first opportune time.

The fall had broken more than Tasha's arm. Her sunglasses were now in a mangle, and she tossed them aside, blinking against the stinging wind.

The fall had broken more than Tasha's arm. Her sunglasses were now in a mangle, and she tossed them aside, blinking against the stinging wind.

Becky said, "Missteps can be devastating, wouldn't you say, Tasha?"

Through wincing eyes, Tasha glared. "Give me your sunglasses."

Becky stood defiant.

"I said give them to me."

Reluctantly, she removed them, dropped them at Tasha's feet, and turned back to the wind-ravaged ridge to resume her climb. Blinking painfully into the sleet, she noticed Hank move to her side. He pulled off his own glasses. "Take mine."

Becky knew better than to argue with him. She accepted the gift, and the group moved on.

Half an hour later the ridgeline came faintly into view, but conditions had made the climb seem an eternity.

She and Hank crested the top, followed quickly by Viktor and Fedor. Each turned their backs against the pulsing, snow-fed gales, settled into a huddle, and waited for Andrei and Tasha, whose pace had greatly slowed.

When they finally arrived, pausing to regain their strength, Andrei instructed Fedor, "Distribute the protein bars. Ten minutes and we continue."

Fedor dug into his backpack, counted out six bars.

"Return two of those to your pack," Tasha demanded. Her stare was fixed firmly on Becky.

Fedor looked to Andrei, who nodded assent.

"You'll forgive the impropriety," he said, "but a weakened Hank Guthry is a far less dangerous Hank Guthry."

"Well at least give a little something to Becky," Hank said.

Andrei looked to Tasha who, with a pained smile, gave a curt nod no.

And the four Russians proceeded to eat. Minutes later, packs slung, they began descending the western slope.

As Becky moved forward, she imagined the scene ahead. Far below, she knew, a great valley stretched out before her. This knowledge, however, was based solely upon Hank's earlier description to her, not upon what she could actually see, for what should have been a gorgeous panorama remained a bleak whiteout.

The trek down the mountain required far less stamina than the climb up, but Becky knew that with each step, great care must still be taken. Snow-covered debris and uneven terrain were common to both the eastern and western slopes. Movement was always a risk. No doubt, Tasha had been lucky to escape her fall with only a broken arm.

Soon, Hank stabbed a finger ahead, indicating the direction of a possible campsite, and an hour later the treeline dimly revealed itself. Hank led the group to the base of a tree-studded scarp. Becky could see it was an excellent location. Under the conditions, it would act as a natural bulwark against the wind and driving snow. She dropped her pack, then herself onto her pack, and sighed wearily. Weakened by hunger and fatigue, she scooped up and chewed a handful of snow. Never a good idea. The practice, Hank had taught her, actually robbed the body of heat and if done frequently could lead to hypothermia, but under the circumstances, she needed to chew on something and couldn't quite help herself.

The others lowered their backpacks, and after a brief rest began the task of pitching camp.

"Hank and Fedor," Andrei said, "you two collect dry wood and build a fire. Viktor, you erect the domes. I'll tend to Tasha's arm. Rebecca, does your first aid kit contain materials for a splint?"

"It does."

"Good. Retrieve it for me please, then help Viktor with the domes."

Each moved to begin their chore, except Hank, who remained firmly planted.

"I believe I gave you a directive, Mr. Guthry. Let's not make this unpleasant."

"You took my knife and axe. How do you propose I gather up and strip wood without a tool?"

"Yes, of course," Andrei said. "Viktor, if you'll be so kind as to give Fedor the axe."

Tasha said, "Brother, there's bad blood between the two. Is it wise for them to be together?"

Andrei paused. "Perhaps you're right. Hank and Fedor never did quite hit it off, did they? Rebecca, you're proficient collecting combustible wood, are you not?"

Hank stepped forward, "Now wait a minute, I should be the one—"

"Fedor, you and Rebecca shall recruit wood and build the fire. Hank, collect the splint and then assist Viktor."

Hank's eyes darkened. "I'll not have it, Beck alone with that sack of shit."

"Don't worry," Becky assured him, "I'll be fine."

She turned to confront Fedor. "Listen carefully, because I'm only going to say this once. I'll collect the wood. I know best from where to trim it. While I'm busy, you collect plenty of brown fir and pine needles, cones too, and snap off dry twigs from dead branches. Use your knife to shred and split them open. That'll be our tinder. You think you can handle that?"

She didn't wait for an answer, just turned, grabbed the axe from Viktor, and stormed off toward the woods.

Frowning, the hulking Russian unsheathed his knife and followed.

•   •   •

Slowly, the chill night cooled the heated stones at the foot of Cody's sleeping bag. And now his drowsy mind felt himself begin to shiver. He awoke not to the howling of wind, nor to the pealing of thunder, but rather to complete and utter silence. Around him, darkness filled the dome, the kind of darkness kissed by the first light of dawn—an indigo so deep as to be nearly black.

Cody sat up and listened.

The silence hadn't been a dream, after all. No wind lashed the dome; no sleet pounded the nearby krummholz. All was deathly still. He shifted in his sleeping bag and at once suffered the pain of a man recovering from severe fatigue. Each muscle protested his slightest movements. Realizing he needed hydration, he crawled from the sleeping bag, snatched up a tin, and stepped from the dome.

And directly into a deep, pre-dawn freeze. A horrible, tortuous freeze that had replaced the storm and nestled itself mercilessly over the stark white landscape. Cody shook uncontrollably, and his face stung like the dickens.

He knelt to scoop up a tin-full of snow and quickly retreated inside the dome. There, he fired up the heater and, with the tin set firmly next to it, melted the snow. If only he had the means to heat it to a comfortable tea-like temperature, he thought wistfully. Oh, how he wished for a good cup of tea—some delicious *Da Hong Pao*, perhaps! And a crumpet with clotted cream. He closed his eyes and savored the thought. And it was there in his imagination he remained until the insufferable cold once again stirred him into action.

Rolling up his sleeping bag and packing his salvaged supplies, Cody considered his predicament. Doubt and uncertainty gnawed incessantly at him. Alone, would he be capable of finding his way back to base camp? Heavy snowfall and the landscape's subsequent transformation concerned him. What if at some point along the way he failed to stay the course and turned the wrong direction? He might very well become lost in this godforsaken place. What then?

Night had given him time to think, and insight enough to realize a better option. Tasha, Hank, and Becky must still be alive. Why else had he not discovered their bodies along with the others? At this very moment, they were likely captives, held by the Russians on the other side of the ridge. If Cody set out now, especially in this calm weather, he would easily crest the ridge and spot the drifting smoke of their campfire. Once he had a fix on their location, he would simply follow them until they neared the extraction point, then with great haste he might slip past them through the woods, gain the ridgeline before them, and warn the helicopter crew of the imminent danger. He along with them would return to base camp and alert the authorities, who would then return and aid the others as needed.

It was a brilliant idea and a courageous thing for him to do.

Cody noticed that the snow in the tin had finally melted. Eagerly, he drank of the delicious water, which had the unfortunate effect of stimulating his empty stomach.

With painful stabs, it began to grumble.

Of all he had hoped to find discarded among the equipment, food was at the top of his list. But there had been none, and so he prepared himself mentally for what was sure to come—severe hunger. The thought tested his resolve, but he shook it away and finished packing. Then, he collapsed his dome, slipped on his backpack and struck out boldly in the bitter freeze.

31

THE NIGHTMARE THAT awoke Becky sat her upright with a start. She listened a moment,
breathed of the cold air, felt her stomach
wrench with the pain of emptiness. Last night, crawling into her sleeping bag, she had believed it impossible to feel hungrier. This morning's pain proved her
wrong. She gathered her senses about her, realizing
she had woken from one nightmare right back into
another. She glanced about at the dome's sunlit nylon walls, then at the sleeping bag next to her, where
last night Viktor had slept. He was now gone. She
heard voices outside—Hank's and Andrei's. She
forced herself up and out of the dome.

The bright blue morning sky took her by surprise, as did the horrible freeze that had settled over
camp. Near the ashes of the fire, Hank begrudgingly
listened to Andrei's directives. Viktor stood nearby,
observing silently.

Becky wasn't concerned about being polite.
She marched forth and interrupted Andrei, "Hank

and I went without food yesterday. We can't do it again. Anyway, it wouldn't be in your best interest to starve us, we'll end up slowing you down, maybe even collapse altogether. If that happens, good luck finding the extraction point." Yesterday, the climb up the ridge had given Becky time enough to reason out why she and Hank were being kept alive. And it sure as heck wasn't because Andrei and his cohorts were reluctant to murder people. Fact was, Tasha had never been given specific coordinates. Hank was needed to lead them, and Becky was needed to keep Hank cooperative. Kill either one of them and these bastards ran the risk of finding themselves lost.

And they knew it.

"You'll be given breakfast," Andrei said. "First, however, you and Fedor will make another foray into the woods for fuel, as the night has consumed our supply. Afterwards, we'll build a fire, eat, hydrate, and be on our way. Acceptable?"

"Of course not," she said. "None of this is acceptable, but do I have a choice?"

Hank said, "I'd ask how you're feeling this morning, Beck, but your sass is answer enough." He winked.

Becky walked past him, touched his forearm and smiled, then took the hand axe from Viktor and once again headed for the woods. Fedor fumbled on his toque, unsheathed his knife, and rushed to catch up.

•   •   •

Yesterday, Becky had found a wonderful spot for dry wood. It was a long curving precipice with a low, overhanging shelf, buttressed by thick fir and pine. Their branches had been relatively dry and the base of the rock shelf acted as a sort of snare that collected twigs, cones, and needles—a one-stop shopping center for tinder. It was perfect, not too far away, and now her current destination.

En route, she decided to take advantage of her time alone with this dimwitted Fedor. She wanted to know who these men were; who Tasha was, really; and what it was they were up to. What could be so important they would be willing to murder good people and bring misery to so many families?

As she led the way through the forest, she addressed Fedor, never bothering to turn. "So clearly you all aren't engineers," she said. "That much is obvious. So what exactly is it you're doing out here?"

Fedor was unresponsive, his heavy footfalls stomping noisily over the undergrowth.

"I mean, you must be up to something. Why else go to all this trouble?"

Still nothing.

"Not in the mood to talk, eh? I can hardly blame you. If I were you, I wouldn't want to talk either. It must torture your mind, knowing the awful things you've done. I guess it's easier for you not to speak about them."

Becky had purposefully prodded, but still no response from Fedor, just the rise and fall of his heavy boots.

"I'm not an expert on abnormal psychology,

but from what I know, people like you do these sorts of things because of a sickness. Your mind simply doesn't function like a normal person's."

"It's time you close your mouth, little birdie. Do you understand?"

Despite the veiled threat, Becky was pleased. For one thing, she had clearly irritated the creep. For another, she had broken through, gotten him to speak. Just a little more work and maybe she could open him up, learn something useful. "I'm just talking, trying to keep my mind off being hungry. Seeing as you've been finding every excuse to feed on our granola bars, you wouldn't understand."

"What I understand is you are a thorn, little birdie. Shut up and suffer in silence."

"I'm not so sure I need to listen to you. I remember Andrei telling you not to hurt me."

"Andrei told me not to kill you," he corrected. "He said nothing about hurting."

"That's right. Andrei told you not to kill me. Andrei forbade you. He's clearly the decision-maker. How long you been working for him?"

"I do not work *for* Andrei," he said. "I work *with* Andrei."

"You can tell yourself that if it makes you feel better, but it's clear he's running things. Heck, I saw your face when Tasha kissed him. You were as shocked as the rest of us. Andrei must like keeping you in the dark. He controls you, doesn't he?" Becky stopped, turned, and for the first time looked Fedor directly in the eyes. "In fact, I think you'd curl up fetal and suck your thumb if he told you to."

Abruptly, the massive Russian lifted his arm and backhanded Becky squarely on the side of her head.

She crumbled to the ground. Her ears rang.

"You will stop talking now, and you will get to work, or the next blow will not be so gentle."

Laid out belly down, Becky moaned, felt a pulsing throb in her head, and as she pushed herself to her knees, her eyes fell upon a startling sight. Inwardly, she gasped.

In the distance beyond the trees, skirting the base of the precipice, heavy tracks in the snow led toward the long, overhanging rock shelf—her and Fedor's very destination. From her vantage point, she could not be certain of the animal that had made the tracks, but given their size and spacing, she had a pretty good idea.

Oddly, though, her instinct to flee was not aroused. Maybe it was because of the omnipresent danger she'd been facing; or maybe it was simply because she had already resigned herself to dying.

Whatever the reason was unimportant, for now all Becky could feel was the cold, calculating stab of vengeance.

The idea that seized her was both sudden and fittingly gruesome. But she didn't care. She had been waiting for such an opportunity.

With renewed vigor she stood, boldly faced Fedor, who regarded her with dark menacing eyes. His bruised face contorted with anger.

"Hank really did a number on you, didn't he?" she said. "Good for him. You're probably not used to getting your ass kicked, are you?"

He raised his arm again. Becky used it as an excuse to cower away, in a direction that would turn Fedor's back to the base of the precipice.

He pivoted and struck with a backhanded blow, and again Becky fell. Pain-filled, her head rang with a shrill peal. On the ground at Fedor's feet, she managed to sit up, shake the noise from her head.

"In Russia," Fedor said through clenched teeth, "our women learn silence after just one taste of the hand. American women, it seems, take two."

Again Becky struggled to her feet, unsteady. His strikes had been somewhat mitigated by the back of his hand, yet still they were obscenely powerful. She feared the next might be a fist—more than she could handle.

She nodded assent, turned obediently, and continued her lead. Staggering through the woods in a roundabout direction, she soon reached the precipice and began skirting its base, her ultimate goal to double back and approach the rock shelf from the opposite direction, away from the tracks. After a minute, her usual gait replaced the stagger, but her head still pulsed with pain. The freeze that had settled over the mountain magnified each throb tenfold. Her toque and balaclava did little to ease the smarting.

Soon, Becky cut toward the base of the precipice, then back in the direction of the overhang.

Fedor must have noticed she had doubled them back. "You brought us too far, little birdie. My affectionate touch must have disoriented you." He laughed robustly.

That's right, Becky thought, keep laughing, draw attention to yourself. She said, "Let's get what we need and return to the others. Same as yesterday, you collect the tinder trapped under the shelf. I'll cut away and strip dry branches."

"You will remain within sight," Fedor cautioned.

"Yes, just like yesterday. We'll move parallel to the base. I chop, you collect."

Fedor nodded his satisfaction, then readied the bag in which he planned to collect the tinder.

Methodically they worked, moving slowly along the base. As they proceeded, Becky noticed the overhang deepening. She called out to Fedor, "Get the needles and cones that are deeper under the shelf. They'll be dry, more combustible. She hacked away at a thick branch, stripped it smooth, but she had no intention of using it for firewood.

As she worked, her hunger ceased, replaced by waves of dizziness and fatigue. Maintaining some degree of strength would be critical, she knew, so she began feigning work, conserving energy and breathing more slowly and deeply. All the while, she watched for signs.

At length, Fedor complained of his back. "I am not built to stoop. What I have is enough."

"Is the bag filled?" Becky called out.

"Half full," was his answer.

"Then we need more."

He paused, turned in a crouch under the low-hanging shelf. "I will decide how much is needed, not you, little birdie."

Becky didn't argue, simply pretended to work.

Then in the distance, nearing the overhang where the snow began to thin, she again saw tracks. As she had predicted, closing in from this direction had hidden them. Fedor would be clueless. Her eyes searched the darkness under the natural cavity of the overhang, and about forty feet ahead of Fedor, she could make out heaps of dirt and foliage haphazardly strewn away from the shelf, the first critical sign of a den.

•   •   •

From the safety of distant trees, Cody huddled in the morning shadows and watched Hank collapse the domes. Cody had seen Becky, as well, until she disappeared into the woods with Fedor. Cody had been right all along in his assessment. Tasha, Hank, and Becky were still alive. Strangely though, upon first seeing them, upon observing them walking, talking, and indeed breathing, his heart felt nothing—no joy or relief. Just apathy. Which was strange. Cody knew himself to be a caring man, so he wondered why it was he felt that way.

The answer became immediately clear. This predicament in which he now found himself, all of this discomfort, this mortal danger, it was Hank's fault—and by association, Becky's! Had they the wisdom and foresight to accommodate Cody's earlier plans, the timing of the production would have been different. They never would have encountered these

Russians in the first place! Simply put, karma had bitten Hank and Becky in their arses! And now here was Cody, a victim of their karmic misfortune.

They deserved whatever they got.

His apathy now understood, Cody maintained his watch, while the morning shadows grew shorter and the freeze deeper. He huddled more tightly, wished for a rapid ending to his nightmare. In the stillness of the creeping shadows, he watched.

• • •

"Look, up ahead," Becky called out, "a heap of foliage. You're in luck. You should be able to pick through it for cones and needles, enough to fill your bag and be done. Fedor, are you listening to me?"

Indeed, Fedor was listening, and he had had about enough of this insufferable American woman and her constant barking, as if she were his handler. Another word and he would give her a third lesson in obedience.

Ahead, he could see what she had been screeching about: a scattering of dirt, needles, and branches. Yes, it would greatly simplify his task. Odd, though, how it all lay in a conical pattern, as if something had ejected it from under the overhang. He moved closer to the foliage for a better look, stared down at it, and when he saw the enormous prints that traversed the heap, he tensed. The tracks led to the rock shelf and into a hollowed cavity, a mere twenty feet away. There his eyes resolved in the darkness a stirring form, a golden, hulking mass of

muscle and fur. And next to the thing, in the darkness, two blinking eyes watched, small and curious,
peering at him from a tiny feral face.

The mass next to what Fedor knew to be a
bear cub scuttled rearward with surprising speed,
and before he could react, it emerged from the den
and turned to confront him.

It was a monstrous beast, in size and in sheer
ferocity. Not just a bear—a grizzly!

Ears laid back and slavering jaws snapping, it
reared onto its hind legs, brandishing its claws like
knives. Its guttural cry echoed sickly from the rock.

"Whatever you do don't run," he heard the little birdie say from behind him, "just back away slowly. Flee and you'll only trigger her instinct to attack."

Fedor heeded the advice and backed away
cautiously, his eyes never straying from the beast's
menacing form. It clawed into the air and, at nearly
nine feet tall, staggered forward on its hind legs like a
baby first learning to walk. Then it dropped onto all
fours and approached with an agitated gait.

"Use your jacket to enlarge your form," the little birdie was urging. "Look, the way I've done."

When Fedor stole a glance behind him, he saw
the American standing at arm's length, gripping a
thick branch, cocked as if to strike.

"You murderous prick," she suddenly ex-
claimed, fury in her eyes. "Meet mamma bear!"

Fedor pivoted, raised his arms in defense, but
he was too late, the little birdie too fast. In an explosion of speed, the branch cut through the air in an
upward arc and cracked solidly against his chin. He

felt his jaw split, his balaclava run cold with blood. A blinding light flashed before him. Intense pain replaced thought. And he never felt himself hit the ground.

Confused and disoriented, Fedor peered up to see what at first he thought to be shadow. It wasn't until the full weight of the frenzied beast was upon him, until wicked snarls hammered his eardrums, until his throat felt the pressure of tightening jaws that he realized he was doomed.

32

C ODY KNEW BECKY would have to emerge from the forest at some point, but the manner in which she broke from the treeline into the clearing startled him to his feet.

Running breathless, she appeared frantic. Fedor was not with her, which only confused Cody. If she had fled from him, why return to Andrei and the others?

It made no sense.

Now, Hank had his arms around her, consoling her. She was pointing into the trees. Andrei's and Viktor's pistols appeared in their hands, and they studied the fringe expectantly. Tasha, her splinted arm in a sling, remained reclined against their assemblage of gear.

Still, everyone watched the trees.

Moments later, Andrei approached Becky, pistol brandished, and spoke briefly. She dropped the axe, which he quickly collected and handed to Viktor, then he began a careful inspection of her person, as if searching for something. This, she seemed to allow willingly.

For Cody, the pieces of the puzzle were now coming together, and a rough image of events formed in his mind. He concluded that Becky and Fedor had met with some unexpected difficulty in the woods, a difficulty which prevented Fedor's return. Having come back without him, Becky aroused suspicion, and Andrei thought it prudent to check her for Fedor's pistol.

Yes, it all was clear now. All, that is, except the exact nature of this unexpected difficulty.

•   •   •

Continuing to feign panic, Becky clung to Hank with her face pressed close to his chest. Away from the Russians, who were busy discussing a course of action, she finished explaining under her breath, "...and so I saw an opportunity and I took it."

Hank spoke likewise, "You did the right thing. That was gutsy, Beck. Real gutsy."

"I'm sure they'll want me to lead them back to confirm what happened."

"And we can do that. They want to see what happens when you surprise a grizzly and her cub, they're welcome to it. Ain't going to be pretty."

"No, it's not—"

Hank poked her to indicate the others were coming.

Becky broke away, head down, shoulders slumped. "I think I'm going to be sick!"

"It'll have to wait, Rebecca," Andrei said. "I first would like to see where this supposed attack occurred."

"She looked up, panic-stricken. "Take you back there?"

"That's correct. I must see with my own eyes."

She took a deep breath, gave a terse nod. "Alright, but I've got to warn you, it's going to be messy."

•   •   •

And twenty minutes later, leading Andrei and Viktor through the forest with Hank at her side, Becky saw an area of bloodstained snow and a portion of a dismembered arm, the first sign that her plan in fact had had the desired result. She turned away from the gore and said to Andrei, "Up ahead. Remember, you're the one who insisted on seeing."

Hank blew a whistle, as he had been doing periodically while the group threaded through the thickening trees. "Andrei, you and Viktor ought to remove the suppressors on your guns. If this animal is nearby, a louder report might help to scare it away."

"Will the rounds be effective against such a beast?"

"If it comes to that, they'll probably just piss her off."

Andrei nodded understanding, and he and Viktor removed their suppressors.

Hank and Andrei continued a bit farther, while Becky remained a short distance away with Viktor. A weakening Tasha had stayed at camp to conserve strength.

"Well ain't this a mess?" Becky could hear Hank saying in the trees beyond.

A moment of silence before Andrei asked, "Is this kind of savagery usual in a grizzly encounter?" For the first time, Becky noticed his voice missing its cool edge.

"Not usual, but then again, most encounters don't happen at the den, with a cub inside. She was just protecting her own. That's what mothers do. You'll notice pieces of him, but nothing seems to be consumed. That's because she's already fattened up for the coming months. Probably just begun over-wintering. No, this was purely defensive."

Through the trees, Becky could see Andrei was kneeling, searching. Then he stood, Fedor's knife and pistol in hand.

Hank lit his pipe, surveying the carnage. A frozen breeze brought to her nose the sweet scent of tobacco.

Andrei carefully surveyed his surroundings, then said to Hank, "I suppose what has happened here pleases you."

"You suppose right," Hank said. "It's a good start, anyway."

"Yes, well, I have what I've come for. Let us return, gather our things and move on."

"Whatever you say, comrade. You're the one with the gun."

33

W ITH THE STORM behind them, movement for Hank and Becky through sub-alpine had become much more manageable. The same, however, could not be said for Tasha. Her condition had deteriorated considerably, and now she and Andrei walked abreast, his arm and hip securing her at the waist.

Yet Becky felt no sympathy.

Andrei had kept his word and allowed Becky and Hank a tin of oatmeal, and never before had such bland food tasted so satisfying. So, too, was she satisfied with her handling of Fedor. The man was an animal—plain and simple. Maloney's murder was testament to that. Though her head still throbbed from his blows, the satisfaction of having evened the score helped to endure it.

The sun was nearing transit when Becky and Hank led the Russians out of the dense forest of towering fir and spruce and into a frozen meadow. From here the valley at last unveiled itself, and Becky caught her first glimpse of it below. In the far distance to her right and left, it narrowed into high sheer cliffs, natural barriers that closed the ends as immense impenetrable walls. Ahead, the mountain descended to a broad expanse crisscrossed by frozen rivers that disappeared and then reappeared across its sprawling, tree-clad reaches. At the opposite end, the valley began to rise again, splitting into three distinct peaks, each rising sharply against the cloudless sky. The crest of one of those peaks was their ultimate destination. She studied the valley with growing apprehension. She knew, as surely did Hank, that once they crossed it and revealed which of the mountains they must climb, they would be summarily executed and their bodies discarded, just like the others. Before reaching that point the Russians would in one way or another have to be dealt with.

Andrei appeared between them. "Which of those peaks is our destination, Mr. Guthry?"

"You'd like to know that, wouldn't you?"

"I would not have asked otherwise."

"Well I'm not going to oblige, because we both know what that means."

Andrei smiled. "Your trust is difficult to secure. As I've already assured you, once we reach the extraction point, you and Rebecca will be released unharmed, as will those in the helicopter who come to escort you home. Of course, you will all have to manage your way back to base camp, but that shouldn't be too difficult, not for someone with your skills, Mr. Guthry."

"You almost sound convincing, but if what you

say is true, you don't need Becky. I'm the one who'll get you where you want to go. Let her leave now. Give her a dome, a knife, enough food to make her way back to base camp. We're a day out to those peaks, but she's several days back in the other direction. You'll be long gone before she ever has a chance to alert anyone."

None of what Becky heard Hank say surprised her. He would forfeit his own life for hers in an instant. That she knew, but leaving him alone at the hands of these butchers was something she had no intention of doing. "Hank," she said. "I'm not going anywhere. You and I are in this together."

"Indeed," Andrei said. "If we free Rebecca, you will never lead us to the helicopter."

"Don't think so, huh?"

"No, Mr. Guthry, I do not. I'm quite skilled at reading the hearts of men, and yours is a hardened one. I suspect you would sooner die than give us what we want. Rebecca will remain with us, for you're not as casual with her life as you are with your own."

Hank didn't answer. He stared broodingly at the distant peaks.

"So it's settled then. You will keep our destination a mystery, and I shall keep Rebecca. It'll be interesting to see how things work themselves out. Lead the way, would you Mr. Guthry?"

Andrei went to retrieve his pack. Becky laid her hand on Hank's shoulder. "I appreciate you wanting to protect me—"

"And Gracie," Hank added.

"And Gracie," she said. "We both love you, but I'd never sacrifice you for anyone, not even my own daughter."

"I'm not asking you to sacrifice anything. I just want you to promise me that when the time comes if I tell you to run, even if it means leaving me, no matter what your heart tells you, you'll listen and do it. Will you promise me that, Beck?"

Hank was beginning to sound fatalistic, and what he was asking of her made her stomach turn. "You know something, Hank, that's a helluva thing for you to ask me to promise. I'm not going to do it." And she hefted up her backpack and set out for the valley below.

•   •   •

They were on the move again. Cody wished the break had been longer. He was exhausted and the lack of food was beginning to take a toll on his system. He never realized roughing it could be so difficult.

Still, he had a goal to accomplish, and he would stick with it, right to the end. In fact, the time for him to overtake these wankers was drawing near. He looked out over the valley, with its abundance of trees and dense undergrowth. He looked beyond toward the three peaks, each a rocky behemoth stained with dark patches of stunted trees and krummholz. It was the perfect place to pass them undetected.

Like the others, he slung on his backpack and prepared to descend.

34

Hank and the others had reached the valley floor with little effort and minimal discomfort—all, that is, except for Tasha. Her arm had swelled up something fierce, and her legs had begun buckling at times, carrying her with growing uncertainty. Little did she complain, though. Hank had to give her credit for that. Still, he wasn't sure she'd make it to the extraction point without more help than Andrei's arm could provide. She would need something to help move her along, a travois maybe.

Because of her worsening condition, they had stopped prematurely to pitch camp. Andrei was tending to her in his dome. Protectively, Hank sat next to Becky at the fire, smoking his pipe, studying the distant terrain. The conditions high on the opposing range were ripe for an avalanche, he thought approvingly. Yep, they were all there: recent heavy snowfall, slopes that inclined just enough to hold it, and ridgelines with cornices so pregnant with the stuff that the slightest trigger would send it all rolling.

And Hank had that trigger girt securely around his waist. All he needed to do was figure out a way to lead the Russians into a track without involving Becky.

He dragged thoughtfully on the chewed bit, exhaled smoke into the frozen air, picked a piece of tobacco from his tongue and flicked it into the fire. The answer would come to him. He was confident of that. What worried him more was Becky's insistence on handling these men together. Hank wouldn't stand for it. Somehow, someway, he had to convince her to do the right thing and, when the time came and he told her to hightail it, she would do just that. Her bushcraft skills were sufficient to carry her safely back to camp. Of that he was confident. Darn her for being so stubborn. She had Gracie to think about.

Hank noticed Viktor staring at him. It was like the asshole was trying to read his mind, which of course he couldn't because while sitting here Hank had wished death upon the sonofabitch a dozen times with never a visible reaction.

He turned his mind back to the problem, searching for weaknesses in the Russians he might exploit. With Fedor out of the way and Tasha's arm in a mangle, Andrei and Viktor were the only two real threats. Actually, it was them holding guns that were the problem. He just couldn't figure a safe enough way to disarm the both of them that wouldn't get him or Becky shot. Even the sleeping arrangements worked against them. Hank might've been tempted to make a play against Andrei in the wee hours, but

Viktor had been given instructions to kill Beck if he heard the slightest disturbance. Hank couldn't risk it. He continued brooding.

Soon, shadows swept over the fire as the sun touched and then dipped behind the western ridge. He and Becky sat in silence, each knowing the subject of the other's thoughts. Viktor, who had been standing huddled in the orange glow of the campfire, still kept his eyes fixed upon them. Now and again, Hank would smile and salute, just his way of saying, *kiss my ass.*

At length, Andrei emerged from his dome and stared regrettably at Viktor, then looked to Hank and Becky before joining them at the fire.

"Tasha's condition is deteriorating," he said. "She's begun to fever, and it seems the swelling has restricted blood to the arm. All of this exertion has only exasperated the problem. She's weak, very weak."

Good, Hank thought. It would give these pricks something to keep their minds busy. Every little distraction helped.

"Further aid is beyond my ability, I'm afraid. What do you know of treating such injuries, Mr. Guthry?"

"I know that when a mule in the Sonoran breaks its leg, folks there put a bullet in its head."

Viktor's eyes swelled crimson in the firelight. He reached for his pistol.

Becky said, "Now wait just a minute!"

Hank swiped the pipe from his mouth, pointed it at Viktor. "That gun for Tasha? Like my idea you asshole?"

"Andrei, we needn't keep him around. I've had enough of his incessant taunting."

"Too bad, you're going to have to deal with it," Hank said. "Look at that western range there. You got three separate peaks, each ridgeline a mile long and broken at a dozen points in between. Kill me and you'll never know which slope and which section to climb."

"It matters not," Viktor said icily. "We can climb any one of them and build a signal fire, draw the helicopter to us."

"You could do that," Hank said. "Problem is only one of those ridges has an area safe enough for a chopper to land. It's why I chose it."

"We'll risk it." Viktor raised his pistol.

"You'll lower your weapon," Andrei said. "We've come too far and will risk nothing. You're a pilot, Viktor, you should know better than any of us. If the extraction team cannot land, they won't. And even if they could, there is no guarantee the weather won't worsen, making a distant signal fire impossible to see."

"In either case," Hank added, "they'll radio for a search and rescue party. Multiple helicopters, plenty of airmen. How do you plan to deal with that?"

Viktor lowered his pistol.

Andrei said, "There'll be no more discussion on the matter. My immediate concern is Tasha. Something must be done."

"The only thing that can be done," Becky said, "is for her to seek medical treatment. I've seen the arm. It's beyond any kind of backcountry medicine."

"Agreed," Hank said. "And frankly, the way her health is declining, I suspect there's more to the injury than a broken radius. I'm not so sure she'll make it up the mountainside."

Andrei became thoughtful, his eyes a window into his mind. He was wrestling with a tough decision.

Hank waited to hear it.

"Perhaps it would be best if she didn't attempt the ascent at all, Mr. Guthry."

Hank raised an eyebrow.

"I would like you to construct a sled for her transport. Once we reach the end of the valley, we'll find a clearing large enough for a helicopter to land. There we'll establish camp, build a fire, feed her, give her water. She will remain. We'll climb without her."

His directives were met with silence.

"We must make up for lost time," Andrei continued. "Tonight we bed early. At dawn we depart."

"And tonight's arrangements?" Hank asked.

"As before," Andrei said.

"If you don't mind, I'd much rather pair with Beck. No offense, But I can't sleep much next to the likes of you. I'm sure Beck feels the same about Viktor."

"There will be no changes," Andrei said. "Viktor will pair with Rebecca, and you with me. Tasha shall have her privacy."

Hank looked at Becky, then back at Andrei, and he sighed. "Whatever you say, comrade. As I said before, you're the one with the gun."

35

TASHA WOKE FROM her sleep—if being roused by fitful turning and restless repositioning could be called such—and found her thermals drenched in sweat. She had earlier withdrawn from the confines of her sleeping bag, but it had done little to ease the insufferable heat. What she needed was fresh air. Cold, clean, fresh air.

She unzipped the dome and parted the flap, peeking out wearily into the starlit clearing. In camp nothing stirred, the fire long dead. And it was just as well, the sight of flames would only sicken her. The effort of gaining her feet brought about a wave of dizziness. It unsteadied her, but still she managed afoot and staggered outside, breathing greedily of the cold air. Her body craved it as an addict craved drugs.

A few minutes out of her tent—she was sure—would remedy the intense discomfort. Under the dark dome of a sparkling pre-dawn, she staggered across the snow, but still her head fevered and her skin burned. Perhaps a moment sitting under a tree would help. She stumbled onward and reached a nearby aspen, steadied herself against its scratchy trunk, and eased herself to the ground. But still she burned. It was the damn turtleneck. Its tightness was constricting her neck and chest. She clawed at the fabric to ease the pressure, but even such trivial motion required tremendous effort. She let her good hand drop to her side; the other she could no longer feel.

A glimpse of the stars that studded the purple sky reminded her of the diamonds Andrei had revealed to her. So many diamonds, and so beautiful, and so valuable. A few more days and she would be back in the States beginning a new life. *A prosperous life.* Excitement swelled her burning breast. Oh, the sprawling estate she would own, the cars she would drive, the wardrobe she would assemble. Her sigh at the thought of a carefree life was so very faint.

She tired more, much more. But it was good, a few minutes to subdue this deplorable fever and she would return to the safety of her dome, the comfort of her sleeping bag.

Just a few more minutes.

In a dreamlike haze, her head began to loll. Her eyelids became heavy. A frozen wind swept her damp hair, yet still she burned. One more minute would cool her. She was certain of it. Just one more minute....

•   •   •

It was Viktor's urgent call that roused Andrei out of his dome. Dawn had arrived, and its lavender light was enough to reveal Viktor standing far from the circle of domes, at the apron of the aspen-fringed forest.

Andrei's lope turned to a sprint when, by the twilight, he saw his sister's motionless form. She was slumped at the base of a tree. Upon reaching her, panic turned to grief, for he knew immediately she was gone. He knelt at her side, reached out, but could not bring himself to touch her pale face. It was a visage frozen in quiet slumber, her darkened eyes gently closed, her blue lips slightly parted. Andrei took her hand in his and hung his head.

"Watch the others," he quietly ordered.

Viktor turned to obey, and then came his startled cry, "They're fleeing into the forest!"

Andrei wheeled up and around. "Where!"

"There!" Viktor had already broken into a sprint, pointing with his pistol.

Blyat! In a moment of weakness, Andrei had allowed Hank and Becky to seize the opportunity and steal away to the far end of the meadow. Dimly, Andrei could see them charging into the aspen. He pulled his gun and pursued.

●　　●　　●

Becky's mind reeled at the thought that any moment she and Hank might be shot in the back. She had to keep her wits about her, couldn't afford to panic and make a mistake. She focused on form, her legs carrying her deftly over snowy shrubs and fallen branches. Her breathing was rapid. Hank remained at her heels, urging her along confidently. At his say-so, they broke left down a jagged escarpment and toward denser forest.

"We're leaving plenty of tracks," Hank managed to say between breaths. "I remember a river somewhere up yonder. We'll skirt it, look for a place to cross."

Becky blazed a path through increasingly heavier trees and undergrowth, ducking under larch boughs and slapping aside low-hanging branches.

"Stop," Hank said.

And when she turned to see the problem, he was heaving for breath.

"You okay?"

"I'm fine." He was peering behind him for signs of pursuit. Becky watched the trees and listened. "Did we lose them?"

"No, impossible in this snow, but I have an idea to slow 'em down."

"I'm listening."

"The montane is plenty dense here, and we've reached a lot of crowding larch. You'll notice the snowfall is heavy between them, but minimal under their canopies. If we time our strides, we can avoid the heavy snow and keep to the thin. It won't hide our tracks completely, but it'll slow them down at points while they stop to confirm our direction."

Becky nodded.

"Let's do it," Hank said, and the two restarted their sprint, this time loping from island to island.

36

BESIDES THE BROKEN arm, he could see no trauma, no gunshot wound or serious head injury, so Cody couldn't figure out how exactly Tasha had been murdered. It looked like she simply froze to death. Stranger still was the way Andrei had knelt sorrowfully by her side, with his head lowered, almost as if in mourning.

It made no sense.

But then again, none of this nightmare made any sense. He glanced again at her frozen corpse. Poor, poor Tasha, he bemoaned inwardly. Cody was an impeccable judge of character and knew she had been the only true innocent among them.

He pulled himself away and turned in the direction of the domes. Everything was there: tents, backpacks, even a crudely fashioned travois.

Another glance at the margin of trees into which everyone had disappeared and Cody scuttled into the domes to check the backpacks. A couple of minutes were all it took for him to find the stash of food. At least, what was left of it. Protein bars were gone, as were the dried beans and noodles. No coffee or oatmeal either. Just a bag of trail mix.

Still, it was better than nothing. He stuffed the find in his pocket and hurried back into the trees to await the inevitable return of the others.

Once safely from view, he sank against a trunk and began devouring the peanuts and dried fruit. Ten minutes produced an empty bag. He split it apart and licked away the salt. He moaned euphorically. Oh, it was pure heaven.

•   •   •

The river appeared ahead. But to Becky, it didn't look crossable. She halted, hands to knees, frosting the air with rapid breaths, glancing left, glancing right. At its narrowest point, the river spanned fifteen feet. The icy water tumbled eastward over sunken bedrock.

Hank reached her side, sucking long drafts of air.

"Now what, upstream?" she asked.

"Yep, search for a place to cross."

"Let's do it."

"Wait, Beck. Make sure to skirt the bank, but stay well clear of the edge. What looks like solid ground is just the river icing up and light snow resting atop it. One misstep and we're in the drink. Under these circumstances, that's a death sentence."

"Understood." And she bolted off upstream.

•   •   •

When the Russians reached the riverbank, Andrei stopped to study the tracks. Hank and Rebecca had paused here, likely to settle upon a course of action, then turned west and headed along the river toward the eastern face of the mountains.

He gazed toward the peaks and breathed deeply of the cold air, becoming contemplative. This pursuit should have been unnecessary, he knew, and he cursed himself for having let his guard down in the first place. Had he the discipline to control his emotions, he would not have made such an amateur lapse in judgment; he would have first cautioned Viktor to guard Hank and Rebecca. None of this would now be necessary.

But what was done was done, and with changing circumstances, he knew there was no time for grief or regret. Only action. He resolved to put his sister's passing behind him and move forward, to finish what he had set out to accomplish in the first place. Her death would not be in vain.

"With Tasha gone, and Hank and Rebecca in flight we must adapt. Once we overtake them, we no longer move to capture. We move to kill."

Viktor stared back. "What of the extraction?" he said. "Your points yesterday were well taken."

"I'm certain by now Hank has revealed to Rebecca their destination, had he not previously. When we reach them, he is to become our target. Shoot to kill."

Viktor's blue eyes gleamed.

"Alone, she could be made to talk."

"And if she refuses?"

Andrei looked to where Viktor kept his knife. "If she refuses, there are ways to persuade her."

Viktor turned a smile.

"Then it's settled." Andrei gripped his friend's shoulder. "The two mustn't be allowed to escape these mountains. We'll begin with Hank." Andrei turned back to the tracks. "It's clear they fled west. Their destination remains extraction."

"It's a destination they'll fail to reach," Viktor said confidently. "We shall see to that."

•　　•　　•

In hiding and waiting for the others to return, a new thought panicked Cody, a sudden realization so apparent he wondered how it had escaped him in the first place. In the event Hank and Becky eluded the Russians, they would never dream of returning here. The Russians might, of course, but what good would that do him? Those losers had no clue where to go.

Without Hank and Becky, he'd have no one to follow; he'd never know which summit to climb to reach the extraction point. He would be left behind in this wilderness hellhole. If he didn't starve first, he would freeze to death!

The stark realization stood him to his feet, and he concluded, reluctantly, that he would have to find Hank and Becky himself.

His belly satisfied from the trail mix and his

body hydrated, he began sucking out peanuts from between his teeth and proceeded to scout the area for their tracks.

Locating them, fortunately, took little time and effort, as they had been made recently and without regard for concealment. The pursuing Russians had further disturbed the snow so that now only a blind man could fail to follow them. This was splendid, Cody thought. He would simply follow the tracks. Once Hank and Becky began ascending the extraction peak, he would surreptitiously overtake them using the krummholz as cover and beat them to the helicopter.

As he forged along the trail, sucking and slogging, his mind once again turned to the subject of his career, specifically to the disastrous outcome of this production. Escaping from these mountains was indeed critical, but so too was salvaging the all-important finale. But the cameras had been destroyed, and the SD memory cards burned along with them. No record of his daring exploits remained to be aired. How could it be done?

Brooding as he walked, he could feel the stress of dilemma mounting in his breast, his throat tightening with anger. All of his hard work, all of his ingenious planning, all of it lay in a smoldering heap. Oh, the unfairness of it all!

It was twenty minutes of painful hiking before the solution finally came to him. But come to him it did, as he had expected it would. Sure, the production had now become a bust, but why not simply produce another finale? Only this time, instead of focusing on generic, run-of-the-mill survival scenes, as he had been doing, why not film a re-enactment, a tale of the horror that this finale had become? Yes, it was genius.

He would lead camera crews along on a journey that would take his viewers from the mine where he first encountered the Russians to locations of gruesome murders. He would treat his viewers to a drama-filled re-enactment of how he himself had exposed the Russians as ruthless killers, and how, despite his own best efforts to protect everyone, they had been murdered anyway. He could point out the very spot in which Maloney plunged to his death, the clearing in which Marshal and Kilpatrick were shot to death, and the shallow graves in which their bodies had been discarded. It would be bloody fantastic. Almost as if the Lord Himself had blessed Cody by staging events.

If a show of such gripping magnificence didn't top the ratings, nothing would.

Now, following deep prints in the snow and covering much ground, Cody mused over how best to maximize his newfound solution. And to his delight, the ideas continued coming. In addition to the re-enactment episode, he would pen a tale of heroism and survival and title it: *FROM HOLLYWOOD TO HELL! A STORY OF ONE MAN'S FIGHT TO SURVIVE.* He would weave a narrative so gripping it would become an overnight sensation, a national bestseller even. There would be network and cable television interviews, magazine exposés and, naturally, the Hollywood party circuit. He would leapfrog his success into the next season of

The Survivalist, and with his career back on track, life would be good again, better than ever, in fact!

Funny, the ups and downs of fortune, Cody thought, and inwardly he began humming a silent tune. It eased his nerves and passed the time. A few bars into *I Can See Clearly Now* and he stopped dead in his tracks, a horrible thought having just occurred to him.

There was one glaring problem with his plan.

Two problems, really.

Hank and Becky.

They would undoubtedly offer up conflicting accounts of events, lies that would cast suspicion over the truth and authenticity of the production, lies that would get in the way of his successful foray into publishing.

In the event the Russians failed to find and kill them, something needed to be done—something bold and decisive.

And the answer came swiftly: Given that this entire debacle was the result of Hank's and Becky's constant meddling and insubordination, a little back-country retribution would not be unjustified. If Cody were to come upon them first, why not fix the problem himself? Having reacquired the explosives, he was in a position do so. Excited, his heartbeat quickened, and with the decision made, he forged ahead boldly, following the others' tracks.

37

BECKY PAUSED, AS much to catch her breath as to discern something she could see ahead. "Look, there!" She pointed excitedly. "A fallen tree."

Hank was stooped over, hands to knees, inhaling long deep breaths. "I'm too old for this shit."

"Maybe so, but you're too young to die."

He looked up, nodded at her.

"What do you think?"

He studied where Becky was indicating. It was a point far up along the river, beyond where the rocky banks rose sharply into vertical walls. There, a tree had fallen, linking one side of the river with the other. "I think you found a solution."

"We can cross the trunk and push the other end into the river," she said. "They'll have no way to follow."

"Right. Not here, anyway. Let's do it." They ran forward.

When they reached the crossing, Becky saw

that the tree was a larch. It had been rooted close to the bank. Erosion and the recent storms had downed it, making it a natural bridge to the other side. Ten feet below, the river streamed over a bed of scattered rocks and boulders.

She studied the trunk. It was long and thick and would likely hold their weight. It extended twenty feet across the river and ten or so feet beyond the opposite bank. The problem was the tangle of stripped limbs that jutted out haphazardly from its trunk. On the one hand, they would offer plenty of handholds, but on the other, they would act as obstacles. Walking its length would be a tricky feat.

Becky stepped up to the tree, but Hank gently restrained her. "I'll go first, make sure it's safe."

She knew better than to argue.

He grabbed a limb and stepped onto the trunk, which was still partially rooted. The tree held without rolling. Carefully, yet deftly, Hank shuffle-stepped the twenty feet to the opposite bank, sometimes swinging his feet around limbs, other times kicking at them to break them off.

When he reached the other shore, he nodded to indicate that he hadn't found it too difficult. She followed, mirroring his steps and snatching at branches for balance. Midway across she looked down to see the river below. It rushed and roiled over menacing rocks. She tried not to image the consequences of falling.

Apparently, Hank had noticed her sudden apprehension. "Don't you worry about the height any," he cautioned. "Keep your eyes on the trunk and your feet. Step carefully."

She took a deep, calming breath, imagined herself crossing successfully, and forced herself to continue. Soon she was over and her fear eased.

"Atta girl," Hank said as he helped her down. "Now all we got to do is push this baby into the river."

"Easier said than done. It's still somewhat rooted."

"Plus, snow has accumulated high around it. No time to clear it all. We'll just have to give it our best."

Together they grasped what thick limbs they could reach and pulled with all of their strength. The strain heated her neck and face. The tree began to slide, but only by degrees. "We can do this," Becky said. And they heaved again.

More slight movement.

The branches scratched and poked at her when she drew herself closer for better leverage, and the two of them pulled once more, Hank's deep grunts encouraging her. She clenched her teeth, dug her feet into the snowy soil, and heaved again.

And again she felt a welcome movement. They were making progress, but had a long way to go, and Becky worried they'd run out of time.

They heaved again.

A gunshot startled Becky, and Hank's pain-filled yelp turned her. She looked across the river and saw Andrei and Viktor. Andrei was positioned in a firing stance, his pistol leveled.

"Drop for cover!" Hank growled through viced teeth, and together they dropped in a crouch against the trunk.

Another shot sounded and the round bit deeply into the trunk near her head. "Hold for a better shot," Andrei called out to Viktor.

Becky saw Hank pressing his stomach. "My God," she said in a panic, "you're hit!"

"Forget it, it just winged me."

Over the hum of the river, Andrei called out again, "Hank, Rebecca, we needn't make this any more difficult than necessary."

"Fine idea," Hank called back. "Why don't you fellows drown yourselves in the river, make life easier for all of us."

"Save your strength for the woods," Becky told him.

"C'mon, Beck, I'm just having a little fun." He winced.

"There's nothing fun about you being shot. We need to lose them, have a look at your wound."

Hank searched about, his pain-filled eyes assessing. "Beyond those aspen there's a meadow that abuts a stretch of dog-hair pine."

"Dog-hair?"

"It's just lodgepole, really, but the darned things grow so close together it's like moving through dog hair. The narrow spacing there shields the forest floor. There'll be little or no snow on the ground. No tracks to follow. Perfect for losing them bastards."

"Great," Becky said feeling a renewed sense of hope. "All we have to do is get you mobile, make a break for those trees and get ourselves in cover. We'll lose them in the dog-hair, find a place to assess and treat your wound."

Hank became quiet and looked at Becky with an expression of a doctor delivering bad news.

"What is it?"

He looked down at his stomach, where he had been holding his hands. Becky could see blood beginning to spread over his parka above his waist and knew he hadn't been winged. Instinctively, she understood it was bad.

"Sorry, Beck, I lied."

"Oh, Hank!" Becky's eyes suddenly filled with tears. Her hands touched his.

"Don't cry, girl. You're gonna fight on, get to the extraction point, get the hell out of here and home to Gracie."

"And so are you!" she said defiantly. She wasn't going to let Hank give up. He would be okay. He had to be okay. She needed him to be okay. Grief clutched at her heart.

He looked down at his parka. The blood was spreading quickly. "For me, this is the end of the line. The slug in my gut hit something awful, I can feel it. I'll only hold you back. This is where we have to say goodbye."

"To hell it is."

"When I give the say-so, we make a break for the trees. Those there are only about fifteen feet away." He began to cough, sputter a bit. "We can make it. I want you to run ahead of me."

"Then we're continuing on—together."

"You ready?"

She nodded.

"Let's go!"

And the two scrambled to their feet, keeping to a low crouch. As they covered ground, Becky knew they were open targets. She prayed for a good outcome. They dashed desperately for the aspen, Hank following her close as a glove.

Again, shots rang out.

Becky could hear them speeding past, hear them striking the trees. Her heart raced. She felt it fill with the weight of sorrow and fear. She and Hank were now close to cover. Then more shots, and Hank stifled a cry.

And they were behind the trees, heaving with deep, frosty breaths.

Hank remained doubled over, coughing, spitting blood into the snow. "Bastards caught me in the shoulder." He straightened with a painful effort, leaned into a trunk.

Becky's worry for him reached a sickening depth. She cursed herself for not knowing what to do. She had to help him, had to get him to safety. She looked back through the trees to the river. Andrei and Viktor were now preparing to cross, testing the fallen larch for soundness.

Hank was favoring an arm. With his other he removed his cap, pulled a cord from around his neck, where hung his FireSteel and striker. "Take this, you'll need it for fire. I'd give you my lighter, but I have plans for it. Take my cap, too, give it to Gracie and get her to a Mariner's game, for chrissake."

"You can give it to her yourself," Becky said becoming firm in voice. "I told you we're leaving here together."

"And I told you that ain't possible. Now listen to me, Beck, I'm gonna try leading them away. You head to the dog-hair like we discussed. Lose them there, get to the extraction point, get home to Gracie."

"That's exactly what *we're* going to do."

"Dammit, Rebecca, I don't have time to argue with you. Listen to me! I'm losing blood, haven't got much longer. You're going to have to accept that, whether you want to or not. Do what I say and don't argue, and don't follow me. I'm going another direction, leading them away. They're too smart to both follow me, but I'm sure I'll draw away one of them."

"No, they'll kill you!"

"They already have," Hank said soberly. "But trust me, I don't plan on going out in a whimper. Now get, before I turn ornery."

Becky looked through the aspen in the direction of the meadow.

"Go, or I'll die angry with you."

"Hank." She could feel tears rolling down her cheeks.

"I love you and Gracie both. You tell her that for me."

"Hank."

And he staggered off in another direction along the bank's margin of trees. Deeper into the woods would have been safer, but Becky could see him skirting at a point where the Russians would be sure to see him.

She watched him go until he was no longer in

sight, and never did he look back. It was the voice of Andrei that turned her toward the river. Through tear-filled eyes, she saw that Viktor had mounted the trunk and was beginning to cross, while Andrei remained on firm ground, his pistol at the ready, awaiting his turn.

Becky wiped the tears from her eyes, collected the things Hank had given her, and turned away from the river in the direction of the meadow.

•   •   •

Hank regretted having had to raise his voice with Becky. But the girl could be as hard-headed as he. Best she saved that stubbornness for survival.

From his vantage point in the trees, Hank leaned numbly against a tree and watched the Russians. It took them only a short time to cross to his side without mishap. Once over, they began scanning the woods. Viktor pointed in Hank's direction before the pair split, and as Hank had suspected, Andrei ran into the trees after Beck and Viktor made a bee-line for his own position.

With a grunt of pain and finality, Hank pushed away from the aspen and began his trek into the bush.

His movement was slow and erratic. Blood dripped from his parka, staining the snow. He found himself having to follow a course based on the spacing of trees, as he needed them every few steps for support. He lunged from one to the next, becoming dizzier with each passing tree.

He knew Viktor had to be closing.

A few minutes passed and Hank decided this was as good a place as any to take care of business. He reached for a nearby aspen, a fine-looking specimen aspiring high into the misty sky. He turned against it, and slid onto his haunches.

Breathing deeply, painfully, he waited.

•   •   •

Ahead, Viktor could see the blood trail leading directly to the American who, forced by weakness, had stopped and slumped against a tree.

Viktor approached slowly. Hank hadn't time to set a trap, he knew, but caution had become habitual.

At ten feet, Viktor stopped.

"Afternoon, comrade," the stubborn American said.

Viktor smiled. "You do understand, this was inevitable."

"I suppose." Hank pulled his pipe from his pocket and chuckled painfully. Blood filled the gap between his lips. "After you finish me it'll be one-against-one, eh comrade?"

"Two-against-one," Viktor corrected him. "You err in your arithmetic."

"My money's on Beck," Hank said before spitting blood to the ground. "Hey, you're not still pining over my donkey comment, are you?"

Viktor stepped closer to observe the American's wound. The blood soaking his parka was dark, almost black, indicating a liver shot.

"You wouldn't begrudge a fellow a last smoke, would you?"

Viktor nodded to the pipe.

Hank brought it to his lips, fumbled with the lighter.

Viktor assisted, scratching the wheel and producing a flame. He brought it to the bowl, and Hank dragged deeply, pulling in sweet-smelling smoke.

"Much obliged."

Viktor pocketed the lighter. "You'll no longer be needing this, I'm afraid."

"All yours. Consider it a parting gift."

Viktor nodded. "Yes, a gift. I thank you." He stared into Hank's eyes, saw the pain in his expression. "You don't bellow as would a woman, you're cheerful in your end. I respect that."

Hank chewed the stem from one corner of his mouth to the other, and took another drag, then, greatly weakened, removed the pipe and dropped his hands to his side. "Oh, you sonsabitches, what's this all about? Why'd you kill all them decent folks?"

"Tell me, Mr. Guthry, which summit must Andrei and I ascend?"

"I asked why you did it?"

Now, Viktor's knife was out. He knelt at the American's side. "Diamonds—a fortune in precious diamonds."

Hank nodded his understanding and again grimaced.

"My round penetrated your liver. You've little time."

"Go figure, you and I got something in common."

"Which summit, Mr. Guthry?"

"Did you know I used to be married?"

Viktor listened with tested patience.

"Her name was Edith, love of my life. She's passed now, some years back."

"My condolences. Which summit?"

"You know, the only good to come from losing the woman you love is you stop worrying about the end yourself. Hell, sometimes you even look forward to it. You see, my end with you is just a new beginning with her."

"I've been patient with you," Viktor said, turning his knife. "I'll not tolerate much more."

"What are you gonna do, kill me twice?" Hank coughed painfully. "By the way, there was nothing wrong with my arithmetic. When I said one-against-one, I meant it. Those are the odds, and my girl Beck is a survivor. She'll win this game of yours."

It was after he noticed the American had moved his pipe from view that the hiss of a fuse came faintly to Viktor's ears. Alarmed, he threw aside the dying man's parka and tensed at the sight of a lit charge, its hissing fuse nearly consumed!

Viktor had sprung to his feet and taken his first stride in retreat when Hank Guthry, in a savage death knell, lunged out and grabbed him by the legs. "Thanks for the light, you Russian bastard!"

Legs in a grapple, Viktor toppled and slammed to the ground, the impact flinging his knife into the bush. Dazed, he tried desperately to scramble away, but Hank's hold was fierce. The explosion came just as Viktor realized the American's artful deception.

38

SNOW-COVERED BRUSH snapped underfoot as Becky darted through an ever-narrowing stretch of woods. The meadow had to be near, and beyond it, the dog-hair pine. Her route became erratic as she found herself scrambling over uneven ground and up steep inclines. More though than the physical terrain, she struggled with the emotions of leaving Hank. She had left him behind. Alone and bleeding. Just left him. The guilt was an acid that ate at her stomach. She cursed silently for having been given an impossible choice.

Now, to cope, she focused on Gracie. She had to survive for herself, but more importantly for her daughter. She had to make it home. A sudden explosion sounded in the distance, stopping her cold. Exhausted mentally, physically, she stooped over.

Hank.

She brought her hands to her face. She wanted to weep, but couldn't, she had no more tears. She straightened. Her mind again focused on the threat.

She searched around for signs of the Russians, and noted the palpable silence. The explosion had quieted the woods.

The explosion. What exactly had happened? Was it possible Hank had drawn away both Viktor and Andrei? And if so, had he led them into a trap? The blast could have meant any number of things, including the end of Viktor and Andrei, which would leave Hank alone and in need of her help.

The thought that he might still be alive and suffering stabbed like a knife at Becky's heart. She couldn't just ignore the possibility. She had to know for sure. Plagued by the uncertainty, she decided to double back and learn exactly what had happened. If Hank were alive and in pain, she had to be there to help him.

Backtracking would be too dangerous, as it increased the chances of stumbling upon Andrei or Viktor. She would have to be smart about returning, not act stupidly in her haste. She decided to gain the dog-hair—it couldn't be that much farther—shed herself of tracks, then double back toward the river obliquely. From there she could pick up Hank's trail and, ultimately, confront the reality of what had happened.

Her decision made, Becky sprang into action.

•   •   •

Cody had emerged from the woods and was nearing a river when the unexpected explosion sent him diving for cover. He lifted his head from the snow, spit away a mouthful, and searched in the direction of the blast. It had come from across the river, somewhere in the depths of the woods.

He remembered his own charges, remembered how one had been missing from the case, and quickly put two and two together. But who had detonated the thing, Hank and Becky, or the Russians? With a little luck, the whole lot of them had been blown to hell.

He willed himself to his feet and narrowed his eyes upon the snow, re-acquiring the tracks. They led along the bank and disappeared beyond a rise. Somewhere ahead had to be a crossing, and he hurried to find it.

●   ●   ●

Andrei now faced a dilemma: continue his pursuit or investigate the explosion. Its unexpectedness had come as a mental jolt. After some deliberation, he decided it unwise to continue pursuing. With the introduction of this variable, there existed too many possibilities which demanded explanation. Had Hank lured Viktor into a trap? Or, despite their remote isolation, had newcomers arrived? Andrei needed more information. He would return to reacquire Becky's tracks later. He broke off pursuit and started back toward the explosion.

●   ●   ●

As usual Cody had been right. The crossing was just ahead, a fallen tree that spanned the breadth of the river. Here, the water cut into the earth ten feet below, churning and slurping over icy rocks and boulders.

At the root of the tree Cody stopped and assessed. From afar, the distance across had seemed negligible, but now, standing at the edge and hearing the din of water below, the opposite shore looked light years away!

Had Becky and the others seriously crossed this? Cody looked out over the length of the trunk, where he saw cleared snow and broken branches, indications others had been before him.

He moaned, unsure whether or not he could manage it. His instinct was to call for Kilpatrick, but as quickly as the urge came, so too did the memory of his stuntman's frozen corpse. The plonker had picked an awful time to get dead.

Cody would have to do this himself.

He mounted the root system, picking his way toward the portion of trunk at the bank's edge. There, he took his first step. But looking down over the moving water, eyes focused on a heap of sharp rocks, he was forced by prudence to quickly draw back. He couldn't do it, couldn't bring himself to take the risk. His life was far too valuable. Anyway, attempting it would be selfish. He had his fans to think about. Unsure what to do, he knelt and straddled the trunk— and from this position had a brilliant idea. Why not simply lie flat and inch-worm his way across? Little by little he could scoot himself forward, embracing the tree as he would a London harlot, and by degrees maneuver the obstacle course of scaly bark and protruding limbs.

Sure it would take some time to cross, but the alternative, he knew, was a plunge into freezing, rock infested water.

•　　•　　•

It was nearing mid-afternoon when Andrei peered skyward through the trees. Clouds had once again begun to amass, crowding and pushing their way toward the eastern peaks. These, in embryo, were the sorts of fierce storms they had battled crossing the summit.

Andrei forged ahead and soon reached a pair of tracks, which he quickly concluded belonged to Hank and Viktor. His pistol ready he turned and followed, and after a short time found himself entering a scene of utter carnage.

Strewn before him in a radius of flesh and blood was the culmination of Hank's and Viktor's animosity. At the center, in a pulpy heap, were the remains of the two men. Much of the damage had been localized, as it appeared Hank had forced himself atop Viktor prior to detonation.

Andrei pulled aside the bodies, arranging one bloody mess next to the other. He searched Viktor's shredded remains and found his pistol and axe. The knife was nowhere to be seen. Examining the pistol, Andrei found the muzzle to be dented inward. It was now useless. He discarded it. The axe, too, had been damaged, the handle blown into fragments, which came loose from the head when he shook it. It, too, he tossed away.

He stepped back and surveyed the horror, gazed upon Viktor, who had been his only true friend. As he stared at his pulverized remains, anger began to build. Inside himself, Andrei felt the heat of a growing fire. Sergey had been expendable, as had Fedor, but with the death of Tasha, and now his longtime confidant, Andrei found himself scarcely able to contain the festering rage. It rose with geyseric force.

In a moment of unbridled fury, he swung in a turn and bellowed toward the heavens. His lungs voided of air. He breathed deeply and bellowed again, and yet again, until his throat convulsed with pain. His screams soon gave way to words as his mind began forming coherent thoughts. "Rebecca! Rebecca! Can you hear me! You've nowhere to hide—nowhere I'll not find you! Can you hear me! Rebecca! I'll find you, and you'll pay for Hank's sins!"

He dropped to his knees and breathed deeply of the bitter cold air. His chest heaved. His pulse raced. And now Andrei Kovalevsky had more than just a plan to execute.

He had a vendetta to fulfill.

39

THE SCREAMS CAME clearly to Becky's ears through the snow-laden woods. The distant calls were Andrei's, and she stopped to listen. They were the ravings of a lunatic delving deeper into insanity. The threats were clear enough, yet Becky felt no fear.

Her resolve had hardened to the point of steel.

Still, she could not be foolish. She listened from behind a tree, listened and waited. Soon the howling ceased and a long silence followed.

Andrei's expression of madness must have had a catalyst, she surmised. No doubt he had reached the scene of the explosion, and his anger revealed a welcome fact: Viktor was dead.

But what of Hank?

More determined than ever, she pushed through trembling aspen, pushed past winter-dead thickets, pushed herself faster and harder until at last she emerged into a snowy meadow. In the middle distance, at the meadow's far fringe, woods continued. But these were not the aspen behind her. These were towering lodgepoles growing narrowly apart.

This was the dog-hair of which Hank spoke.

A renewed sense of hope forced Becky into a run, but hunger and fatigue made it impossible for her to maintain. She slowed and plodded, and at times her legs planted knee deep in the soft snow. The tracks here in the meadow would be apparent enough, but even from this distance with gray clouds pressing overhead, she could see that the dog-hair remained relatively free of snow.

Reaching the woods she had a clearer look. Hank had been right. Spaced so closely, and with limbs knitted at the treetops, little snow found its way to the boreal floor. Here, concealed movement would be easier and impossible for the non-expert to track.

Now what remained was a careful hike through the pines and an oblique return to the river.

Becky wasted no time.

•   •   •

Skirting the trees along a stretch of riverbank, Cody kept to the tracks, which soon shifted direction into the woods, toward the blast. As he crept along, his tongue searched the recesses of his teeth for fragments of nuts. Hunger gnawed at his stomach. It and the frozen air, he lamented, conspired to test his resolve. Oh, at this moment how he wished he were at *Oliver's*, dining on a meal of steak and potatoes. But the thought only worsened his discomfort.

Then from somewhere up ahead came an awful wail. Cody stopped and crouched behind some trees. The hoarse cry was indistinct. He wondered who had made it.

The answer followed quickly as the voice of Andrei began calling for and taunting Becky. The anguish in his voice told Cody tragedy had befallen him. Of the Russians, only Viktor remained, so Cody assumed the worst had happened to him. It was righteous news. One less threat to deal with.

Cody decided to move off the trail and remain still for a while, give Andrei time to clear out. The fact Cody had closed the distance renewed his faith in his plan. While he knelt in the brush, his right hand reached to the small of his back where he had tucked away the charges. Their touch was reassuring. After a time he continued forward. Best not let Andrei get too far ahead.

Ten minutes brought Cody to a repulsive scene. Ten more and he was able to stop his bile-filled vomiting. Wiping his mouth and looking away from the carnage, he again found tracks, this time of a single man. Andrei, presumably. Pleased by his power of deduction, Cody moved to follow. And as he did, his sight fell upon something startling.

Hello! What was this here?

He knelt down, reached into the snowy scrub, and snatched up a shiny black pistol. It must have been Viktor's, tossed away by the blast. He smiled. Andrei, the idiot, had overlooked it. Once again, fate had sent Cody a message: this is your battle to win!

•   •   •

Becky tried to prepare herself emotionally. Ahead, beyond the trees she could see signs of a brutal conflict. She saw blood. She saw bone. And her heart sank when she saw bodies. There were two lying abreast. Given her distance, given the blood and failing light, she couldn't tell Hank from Viktor. But there were two bodies.

Two.

She couldn't ignore the conclusion.

Hank was dead.

She had come in hope of finding him alive. She had prayed that he had exaggerated his wounds. She had wanted to believe that what she knew to be so, wasn't so at all.

But the stark reality lay before her.

Hank was dead.

Her instinct was to look away and retreat afar, to purge the image from her mind and pretend Hank had escaped this evil and was at this very moment sitting under an aspen somewhere smoking his pipe and enjoying a deep blue sky.

But to ignore this reality wouldn't be fair to him. It wouldn't be right leaving him there in the snow, resting next to a cold, callous man—a murderer. No, Hank deserved better. She decided to face his death head on. She would tend his body and cover him with the dignity he deserved.

Fearing an ambush, her eyes searched the trees. She studied the branches and the brush for any signs of unnatural movement. She waited. And once she felt sure, she crept forward into a scene of unimaginable horror.

Here, a barrage of conflicting emotions struck her like an avalanche. Repulsion, fear, anger, grief, they were all present in force. But grief trumped all. Grief brought Becky to her knees and more tears to her eyes. In a crouch next to Hank she grieved.

But soon thoughts of her dangerous reality returned, and Becky reminded herself of her obligation to Gracie. She fought to bury the grief, and began the somber task of taking care of Hank.

The work of fifteen minutes brought it to an end, and she was just completing her duty when, sidelong, a glint of steel from in the scrub caught her eye. She turned for a better look. The glint was gone. When she stepped forward it returned, this time exposing itself from a mesh of woody underbrush.

The knife Viktor had taken from Hank.

The very act of touching its handle brought about a change in Becky. She lifted it, turned the blade, stared hard at its razor edge. And in her mind something changed. In her mind the answer became clear.

Until now she had adopted an attitude of prey. She had fled the Russians in hope of escape. She had longed for the safety of home and the peacefulness of Gracie's company. But no more. She could no longer afford dreams. She had outwitted Fedor, and Hank had ended Viktor. Now all who remained was Andrei.

No longer would Becky be the hunted. She glanced at the mound of snow now covering Hank's body. Her eyes narrowed again on the knife's razor edge. She buried deep inside herself the longing to return home, the longing to be near Gracie. And she breathed deeply, resolutely.

No more would Becky act the part of prey.

From here forward, she would be the hunter.

40

HANK'S UTILITY KNIFE was a blessing. With it, Becky knew, much was possible—including the fashioning of the trap that would kill Andrei Kovalevsky.

In the late afternoon, long deep shadows came gliding from the west, deepening the bitter freeze. Collecting firewood and building a shelter before nightfall was essential, and so deep in the dog-hair Becky went to work. First she found a large fallen limb and dragged it through the brush to a tree with a low fork. There, she anchored it from ground to fork, creating a spine from which to build. Smaller limbs she hacked away from trees and leaned perpendicular from ground to spine and finally, after pruning smaller more supple branches, she weaved them between the ribs. This formed the skeleton to which she packed all the loose foliage she could find: twigs, pine needles, and feather moss.

Shelter complete, Becky stepped back and admired her work. It wasn't bad. If Hank were here, he would tell her in a gruff voice, "It'll do for the night."

She peeked into her crude little hovel. She knew that once inside, her body heat, coupled with a nearby fire, would help to give much-needed warmth. The frozen ground would be the real thief. Becky knew it drew cold from a resting body much quicker than did the bitter air. To counter the effect, she covered the earth with layers of needled branches topped with more feather moss. After a short rest, she moved on to the fire.

It concerned her. With the FireSteel Hank had given her, making one would be possible, but moisture in the branches might produce too much smoke, and too much smoke could give away her location. The fire had to produce it at a minimum.

She recalled Hank's teachings, the methods he had shown her for harvesting dry, high-grade fuel. She set about searching for dead, low-growing branches. Her eyes fell upon many. She chose the best and set the knife's blade perpendicular against it. With a scavenged limb, she began pounding the blade's top edge. Each strike produced a blunt thud. She knew the dense forest would prevent the sound from carrying far. The steel blade cut deeply and quickly. The branch fell. She moved to the next and repeated the process.

As her body heated from exertion, she paused to cool herself down and reduce sweating. Then she continued, ignoring the ache in her arms and legs. In time, she had collected enough limbs to maintain what she estimated to be a six-hour fire. She hauled the bounty back to her shelter and stacked it into a pile.

Next to it Becky sat and at each knot-end examined the branches. Dying daylight made finding one with pitch wood difficult, but eventually she did. This would be the starter. She remembered Hank's long ago demonstration, recalled their conversation.

"Got a nice little harvest here," he had said after the two chopped away what felt like a cord of wood, "but now you got to set 'em ablaze."

"Why?" Becky said. "That's what I have *you* for." She smiled and nudged him with an elbow.

"And when you're camping with Gracie and I ain't around? What then?"

"Lighter fluid and matches, of course." She smiled.

He looked down, shook his head pathetically.

"Alright, mister know-it-all, what do we do now?"

"We find the fatwood."

"I'd find it if I knew what it was."

"The pitch that runs from the knot of the branch. A few limbs will have it, but not all."

"Show me," Becky said curiously.

He sifted through the limbs until one caught his attention. He turned it to show Becky. "See here where we made the cut? See the light-colored wood?"

"I do."

"See the dark, resin-soaked stuff inside it?"

Becky saw it and smiled because she had learned something new. "Resin is flammable, right? Is that why we're after it?"

"It's exactly why we're after it. We'll shave away the surrounding wood. What remains is the pitch stick, which we'll rest atop the kindling. Spark it with the FireSteel."

Becky sorted through the limbs, found one that fit the bill, showed Hank.

He nodded approval and began hacking away wood.

She did likewise with hers.

"Now when you're camping and need fuel, you'll know just what to do. Make sure to show this to Gracie. Don't let her do any of the cutting just yet, but teach her the process."

"I'm her mother, Hank. You think I'd have her handling a sharp blade?"

"I'm just saying." He showed the expression of someone who feared having given offense. "I wouldn't want her to nick her little fingers is all." He continued shaving away wood to change the subject.

Inwardly, Becky smiled. There wasn't a conversation the two ever had that didn't end up with Hank talking adoringly about Gracie. It touched Becky how much he cared for her. She watched him as he stripped away thin layers from the branch. Her eyes turned to his face, blinked at his grizzled beard, studied the deep lines that creased his forehead. He loved doing this, loved everything about the outdoors. Most of all, Hank loved the freedom. Becky admired him.

Nearly cutting a finger shook her from her reverie. She noticed tears had stained the branch in her hand. She told herself to focus on the here and now, continued stripping away thin layers. Soon she reached the fatwood. It was a good size, four inches in length. The fire would start easily and burn hotly. Best of all, dry wood and very little smoke.

Finished, she stored the wood and the kindling inside the shelter, huddled herself next to it, and set about the more grim task of devising a trap. Her first thought was a shallow pit, maybe a foot or two in diameter. She could sharpen spikes, drive them angled up into its sides, and lure Andrei along a path where he would be sure to step in it and impale his calf. But even with the knife, a testing of the frozen earth proved the task nearly impossible. She hadn't the proper tools to construct such a thing.

Becky searched high into the trees. At their tops, blankets of tightly woven foliage hid the sky, but still the ever-darkening woods revealed that night was upon her. The chore of collecting firewood had stolen the day's remaining light. Tonight, she realized, would be her last in the mountains. Whether tomorrow afternoon she reached the summit for extraction—or whether she didn't—Becky understood that one way or another, all of this would soon end.

Her mind turned next to a direct attack. She could conceal herself in the bush, draw Andrei near, and spring upon him in surprise. But this, also, Becky rejected. Too many factors worked against her, most important of which was her lack of martial training. Gaining surprise, swinging a knife, these feats she could accomplish, but one mistake and she would find herself face-to-face with an armed madman more capable of self-defense than she.

Becky lowered her eyes from the treetops, and in so doing quickly looked back up. The answer came to her suddenly. She would use the one force that was sure to be effective against him, effective really against anyone. She would use gravity!

On her knees she scurried from the shelter, then stood to her feet, determined even in the frozen darkness to find and collect the materials she would need.

41

THE HARSH ENVIRONMENT had taken its toll. Darkness had complicated the task. But unwilling to concede defeat, Becky had fought away the pain, had worked through hunger and near dehydration to build a fire and collect the needed materials to fashion a trap.

She had searched through frozen groundcover, sometimes on hands and knees, until a boulder of appropriate weight presented itself. Her find was twenty pounds, give or take. It was rounded, but with a single flat edge, and slightly depressed. It would serve two purposes: the depression would act as a bowl in which to melt clean snow for drinking—she needed desperately to rehydrate herself—its second use would be as the moving force of her trap.

So, too, did Becky cut away and strip branches, one inch in diameter, eight inches long, sharpening each to a painful point. And finally she unbundled the thermal layers she had peeled from Viktor's corpse and cut away long thin strips.

It was sometime after midnight, she estimated, that all materials were collected and readied for assembly. By this time, however, her body had begun to falter. Pain kneaded at her musculature; cold stiffened her tendons; dehydration hammered her brain. All were working together to thwart her efforts and shut down her body.

Becky realized she could no longer ignore her suffering. Her body needed rest and warmth. And, most critically, her body needed water.

She pushed aside the materials and, having too long neglected herself, huddled near the fire at the shelter's opening. There, she warmed her aching bones, began to relax, now and again starting from noises she couldn't account for.

Slowly, heaviness crept into her head.

Sleep came unexpectedly.

•   •   •

Travel at night would be impossible, Andrei knew. And nightfall approached quickly. Becky would be forced to camp somewhere below the angling slopes, for travel up them would be far too menacing in the dark. The same limitations he faced as well.

Deep in the aspen, he regretfully cut off pursuit—deciding to return before first light—and hiked back to camp on the far side of the river. There, he collected what minimal supplies he would need, ignored the rest. He revived the dead campfire and readied his backpack for immediate departure in the pre-dawn. After warming himself near the shifting flames, he crept into a dome tent. There, he rested and, taken by a sudden desire to sketch, removed his pencils and pad.

•   •   •

When Cody emerged from the aspen into the snow-blanketed meadow, he stared hard at the woods beyond it. The trees were different there, different from the ones next to which he stood—different in kind and different in arrangement. They grew much more densely. He saw that the tracks crossed the meadow, leading toward the opposing woods.

Earlier, the high peaks had brought the valley into early shadow, and now the purpling skylight revealed an unseen sunset. Cody shouldered his pack and continued ahead. It was only as he neared the far woods that he looked closer at the tracks and realized they had become fewer in number. He stopped and stared at the deep impressions. He turned and studied those he'd already passed. He looked forward again. *Behind him, ahead, these were not the tracks of two people. They were the tracks of one!*

The discrepancy confused him. What had happened to the other, he wondered? Cody had been following a pair of tracks for so long, he'd taken for granted they were of Becky and Andrei *both.*

Now, having paid more attention, he knew differently.

He squatted and gaped at the deep impressions, hoping the size and depth would reveal who had made them. But the tendency of the loose snow to shift and crumble made the task difficult. He hadn't a clue. He paused and thought. Becky was the bird in flight. Logic dictated the tracks belonged to her. He decided to continue forward.

Each step he took seemed to beckon the darkness. He quickened his pace, the cold air stinging his lungs. Soon he reached the edge of these new woods. And here he stopped, gaped at the earth between the trees. Where was the snow? Sure, there were clumps here and there, and much hung above him in the meshwork of branches, but under his feet there was precious little, certainly not enough to leave noticeable tracks.

Through his balaclava, Cody scratched his head and thought of the implications. Without tracks to follow, how would he shadow Becky to the extraction point? How would he know which summit to crest? Three separate mountains rose at the valley's terminus, and each would be a real bear to climb. He couldn't simply pick one and hope for the best.

And there was this little matter of backwoods justice. He couldn't very well assume she would perish in the wild. He had to make certain of it. His hand felt the length of the gun's barrel in his jacket. He had to find Becky.

But the loss of daylight limited his options. In fact, they gave him only one. He needed to erect his dome, spark up the propane heater, and melt snow for drinking water. He couldn't hope to do those things in the dark.

He hiked through the trees until a suitable

spot presented itself. Here, he shrugged off his pack and set to work. Now practiced, he assembled his dome quickly. For warmth he turned on the heater, twisted open its propane valve, and triggered the igniter. It sparked, but it didn't ignite. He tried again, and once more it produced only a spark, no ignition. He lifted the heater, put the cylinder side to his ear, and listened for the hiss of gas. Nothing. He couldn't smell it either. He double-checked the valve to make sure he had opened it, which he had. Realizing he was out of fuel, he tossed the whole bloody thing aside. "Blimey!" he shouted aloud. "Blimey, blimey, blimey!"

Without the heater, his level of comfort—already compromised by circumstance—would reach an intolerable low. Indeed, he might even freeze to death! He sat in his dome and considered the problem, but rather than solutions, the only thing that came to Cody was a growing awareness of thirst and fatigue. He needed water. His body demanded it, especially now since he'd been forced like a common production assistant to carry his own supplies. The more his mind focused on water, the more his body craved it. He remembered Hank telling him and the crew not to eat snow for hydration. A chew now and then, the big oaf had said, wouldn't hurt, but excessive consumption was a big no-no. *Why?* Cody wondered. What could possibly be the harm? His body needed water, and snow was simply water in solid form.

Having sufficiently proven the myth rubbish, he emptied his pack, left the confines of the dome,

and hurried back to the nearby meadow. With powdery snow aplenty, Cody began scooping and filling
his pack. With it he returned to the dome and made
himself as comfortable as humanly possible. Then he
began to eat.

In the beginning, lumps of snow stung at the
membrane in his mouth, but with repeated mouth-
fuls, the sting quickly turned to numbness, and Cody
found he could tolerate it. Indeed, he couldn't stop.
Badly he needed water. He chewed more. Swallowed.
But strangely, in time, rather than feeling satisfied,
he found himself beginning to shiver uncontrollably.
Sitting with his knees to his chest and arms wrapped
about his shins, he squeezed himself tightly and
rocked. Still he craved water and still he shivered.
His breathing convulsed through chattering teeth.
Frustrated, he tossed his snow-filled pack out of the
dome, zipped up the door, and rocked himself violently.

Night had just come, which meant the freeze
would only deepen. Without the heater to warm the
dome's interior, Cody thought bitterly, he was now
only hours away from incalculable misery.

*   *   *

The deep freeze encroached upon Becky's dying fire and into the shelter. The resulting sting
against her face snapped her eyes wide open. She
drew in a startled breath. She had nodded off, but
hadn't intended to. How much time had passed? Her
carelessness panicked her. When she moved quickly

from her huddled position, her head jolted with the throb of dehydration. She had meant only to warm herself and drink water, but instead had fallen asleep. She peered through the shelter's opening. Her eyes searched the canopy. There, heavy darkness remained. Dawn, thankfully, had not yet arrived.

Still, she knew much more needed to be done. The trap she intended to construct would take time. The strips of Viktor's clothing gave her much to work with, but she needed more. The bark she'd stripped and saved was intended for cordage, and making enough for her purposes would require a few hours.

But her tongue had become thick and dry, and she badly needed water. She crawled from the shelter, bringing with her firewood, and teased the orange embers to life. As she dug fresh fuel into them, they glowed and carbonized and lifted into the air. Soon, the fire returned. Near it, she rested the boulder, depression side up, and upon it scooped the freshest snow she could find. The dog-hair greatly reduced its abundance, but some had still found its way through the interlaced treetops.

With the fire near, each scoop of snow melted quickly in the depression. Becky knelt low and slurped eagerly from the rock. The cold water running down her throat and the steady heat against her face brought blessed relief. The comfort addicting, she repeated the process. Then repeated it again, and again, until she'd had her fill, felt her mind and muscles respond gratefully. She breathed deeply of the cold forest air, ready now to face the challenge ahead.

42

UNDER THE WEAK light of daybreak, Becky's contraption appeared shocking. She could no longer see the twenty-pound boulder under the bloodied swathes of Viktor's flannel. She tightened a few more strips. It had taken four or five just to secure one stake. In all, the weapon was fitted with ten, each sharpened to a deadly point. When she was sure all were secure, she stepped back and judged the monstrosity. It resembled the crude mace-head of an ancient warrior—only much, *much* larger. Her instincts as a mother made her feel repulsed by the horrible thing. But her determination to survive had the opposite effect, and she soon found herself smiling with cruel satisfaction.

Becky had spent the better part of the night twisting cordage from bark and pine root, and while she now had enough for her needs, the lack of sleep along with gnawing hunger had begun to dull her concentration.

Remain focused, she reminded herself. *Think*

about what's working, not about the fatigue you're feeling. And though her stomach protested, her muscles had regained much of their vitality. The power of water was near magical. Rehydrating had slowly but surely stolen away her headache, and her stiffness was all but gone. She pressed two fingers against the side of her face. The bruises Fedor had given her were still very tender. Water would do nothing to remedy the result of his heavy-handedness.

Becky's plan now was to locate a portion of woods where the trees formed a natural pathway. It would be simple, as the dog-hair grew everywhere in this sort of pattern, and she had walked many such trails reaching this spot. After finding a suitable location, she would set the trap high in the trees along the pathway. As bait at its end, she planned to build another fire and debris shelter. To the flames she would add dampened wood. The smoke it produced would rise high from the treetops and, with luck, attract Andrei's attention.

Along the trail she planned to conceal a trip-wire, which would release the mace-head and send it swinging high in an arc from behind him. In this way she planned to end this ongoing nightmare.

First, however, she needed to test the strength of the cordage against the weight of the mace-head. That she could do here quickly. Her eyes searched high into the shadowed trees and soon fixed upon two heavy limbs nicely spaced and growing at appropriate angles. Over the first she tossed the end of the cordage. It missed its mark. She tried again, this time sailing it over. She pulled down the end and raised the mace-head. It scratched and dug along the ground, lifted, and swung gently from the force of her pull. Becky hefted it until it was as high as a man's head. She tied off the cordage. Gently, the weapon pendulated. The cordage stretched slightly, the strain causing a faint creaking.

But it held well, pleasing Becky.

Encouraged, she tossed over the second end, this time rounding the limb on her first try. Again she hefted until the mace-head was raised high, suspended between the two limbs. Once Becky located a suitable spot, the cordage she now held would be fashioned discreetly along the length of the tree trunk and stretched as a tripwire horizontally at the forest floor.

Her hands slowly relaxed, and she was just about to release the line when something in the woods caught her attention. Her hand tightened back on the cordage. In a moment of panic, her breathing stopped and she strained to listen. This time she heard nothing. Quickly she tied off the line, then stripped away her balaclava for a better listen. The freeze pricked the flesh of her neck, but only faintly did she notice, her focus now on discerning unnatural sounds.

Then it came again, a rustle.

She tensed, held her breath, listened.

Fear gripped her. She was not yet prepared. The trap had been raised as only a test. It was not set, nor had she concealed it.

Her mind raced with thoughts of possible action. She could flee, try and put distance between them. Would Andrei be capable of following? He had found her here. Maybe he could track, after all. Becky knew little about the man, save his fondness of art and murder.

When a noise sounded again, Becky reeled in shock, for what she was hearing was not the hushed footfalls of a stalking killer, but rather the soft whimper of a man.

Then, chattering and mumbled curses issued from the trees beyond. And there, shadows shifted. Becky could hardly believe it. The words, while indistinct, were accented British. What she was hearing was a cold and frightened Cody!

Fearing he'd pass her without notice, she called out in a hoarse whisper, "Pssst, Cody."

The shadows stopped moving.

"Cody."

"Becky? Is that you?" The voice was weak and defeated, but the voice was definitely Cody's.

"Yes, it's me, come here. Follow my voice."

Moments later Cody materialized from the shadows of the woods. The sight of him made Becky smile. Fedor had announced him dead, had declared him "cancelled." Yet here he was in the flesh. She didn't understand. But at the moment she didn't care. He had survived, that was all that mattered, and now the two could work together. She felt a renewed sense of optimism.

Cody stood with rounded shoulders, his pack sagging low against his backside. Through his open-face balaclava, Becky could see his eyes were red and puffy, as if from excessive rubbing or crying. His pathetic face, below a swollen nose, had begun to beard. She regarded him pitifully.

"Becky." Her name was all he could manage to croak.

"Let's get you warm," she said, and approached him with an outstretched arm.

"You mean you have a fire?"

"In a small clearing just beyond those trees."

"Becky, I'm so thirsty. You haven't any water perchance?"

"Not water, but the means to melt you some. I'll have to find a concave rock, but there're some around." She studied his grime-streaked face. "Your lips are blistered. You weren't eating snow, were you?"

His answer came after a pause, "No, of course not. That would be daft of me."

"Come." She took him by the hand and led him to where she'd established camp, stood him by the fire. "Warm yourself here. I'll find a sipping stone." She dashed off before he could utter a word.

•   •   •

Cody was relieved when Becky returned quickly. With her she carried a large rock. She turned it up, showed him a shallow cavity. She scooped snow from what appeared to be a premade pile, scrubbed it against the rock, then held the cavity side to the fire. A minute later, after she'd rested the rock near the fire and filled the bowl with snow, she smiled to Cody. "It's melted," she said. "Sip slowly. I'll add more until you've satiated yourself."

"Thank you kindly," he whispered hoarsely. He knelt and drank. On its way down, the cold water stung at his blisters, scratched at his parched throat, but ended its journey at a place inside him that stirred a feeling of bliss. He drank more. The sting lessened, but the pleasure inside did not.

"Feels good," Becky said, "Doesn't it?"

Cody drank more, nodding his agreement.

She scooped more snow onto the rock. It melted. Cody drank. The process went on for many minutes, until Cody found the will to sit up and sigh his satisfaction.

"I thought you were dead," Becky said.

"At times, so did I."

She reached out and touched his forearm. "The two of us are all who remain," she said somberly. "Hank and the others are dead."

Cody was sure her words were meant to test him, to evoke feeling, so he did his best to show it. He placed his hand atop hers, lowered his head, and said in his best grief-stricken voice, "I know, Becky. It's awful, isn't it? May God speed their souls to His Kingdom, look after them as a father would his children." Mentally, Cody repeated the last line. Had he overdone it?

"Andrei's out there somewhere," she said. "He's still pursuing me."

"Yes and he'll not stop. We're witnesses to his crimes."

Becky nodded knowingly.

"I came across the remains of the others."

"What happened to you?"

A heavily exhaled breath for effect and he proceeded to recount events, with some elements emphasized—such as his brave return to camp during the whiteout—and other elements left out entirely. Becky watched with hungry eyes, clearly awestruck by his ability to adapt and survive.

"Time's now an issue," she said, when Cody had finished his story. "Extraction's later this afternoon and we have a mountain to climb."

Cody couldn't have segued any better into the one question that he so desperately needed to be answered. Since she had brought it up, now would be the ideal time to ask it.

"Yes, the summit," he said. "Which of the three mountains must we crest?"

Becky's answer was swift and direct. "The right one. Just beyond its summit, there's a natural clearing protected by high shelves of limestone. Safe for a helicopter to land."

The right one, Cody mentally sang each monosyllable. *The right one.* At the moment the sweetest three words of the English language!

"Cody, are you still with me?" Becky interrupted.

"Oh, yes, of course."

"We're going to make it," she said optimistically. "You and I are going to survive."

"Not if Andrei finds us we're not."

"No, no, Cody, don't you see? When Fedor announced you were dead, it was clearly a lie. I doubt Andrei knows you're alive. We can use that to our advantage."

"Fedor said what?"

"Said you were dead. He lied to Andrei. He lied to all of us. Who knows why? Maybe he figured you would die on your own, maybe the weather urged him back to camp before he could find you, or maybe he just became tired of the chase. The reason doesn't matter. Fact is, Andrei thinks you're dead, and we can use that against him."

Cody listened to the wonderful news. The feeling of giddiness raced his pulse. How his luck had finally turned! He had found Becky. He had elicited the location of the extraction point, and now this: Andrei, the only surviving threat, believed him to be dead. Cody couldn't have asked for a more generous turn of events. His blistered lips cracked and bled as he smiled. He winced and licked them, tasting his own blood.

"You hear me, Cody. We can use this against him."

"How do you mean?"

"When we confront him. His belief that you're dead can only work to our advantage. Look, I have a plan, something I'd like to show you. Here, follow me."

"I've a plan myself," Cody said under his breath, and as he stood, he felt the reassuring weight of the pistol tucked at his waistband.

•　　•　　•

Signs of her passage were subtle, Andrei observed, but present. At her point of entry from the meadow into these woods, densely populated with pine, it was clear she'd been indecisive and struggled to choose a direction. But beyond her initial entry point, the signs were much less obvious. Andrei slowly and carefully followed the markings: an occasional heel print pressed softly into the frozen earth, the crushing and flattening of loose twigs and pine needles. Andrei stalked forward in a low crouch, his eyes searching in the dim light. Every so often he paused, knelt, studied. And always he listened for unnatural sounds, no matter how faintly audible.

In this way, he proceeded for the better part of an hour, until a pattern of direction emerged. There was the occasional bend left, a similar bend right, but always the general direction was north, and never far from the margin of woods. This knowledge greatly speeded Andrei's rate of travel, and soon he came to a small clearing. More signs of her indecision, and then a sharp ninety-degree turn right, back toward the meadow. A short walk brought Andrei to a point where she had emerged from the trees and again crossed to the aspen. But here similar tracks in the snow indicated a return trip and Andrei, not fooled, once again entered the pine. Tracks continued west. Eventually, she would have to leave the woods and start the climb up one of the peaks. When she did, the deep snow would make following and closing the distance easy. And Andrei's training blessed him with a great level of endurance, a level Rebecca could never match. He was confident he would soon be upon her.

43

BECKY LED THE way back to her trap, picking through trees and over brush. She was eager to show Cody what she had in mind for Andrei. Better to just demonstrate rather than try and explain.

Her feet pounded the frozen earth with renewed vigor. With an ally here, she felt more emboldened. Confidence burned like an ember inside her. Mentally she stoked it. It wasn't that Cody was a fighter, nor was he a close friend. In both cases, he was not. The confidence, she decided, came from familiarity. Despite all his faults, Cody was a man she had worked with for some years. He was a man, for better or worse, she could lean on to help get her through this terror. They would help each other. They neared the trees where she had set the trap.

"I should think this is far enough," Cody said from behind her.

"No, no, just a bit more, we're almost there."

"I believe this will do," Cody said with a firmness in his voice that turned Becky. "If I take care of business here, I'll not have to look at your corpse as I warm myself by the fire."

Her eyes were drawn to Cody's side. He had removed a glove and was gripping a pistol. "Where did you get that?" she said. "What do you think you're doing?"

"I'm ending you," He said coldly. "I should think it obvious."

"I don't understand. Is this some sort of joke? A stunt maybe for the show? There are no cameras here, Cody. Stop this nonsense. We have a killer on our trail?"

"Correction," he said, "You've a killer on *your* trail. As you pointed out yourself, Andrei thinks I'm dead." Cody beamed.

"And so you're going to shoot me and prove to him otherwise?"

"Not quite what I had in mind. The pressure of this ordeal, sadly, was too much for you to bear. Once Andrei finds your body with the gun in your grip, the victim of a self-inflicted gunshot wound, he'll end this foolish game, and I'll be allowed to reach the helicopter unmolested."

Instinctively Becky began backing away.

"There's nowhere for you to go," Cody said. "You can't outrun a bullet." He crept forward, maintaining the distance.

"I think the trauma of all this, maybe the dehydration, they're impairing your judgment. Please, Cody, think about what you're doing. I'm not the enemy. The enemy is out there."

"Let me tell you something about the enemy." Anger rose in his voice. "The enemy is all who've opposed me from the start, the fools who hadn't the wisdom to trust my judgment. Everyone who had a hand in ruining what should have been an epic finale."

"Whatever your grievances, this isn't the way to—"

"Fools like Hank, who at every turn belittled me and thwarted my efforts. His death in this frozen hell is actually a blessing."

Becky gasped.

"Fools such as yourself who see their career as a means to an end, insurance for a sickly child, and would hinder those of us who understand that in reality a man's career is a calling."

"How dare you bring up Hank and Gracie." Her fists balled tightly. "How dare you talk about them so callously."

"Oh, come off it, Becky. You know as well as I that deep down inside you regret having birthed the little gimp. Your mock distress is nothing more than an appeal for sympathy."

Heat rose in Becky's face. Her mind turned from wanting to reason with Cody to wanting to destroy him. She thought to leap forward and attack the bastard, but with his insult came a leveling of the gun. She backed farther away, where her eyes suddenly caught sight of the cordage tied to the tree.

Again, Cody advanced, maintaining the distance.

"You've done many questionable things,"

Becky said, "but this is a low beyond even you, beyond all forgiveness. You would pull that trigger and put a bullet in my heart, wouldn't you? You would kill me and orphan a child. And you would do it all without a second thought, anything to save your own ass."

Cody looked at her in confusion. "Save myself?" he said. "Is that what you think this is about, saving myself?"

Becky shuffled back a few more steps, drawing Cody with her.

"This has nothing to do with survival, Becky."

"If not to save your own skin, then why?"

"Have you not heard a word I've said? I've no doubt *I'll* survive, with or without you. Indeed, we could leave now and reach the extraction point together. No, Becky, this has nothing to do with survival and everything to do with capitalizing on our failure here."

Becky had now passed the suspended trap and was nearing the second tree. She stopped near the cordage. As expected, Cody maintained his distance. He stopped along the mace-head's pendulum path.

"I have plans to salvage the finale, fix this mess you and the others created. In the not-so-distant future, I shall return here to film a tale of terror and survival. No doubt there'll be book deals, talk shows, magazine exposés, the works. But not with you and Hank around to spread malicious, contradictory lies. And you would, too, wouldn't you? Well, as luck would have it, the Russians did half my work for me. I'll simply finish the rest!"

"Not if I can help it, you won't." Her hand produced the long blade.

"Brilliant. You have a knife. Whatever will I do with only a gun? Oh, my! I'm doomed!" He chuckled. "The future doesn't bode well for you, I'm afraid."

Becky could see his arm straightening, his knuckles tighten white. He was taking aim.

And in a swift turning motion, Becky slashed at the cordage. The blade's razor edge cut easily through the line, and there was movement above as the massive rock swung down in a graceful arc, its staked surface rotating ever so slightly. The cordage groaned from its weight. Becky looked into Cody's startled eyes.

But as the mace-head reached its mark, he weaved deftly to his right. The weapon swung past and he straightened with a triumphant smile. "Ha, missed me! Go to hell, you incompetent tart." His finger squeezed the trigger.

Her eyes tightened shut.

The pistol fired.

Its report was louder than Becky expected, with an explosive peal that echoed through the trees. She dropped the knife as her hands flew to her chest. But she felt no burning impact, no pain. *Had he missed?* And when she opened her eyes, the answer was clear. The gun had misfired and exploded. Cody's hand, now mangled and bleeding, trembled before his paled face. He stared dumbly at his lacerated fingers and had just begun to howl in pain when the mace-head, on its return swing, found its mark.

Becky hadn't time to avert her eyes. She expected the blow to his head to be a resounding crack,
but the stretching cordage had lowered the mace-
head, and the impact came not as a crack to Cody's
skull, but as a splitting slap to the back of his neck,
its force driving an eight-inch stake through his naked throat. From this wound blood spurted in pulses.
His eyes bulged. A wet moan escaped his lips. Thus
impaled, Cody fell to his knees and was dragged forward by the momentum of the mace-head. When at
last he came to rest, his lifeless body remained up-
raised, anchored erect by Becky's instrument of
death.

44

THE FREEZING WIND mounted, raking trees and whistling through branches, stirring Becky from the shock of Cody's morbid tableau. Her mind leapt from the savagery of it to the reality of its consequences. Her sight fell to the pistol. Its misfire had rung loudly through the woods. Unquestionably Andrei had heard it. And if he were anywhere near, he would arrive in minutes.

Fresh panic seized her. The trap, while it had saved her life, had been sprung. It would be impossible to reset it elsewhere before Andrei was upon her. She would have to abandon the idea entirely. Her primary goal now had to be extraction. As for Andrei, she would alert authorities and get her revenge in court. She breathed deeply of the cold pine-tinged air, snatched up the knife, and started west. She stopped abruptly. *Hank's Mariner's cap.* It remained in the shelter. She couldn't leave it. It would take her only a minute to retrieve.

Her boots clapped against the debris-covered

earth as she ran forward and darted through trees. The campfire came into view. She saw the sipping stone. It reminded her to rehydrate. She stopped before it, ungloved, warmed her hands and face. The comfort it provided closed her eyes. She felt tension leaving her body. Then she scooped from the snow pile what little remained and warmed it in the stone next to the fire. Kneeling, she drank.

Her desire was to remain next to the comforting fire; her better judgment told her to collect Hank's cap and leave. Far more powerful, her better judgment prevailed. She tugged on her gloves, crawled into the shelter and grabbed the cap by the bill. Once out, she stood and noticed something folded in its crown. Parchment. *Had Cody meant to leave something behind?* She unfolded it, and what she saw before her made her tremble in quiet panic. It was her portrait Andrei had sketched at the lake. But it had been changed, was different now, grotesque. Her visage embodied death, her skin shriveled, her face skeletal.

"Beauty is fleeting, is it not, Rebecca?"

Her eyes lifted to see the cruel bastard leaning tall and relaxed against a tree, unarmed.

"Sadly," he said, "death must come to us all."

The arrogant ass. Her hand found the hilt of her knife.

"Ill-advised, Rebecca. I could draw and fire my gun before your blade ever left its sheath."

Her hand dropped back to her side. Her eyes glanced sidelong. She thought to flee, but knew it would be useless.

"You were not aware, but I was witness to your conflict with Cody. Frankly, I was shocked to see him."

"Fedor lied to you. Even your own people never respected you."

"Fedor paid the price, didn't he, Rebecca?"

She said nothing.

"It was an effective trap you employed against Cody." He clapped casually. "Bravo."

"I built it for you."

He waved a dismissive hand. "I would not have fallen victim to it. It was poorly concealed."

"I was testing it. I planned to hide it elsewhere, lure you under it. If not for Cody's interference, I would have killed you."

He smiled. "You do realize using it against him was unnecessary."

"If you were watching, you saw I had no choice."

"Certainly you believed so at the time," he said. "What I mean is the fool had retrieved Viktor's firearm. Its barrel and muzzle were damaged in the blast. It never would have fired."

"That would be the same blast that killed your buddy Viktor?" She remembered Andrei's agony and took delight in reminding him.

His eyes darkened. "Viktor, yes. He was a true friend. You'll pay for his death."

"So you made clear yesterday when you were howling like a lunatic."

"Then you heard me."

"Everything alive in these woods heard you.

You're mad."

"I'm wealthy, my dear. A fair compromise."

"Murdering innocent people doesn't make you wealthy, it makes you a monster."

"The deaths were unavoidable."

His rationalizing sickened her. "How is killing innocent people unavoidable, you asshole? How does something so despicable make you a wealthy man?"

"Harsh words, Rebecca, but I suppose you've earned the right to see for yourself." With his eyes never straying from hers, Andrei opened his parka and moved aside his flannel shirt, revealing a money belt. From it he removed a velvet draw-string bag. "In this bag are diamonds. Cut and polished stones of enormous value." He loosened the drawstring, reached inside the bag, and carefully plucked out a stone. Even under the canopy's dull light, Becky could see its silvery glitter.

"So you stole diamonds. You're a thief *and* a murderer."

"I'll not expect you to understand."

"I don't care to understand your pathology. I just want to know why you involved us. I don't get the connection?"

"Phase one of the plan was securing the product. You and the others, Rebecca, were phase two."

"But why us? Why here?"

"The diamonds were to be sold at auction in New York City. My team acquired them en route. Afterwards, we were to return to Russia for relinquishment to our employers. I had other ideas."

"You stole them twice."

"In a manner of speaking, yes. But the men to whom I must answer would never tolerate the loss. I couldn't afford to simply disappear. Their resources are far-reaching. Eventually I would be found. For any of this to work I had to die—we all had to die. The aircraft, the diamonds, they had to be unrecoverable.

"The plan to disappear began long before New York City, soon after Tasha wed Marshal to come to the United States. In the beginning, her work in film was purely vocational. But when she began work on *The Survivalist*, the very nature of the show provided our opportunity. We needed only the right assignment at the right time. When I was tasked with New York City, Tasha contacted me and told me of your production here in these mountains. The tumblers quickly fell into place. The problem had been unlocked. You remember the beautiful lake? At its bottom lies a cold dark secret, a small aircraft. More proof that beauty is only surface deep."

Becky shook her head, wondered how a man could ever become so cold and calculating. Physically Andrei was handsome, but at his core was rot. He was right about one thing: beauty was only surface deep. "All of this so you could buy more things—live in a bigger house, wear fancier clothes, eat at expensive restaurants. Those things are worth killing people for?"

"We all die, Rebecca."

Throughout their exchange, Becky had begun to feel a strange sense of calm. Her hands had steadied. Her pounding heart slowed to a relaxed rhythm.

Given the circumstances, the feeling was strange. It was, she believed, the result of accumulated horrors. For days now, she'd been expecting sudden death, yet at times her desire to live prevailed and she'd fought ruthlessly. The emotional swings had now numbed her.

Andrei returned the diamond. "You and Hank were right to withhold the location of the extraction point. I would have killed you both immediately."

"That's no secret."

Andrei nodded to the fire. "The sketch, I would like it turned to ash."

Becky was glad to do it. She knelt to the fire, which had become a scatter of slow-burning brands. She touched the parchment to one, and it flared from the corner up. Even through the glove, her hand felt an intense heat. Once the sketch blazed, she dropped it onto the fire.

"Very good," he said. "It's as if you never existed."

"Where does this leave us now?"

"It leaves us facing our original dilemma. You know which of the three peaks must be ascended. I wish to have the same information. This time you will tell me."

"We're covering old ground," she said. "In honor of Hank, let me just say go screw yourself."

Andrei unholstered his pistol and stepped closer to Becky. "You die here today, Rebecca. Of that there is no compromise. The questions you must ask yourself now are 'What will become of my daughter and who will take care of her? Will an unknown benefactor establish a fund for medical treatments, or will she die tragically in a house fire?' Think long and hard, Rebecca."

The threat against Gracie quickly dispelled Becky's sense of calm. She felt her fists tightening. The still warmed glove brought her mind back to the fire. Her next move wasn't calculated. It was the result of sheer panic.

45

BECKY'S OPEN HAND swept swiftly into the fire, scooping at spent fuel, following an upward arc toward Andrei's face. Her hand felt the heat, but the glove's protection prevented its burn. A particulate cloud of gray-white ash and red-orange ember, burst before his eyes.

His pistol fired.

A grazing bullet seared the edge of her neck.

Blinking wildly, Andrei stumbled back, swiping at his eyes and face.

Becky ignored the graze. Her grip found a smoldering brand, and she hefted it up, sprung at Andrei with unrestrained fury, thrusting and swinging the burning club.

It struck the pistol just as he fired a second shot. The bullet bit into a pine. The pistol launched from his hand into the brush. She continued forward, lunging with the brand as if it were a spear.

Andrei recovered and his words revealed confidence. "That's it, Rebecca! Harness your anger!

No sense perishing without a fight!" He sidestepped her next attack and struck her wrist with a vicious chop.

Pain coursed up her arm as the brand dropped to the ground.

He leapt back, circled around and squared himself, smiling through a film of ashen grime. "You're well outmatched, my dear. And I'll not take it easy on you."

She went for the brand, but before she could retrieve it, he pivoted at the hips and lashed out with a back kick. His boot struck her solidly in the solar plexus. The blow expelled her air, and its impact drove her backward. Groaning and gasping, she toppled into the shelter, snapping branches and crushing loose debris under her back.

"You take punishment well!" he cried.

His taunts enraged her. She grunted to her knees, tried to breathe, saw him suddenly bound forward.

She met his charge with her own. Maybe he had expected her to turn and run, maybe to cower in fear, for his eyes registered disbelief as she propelled forward. She drew her blade and dove with full extension, landing prostrate before him, driving the long knife through the top of his boot, through his foot, and into the frost-hardened earth.

His cry echoed through the trees. She scrambled onto her knees, looked up and saw his face contort in agony. "Took the taunt right out of you. Didn't it, you bastard?"

He raised a fist and brought it down forcefully,

striking her skull. Again she flattened, dazed and bruised.

She lifted her head, spit away dirt, and through blurred vision was vaguely aware of him kneeling and clutching at the knife's hilt. His cries of pain became screams of rage.

Her eyes cleared. She rolled and scrambled to her feet. Andrei struggled to remove the knife and free his boot. She saw a chance to run and took it. As she loped over tangled brush, her body jolted in pain. Her strides became limited. It felt as if she moved at a child's pace. But still she ran, over moss-covered rocks and past towering pines, heading west toward the mountains. He'd fare no better with the wound to his foot.

Long minutes brought her to the edge of the dog-hair, where she emerged into a sloped meadow thick with snow. Here, her movement would be further impeded. But again, Becky knew, Andrei suffered the same handicap. She pushed forward and covered a hundred yards in the open when a glance back showed him emerging from the pine. His head turned as he scanned the meadow. It stopped when he sighted her. He advanced.

Ahead, the ground leveled then sloped down and branched into three narrow draws, the terminus of each grafting into the folds of an aspiring mountain. She looked right, high toward extraction. There the peak was low, maybe three hundred feet beyond the tree line. The slope, too, was manageable. All were factors that invigorated Becky. She forged on through the draw, picking over uneven terrain and leaping sharp rocks and boulders, moving sluggishly at times but never stopping. Her breathing was heavy and labored. Pain stabbed at her side, but she refused to succumb.

Later, when she finally crossed the draw and reached the slope, she could see Andrei had made up half the distance. Behind him, a faint trail of blood stained the snow. His wound had to be debilitating, yet still he closed. She worried she wouldn't make the peak before he caught her. And what if she did? For purposes of light and filming, transport wasn't scheduled to arrive until late afternoon, just before the golden hour. What would she do until then? She had to keep moving.

Becky's stride up the slope toward the ridgeline felt like a full charge, but the minimal distance she was covering proved the feeling to be an illusion. She searched forward, praying she might see something that would trigger a plan, anything that might give her an edge over Andrei. A break to renew her energy would help. Her body needed it. But blankets of deep snow stretched everywhere before her, and she knew her tracks would lead Andrei to any place she might hide to rest.

Her progress soon turned to a walking pace. She couldn't force anymore from herself. An hour passed as she climbed, but Andrei's failure to close made Becky confident he had begun to suffer the same extreme fatigue. She glanced back every few steps, now and then catching sight of him following between the trees and brush below. His distance remained fixed, fifty, maybe sixty yards.

She topped a rise, and at long last her legs were given brief relief. Here, the slope flattened into a terraced clearing. She crossed the first level and picked her way up a rock slope that rose twenty feet before flattening again. She crossed, and reached another slope, climbed again, reached yet another, this one denser with woods. Threading through the trees, she emerged into a small meadow and had just started to cross when movement turned her head to the right. Her first impression was that of cinnamon fur and palm-like antlers.

Then a moose came into view.

The massive animal rose from its meal of sticks and twigs, clearly agitated by her presence. Becky could see he was a bull from the bell hanging under his chin. He lurched into the clearing, stomping his hooves and bellowing with deep grunts. The animal was truly massive, had to be well over a thousand pounds.

Becky froze.

It was late fall, which meant mating season. The bull saw her as a courting threat. Instinctively, she began a slow retreat, backing up toward the woods. She stopped again, realizing she was returning in the direction of Andrei.

The bull peeled his ears back, shook his enormous head, displaying the wicked tines of his antlers. He charged forward, stopped mid-meadow.

A threat. A challenge.

Becky tensed. Her body quivered from the mixing of fear and renewed adrenaline. She spoke to him softly, put her hands palms out to calm him. "It's alright, boy. I'm not here to steal your girl. It's alright boy." She repeated the phrase as she sidestepped slowly toward the woods at the southern end of the meadow. She had closed half the distance when the bull, still angry, still grunting, resumed his charge.

This time he didn't stop.

Becky's slow, calm retreat turned into an outright sprint. Her eyes searched the woods' fringe for a large tree to duck behind. Nothing she saw looked promising, so she bolted forward, leaving a wake of frosted breath, intent on running as deep into the woods as she could get. She hoped to God the bull's charge was another bluff, that the animal would turn away or stop.

But he didn't.

He was fast, as Becky knew he would be, and when she reached the fringe, she could hear him bellowing thunderously behind her, feel and smell the stench of his hot breath. And then she was in the trees, still running, still heaving and exhaling misty clouds. The grunting faded. The stench disappeared. A glance behind her showed the bull had stopped to watch her flee, satisfied he was the contest's victor. He could have the cow, Becky thought. She just wanted her life.

And then she looked forward again. Her next step startled her when her boot didn't meet the ground. She felt herself falling forward, onto snow-blanketed rock, felt herself rolling painfully down a slope, crashing through brush and over uneven earth. Every turn seemed to land a different part of her body against something hard or protruding. It was as if she were being pummeled by a hundred prizefighters. Then she stopped as she rolled onto level ground and into a swathe of dead thickets. Brambles poked at her body. Some scratched against her face. Pained, she freed herself and sat up, the simple act requiring enormous effort.

Her chest rose and fell with rapid breaths. After calming herself and determining no bones had been broken, she looked about and listened discerningly. The grunting of the bull had stopped. Likely the animal was enjoying his victory and would soon go about his business.

Her main focus returned to Andrei. She listened for him but heard nothing, save the rapid beating of her own heart. She considered his likely actions. Following her tracks, he would soon come upon the bull and be forced to divert, as she had been. Or the bull would now be gone and Andrei would traverse the meadow and appear above her.

She glanced about. Thickets surrounded her, protruding high from the snow. She looked to where she had misstepped and saw that the trees abruptly ended at a slanted deadfall, down which she had tumbled and crushed a narrow path. Andrei was nowhere to be seen. Yet she knew he was closing in, from somewhere. There was no telling his distance. She may have gained ground on him; she may have lost it. This was not the time or place to learn the answer.

She pushed to her feet and turned west to where the terrain, heavy with thickets, curved around the rise toward the far edge of the meadow.

She searched out the area of least growth and forged through it. Dead brush crunched and snapped underfoot. Progress was slow.

Now and again Becky looked back for Andrei, but still he was nowhere to be seen. Eventually the bend began to rise, and the thickets gave way to light underbrush, then finally to dense forest. After some hiking, Becky estimated she had regained a position somewhere west of the meadow in which she had encountered the bull.

Here, she continued her ascent through the montane toward the summit, still leaving obvious tracks, climbing for what must have been hours. All the while she kept vigilance behind her. Eventually montane gave way to sub-alpine. By now, the sky had become cloudless. She looked up high. The sun had passed transit and stolen away the freeze. Despite the glaring snow, Becky's view ahead was clear. The summit loomed. Its growing size encouraged her.

As she bound forward in ungainly stride, her feet punched deeply into the powder. Her eyes desperately searched ahead. Taking her sight from the ground made her stumble, forced her to have to right herself. She knew her divided attention was helping Andrei close the distance. He wasn't burdened by the same desperate need to plan and evade.

Soon, her legs were again rubber. Sporadically, she found herself buckling at the knee. The slope steepened. Her eyes searched. Detail at the summit began to resolve itself. She was getting closer. Her heart raced as she climbed. She stumbled again, corrected herself. Soon, when she looked up, she saw trees to her right opening into a clear track. It gave her an idea. She angled toward it.

When she emerged, she paused seeing the signs she had expected. Upslope to her left, a steep, treeless track rose to a sheer limestone face. From its base running half the length of the track, the ground was convex and heavy with snow. Given the recent storms, the angle of the slope, the treeless track, Becky knew this was prime avalanche territory. Normally she would avoid it like the plague, but given the circumstances she would have to embrace it.

Thoughts of Gracie returned uninvited. In her mind, she saw her daughter young, innocent, brave. She saw her smiling. Saw dimples creasing her pale cheeks. She saw her running playfully in the park. Saw sandy hair blowing in ribbons behind her. Becky wanted to hold her now more than ever.

"You must be near, Rebecca!" came Andrei's call from somewhere behind her in the woods. "Can you hear me? Surely you can. We haven't much time. This shall all be settled soon. You have my word."

His voice had startled her aware.

Damn it! She scolded herself for having stopped and slipped out of focus. She had promised herself she wouldn't. Thinking of Gracie only made her predicament more painful. She ran from the trees and began picking her way up the track, slowly angling toward its center. When Andrei emerged, he was only thirty yards behind her. Had she spent any more time dreaming, she'd likely be dead right now. She cursed her mental slip.

"That's it, Rebecca, lead the way!" he yelled.

Becky drove onward. *Oh, she would lead the way alright. Straight up the center of the track. All she hoped of Andrei was that the bastard followed.*

After a time she looked again. He was indeed behind her in the track, maybe twenty-five yards, speeding his progress by using her impressions as a trail.

She forced her feet harder and deeper into the snowpack, fighting against her failing legs, now and again glancing back hoping for movement of the snow. Each time she looked she saw nothing, save her own deep tracks and Andrei's accelerated progress.

"We mustn't be late for extraction, Rebecca. Keep to task. You're doing splendidly. Yes, you're a fine little *soldat!*"

She tried a new tack. Rather than head straight for the limestone, she would crisscross the field, hoping to create more instability in the snow. She didn't know if it would work, but she needed to try something, anything. She had just begun switching direction when Andrei's call from behind brought her plan to an abrupt end.

"You think I fail to recognize the signs, Rebecca? Risking your own life to threaten mine is brave indeed. What is it you Americans call this? A game of *kuritsa*, of chicken, yes? Forge ahead, see who'll cower first? Well I'm sorry, my dear. Your future may be bleak, but mine, mine is as bright as glittering diamonds." Becky glanced over her shoulder to see Andrei now ascending at an angle, heading back for the trees. He hadn't fallen for the bait.

Her eyes closed. Her hope faded. What now? A look ahead showed the limestone looming near. She had forced her legs deep into the snow, driven each step with a violent thrust in the chance that a plate behind her might dislodge and slide. Yet luck hadn't rewarded her efforts.

When she reached the limestone monolith she turned, crouched at its base, and heaved heavy breaths. She looked left. Andrei, now some distance at the edge of the track, had nearly reached her elevation. He planted himself against a tree, began removing his boot to tend to his wound. She studied his face. Even at this distance she could see it set in raw determination. His eyes narrowed at his bloody foot. The light of the sky glinted from the sweat of his forehead. He probed the wound and grimaced. His pain pleased Becky. All those poor people, her dear Hank, the horror she was going through now, this was the man responsible for it all. Hate swelled inside of her.

"You seek a respite in our game of death," he called out. "Under the circumstances, I approve." His breath frosted the air as he taunted her.

Weariness made Becky groan. She tilted her head against the cliff face, could feel its cold stone through her balaclava. Then a glance up gave her an unexpected rush. There, thirty feet above her, hanging prominently from the rim of the limestone was a massive cornice of snow and ice, protruding three, maybe four feet over the lip. It hadn't been obvious when she was climbing. A sudden idea jolted her with adrenaline and stood her to her feet.

"No, no, sit for a while, my dear. Breathe deeply and invigorate yourself. The fun is yet to come."

Becky began skirting the limestone.

"If it's the gun that moves you, you mustn't worry. I'll not shoot you. I shall need what little ammunition remains for whoever is to become my chauffeur. As for you, you'll be getting the blade. Tit for tat, so to speak." He held up the bloody knife he had pulled from his foot, turned it under the sunlight.

She was now moving in Andrei's direction. She knew he would have to put on and tie his boot. She estimated she could round the monolith and climb its slope before he reached her. But it would be close.

"Respite complete, I see. Oh well, as you wish." He began snugging on his boot.

Becky was climbing the slope and nearing the top by the time Andrei was on the move. He brandished the knife, hadn't cleaned the blade of his own blood.

When she reached the snow-covered cap she could see that it sloped gently upward fifty feet toward the false edge. Beyond and below it ran the avalanche track. From this vantage point the cornice concealed the true precipice, four feet nearer. Now, with no other option, it was do or die. From here she would make a last stand.

She turned her head toward the western summit, could see its long white ridgeline fifty meters above. Just over it, she knew, was the clearing where the extraction helicopter planned to touch down. The sun warmed her face. It was on a downward trajectory, still two hours from reaching the horizon.

Andrei was ascending the slope, nearing.

Becky turned and backed toward the precipice. "Nowhere else for me to go," she said. "You've won. Please, you can't hurt my child."

Andrei reached the top, bound forward, and stopped from her at twenty feet, his chest heaving. Behind him, spots of blood still showed his trail. He stared into her eyes, turned the knife absently in his hand.

Becky faced him directly. "I suppose a final plea would do no good."

"It's fitting that we're here." He swept the knife in a long arc as if to mean the mountains. "The wild, it's a brutal environment, yet it isn't. The animals that survive here do so by killing and consuming other creatures, yet none of it's personal. When the bear savaged Fedor, it was instinct. She had a cub to protect. There wasn't a second thought. No concern about law and morality. It was pure will to survive. I suppose the same could be said for you, Rebecca. Your actions have been to protect your daughter as much as yourself. I understand that. I respect that. I respect you."

"Then you won't harm Gracie?"

"I'm also a man of conviction. When I decide to do something I do it. You were given the choice earlier, before this." He looked down to indicate his wounded foot. "Actions have consequences, I'm afraid."

"And I'm going to pay for them. But not

Gracie."

"You'll be paying for Tasha and Viktor. Gracie is another debt to be settled."

Becky felt a combined sense of worry and rage. "You're a monster."

Andrei limped forward, the knife turning in his hand.

She backed away carefully, closer to the edge, stopped at what she estimated to be a foot or two from the true precipice. "You know I'll fight."

"Indeed, Rebecca, I'd expect nothing less."

"I've decided I don't like you calling me that. It's too personal."

"As you wish. Becky."

"I'm going to kill you," she said.

"That's the fighting spirit." He closed more distance.

He was close enough now for Becky to see the sickness in his eyes. They gleamed madly. He was feeding on her fear.

At ten feet his stance suddenly shifted. He brought in his elbows and lowered his chin as if he planned to end conversation.

Becky tensed. She knew what was coming, but couldn't fight away the tremble in her limbs. Her heart rate rocketed. Her eyes widened to anticipate the slightest of his movements.

And then it happened.

Andrei closed the distance quickly and lunged. The knife lashed out.

Fear and inexperience threw her thoughts into confusion. Yet still she reacted, rolling to her right and away from the edge. She felt the pull of her par-ka, then a hot sting against the flesh of her arm.

She stood and turned, saw Andrei had already pivoted to face her. Hurriedly she circled to put the precipice behind him while her hand flew to her bicep and came away in blood. The sting was intense.

There was no more taunting. She knew he was determined to end it. Light-headed, she lunged for-ward to kick him back, but despite his wounded foot, he sidestepped easily. Her front kick missed. Her boot dropped into the snow, and its impact sent a shudder through the cornice.

And like a calving glacier, a massive shelf of snow and ice cracked and split, went sliding down the edge, leaving a cloud of white powder in its wake.

Quickly she turned to Andrei, saw he stood abreast of the edge, as did she. His eyes met hers. Desperately her hands reached out and grabbed him, found grip on the sleeves of his parka.

But before she could manage her arms around him, the knife swung up, pierced her clothes, found the flesh of her stomach and drove inside her. There came horrible pain. Becky moaned, felt herself losing lucidity.

But fear for Gracie gave her a final rush, and she lunged forward embracing Andrei tightly, crush-ing the knife between them, deeper into her. With awareness fading rapidly and the monster in her grasp, she pulled toward the edge with a strength foreign to her, felt herself teeter, Andrei along with her. He fought to right himself, but a last heave top-pled them both over the brink, flailing, falling.

46

IN THEIR FALL Rebecca had lost her embrace. Rote conditioning made Andrei right himself and land into the snow bank with practiced efficiency: ball of the foot, calf, thigh, and finally his side. It was a paratrooper's landing, learned in the military. The sequence lessened the impact's stress on his body, but still he felt a blinding pain course from his injured foot, up his leg, through his side and neck, into his brain. He endured it, rolling in the direction of his momentum and struggling to stand. But pain and disorientation had forced a mistake, and he realized as his body wheeled and flailed that he had rolled out of the fall in a downslope direction. Gravity fought against him.

He kicked out his legs, punched out his arms, trying desperately to slow himself, but his momentum was too great. He tumbled. Snow slapped at his face, filled his mouth, found its way under his clothes. Then an awkward tumble and he felt his shoulder strike hardpack and dislocate. Vertiginous waves assailed his mind, and it seemed forever before he finally came to rest.

Still conscious, he looked up into the graying sky before laboring to his feet. Once standing, he searched upslope and noted he'd fallen forty or fifty meters. Rebecca lay unmoving in the snow at the base of the monolith—likely dead. He would return and cut her throat, be certain of it. He began picking his way upslope, felt his injured shoulder scream in protest, stopped to attempt to relocate it. And then he heard a deep ominous *whumph*. His eyes fixed worriedly upon the snowpack above him. There, movement began—movement that sent terror pumping through his veins.

Thirty meters above, in an arc stretching from one side of the track to the other, there separated an enormous slab of snow and ice. It appeared to move as if by design, slowly, gracefully. But Andrei knew this was a false impression. In fact there was nothing slow or graceful about it.

He couldn't outrun it. He looked right, looked left, saw both tree lines were much too far to reach. With no other options, he chose left and ran. The deep snow and his injured foot forced an awkward stride. Still he pushed, battling the odds.

The slab picked up momentum.

The ground beneath his feet seemed to jolt as if by an earthquake.

Andrei scrambled in panic.

A sidelong glance showed the slab fragmenting into blocks and granules, sliding and billowing downward with wicked speed. The tree line still seemed impossibly distant. The roar of churning snow and ice descended like jet engines upon his ears. *Rebecca had managed it. She had somehow bested him.* Andrei regretted having underestimated her. His well-made plan had no contingency for this.

Numb and deafened, he turned to face the inevitable, saw his end in the form of a wall of moving snow, tons of it ten feet high—and he embraced it. There came a strange sense of calm as he straightened himself, hands reaching for the feel of his precious diamonds.

And at once, an unimaginable force swallowed Andrei Kovalevsky.

•   •   •

Splayed out on her back, Becky's eyes flew open, and she stared up at the sky's deepening blue. She wasn't sure how long she'd been unconscious, but snow had already numbed her underside. She was alive and breathing, yet felt incredibly feeble. Each breath she took pained her left oblique, where Andrei had so cruelly plunged the blade. She unzipped her parka, tried to pull up her shirt, but found blood had frozen it to her flesh. She let it be for fear she might again start the bleeding.

Where was Andrei? Why hadn't he finished her? Renewed concern moved her. But no amount of willpower could turn her faster than by degrees. With a pain-filled groan she rolled to her side, stared down the shadowing slope, eyes alert for danger. She saw next to her a shallow trench in the snow where Andrei must have landed. It ran downslope ending at what looked to be a drop edge. Must be a trick of the light, she thought, since no step had been there previously. Weak, trembling arms pushed her upright and seated. She narrowed her eyes. When her sight sharpened she knew it had been no trick of the light, no figment of the imagination. She stared disbelieving at what was clearly a drop edge, eight feet down. In fact, its lip curved in a smiling arc from one end of the avalanche track to the other. And suddenly she realized what had happened: the weight of the cornice together with their fall had worked to trigger an avalanche. Andrei must have rolled downslope and come to rest squarely in its path.

After struggling to her feet, Becky stood hunched in a position that offered the least amount of pain. She looked downslope to where thousands of tons of snow had come to rest in a field of white, icy blocks.

And no sign of Andrei.

Inwardly Becky cried joy. Her breath came convulsively as a floodgate opened and waves of emotion swept over her. Trembling uncontrollably, she turned and looked toward the summit, where the sun had dipped by fractions below the crest, tingeing the snow with orange light. In the far distance she heard the faint and steady *thwack* of rotor blades.

Ever so gingerly, Becky Ford put a weary foot in front of her and began the final climb home.

EPILOGUE

"WHAT ABOUT S'MORES, Mom? The doctor didn't say I couldn't have S'mores, did she?"

Becky glanced into the rearview, saw Gracie's worried expression and smiled. "No, honey. The doctor said nothing about not having S'mores."

"You didn't forget to bring them, did you?"

"I didn't forget, honey."

"Yes!" She pumped a small fist. "Because camping's no fun without S'mores."

Becky turned off the highway onto a rutted road that ran down to a wooded lake and a little-known spot Hank had shown her a few years back, when the three had first camped together. Becky drove at a school zone speed, but still the car bumped and jostled. She could see Gracie bouncing in the back, Hank's Mariner's cap fitted loosely and slightly skewed on her head.

Becky looked toward the woods. It was a warm summer afternoon and in the distance, underscored by the car's glistening hood, a distant line of larch trees towered, full and green.

Her cell phone rang on the seat next to her. She didn't recognize the number. An out-of-state area code. She braked off the road, tapped the green phone and speaker symbol. "Hello?"

"Mrs. Rebecca Ford?" A man's voice asked. Static interfered.

"Call me Becky." Since the ordeal, the sound of Rebecca just didn't sit right with her. "Speaking, not sure for how long, though. I'm a bit off the grid."

"That's perfectly alright. I'll make it brief. I'm Travis Williams calling on behalf of Sotheby's in New York City."

Her mind immediately went to the diamonds. Authorities had only just recovered Andrei's body a few days ago. The avalanche's massive snow pile and worsening weather conditions had forced a postponement until snowmelt.

"You'll be pleased to know our people have concluded their investigation and all gemstones have been accounted for."

"That's great news." Becky wondered whether there was ever any doubt.

"To show our gratitude and to honor your efforts, we'd like to fly you and your companions to New York City for a weekend, to enjoy fine dining and entertainment, perhaps take in a show. Whatever you'd like."

Becky smiled. "That's very generous of you. My mother and daughter—"

"—That's me," Gracie called out from the back.

"I'm sorry, Mr. Williams. I have you on speaker. We would be very pleased."

"Wonderful. We shall contact you at a later date then to make arrangements. Again, on behalf of Sotheby's, we thank you, Mrs. Ford."

"You're welcome." After ending the call Becky powered off her phone. "What do you think about that?" She asked Gracie.

"Where's New York City? *York* sounds funny."

"The other end of the country, honey. It's a big place, lots of tall buildings." She could see Gracie staring out the window, considering.

"I'd rather have S'mores."

Becky pulled back onto the road and continued toward the lake. The larch, rustling from a light breeze, turned her thoughts to Hank, each one bittersweet. She wished he were here now, in the seat next to her, going camping. He'd probably be advising her how to navigate the road. She smiled, looked up at the blue sky, then again at the trees. Their color reminded her of the Mariners. The season was here and the Boys of Summer had taken the field in Seattle. She decided to pre-purchase tickets for a few games.

Then she had another thought. "Gracie?"

"Yeah, Mom?"

"One more thing about these S'mores."

Gracie was looking back at her through the rearview.

"You'll have to earn them, do a little work first."

Her eyes widened. "How?"

"By helping me start a fire before sundown. I'm going to show you how to build one, how to collect kindling and use a FireSteel."

She shrugged. "That's not work. That sounds fun."

Becky smiled, met her daughter's gaze in the mirror. "And Gracie?"

"Yeah, Mom?"

"I love you, honey."

ABOUT THE AUTHOR

Dalton Keene is the author of multiple works of fiction, including short stories, plays, and novels. His debut work, *TELESMA*, has been met with high acclaim and is currently available online or in stores.

Visit Keene's website at *www.daltonkeene.com* for more information and to learn about the author's upcoming projects.